ISBN-13 978-0692176986

Printed in the United States of America

Vickie Whitehead is a fiction author and illustrates her books. She is a mother of two adult sons and a grandmother. Teaching children of all ages is her delight. She and her family were missionaries to the Philippines from 2002 until 2010, teaching missionary children. She now teaches fifth graders at a Christian school in Colorado. The dynamic of Drifter was born when she and her husband would tell stories to their sons before bedtime. Having a love for the outdoors and participating in mountain man rendezvous' sparked the idea for the beloved character of Amos and his devoted dog, Drifter. Their adventures along the way should inspire and give hope to all those who love the outdoors and want to strengthen their walk with the Lord.

I dedicate this book to my devoted husband, Bryan, who developed the characters of Amos and Drifter with his creative storytelling ability. Our boys loved listening to the Adventures of Amos and Drifter before they went to sleep every night.

My youngest son, Caleb, spent endless hours editing and formatting my book. He was so patient with me, persevering until the end.

Bradley, my oldest son, gave thoughtful encouragement and advice while helping me see where I needed to make changes.

And most of all, to my Savior, who gave me spiritual life with the desire and ability to write. He will always be there for me with his everlasting love.

The Adventures of Amos and Drifter
(Arctic Dog of the North)

Written by Vickie Whitehead

Cover in Acrylic and
Inside Design By Vickie

Table of Contents

Beginnings

The brisk wind whistled through the forest as the snowfall sent hushed tones to the earth below. Loneliness swept through the valley for a lone husky sled dog. The search was taking him deeper into a world of lost senses. The dog trudged through deep, sharp snow crystals, looking for warm shelter. His journey was sure to end when a sudden burst of energy combined with the longing for survival took over.

Humans were a big part of his life, having experienced their kindness and trust. Living and working among them brought great satisfaction. The idea kept him moving toward comfort. The distractions of the past kept his tired and worn limbs free from the numbing pain beginning to take over when he located a cabin in the visible distance. He sniffed and searched around, looking for a way in, but finding none, he curled up along the back of a snowdrift sufficient to protect him from the gusts of wind. Finally, protected from the harsh wind smacking his face and chilling his lungs, he lay in a deep sleep.

Several days went by since Drifter left the home of his former master. Drifter had been the lead dog for John's dogsled team. They traveled thousands of miles across the beautiful mountain ridges through frozen pine bristles in the rugged Canadian hills of the Rocky Mountains into the Umiat Territory in Alaska. The team's master transported supplies to support a neighboring Eskimo tribe or food to other homesteads preparing for the long winter. Pulling a sled was a hearty, thriving life. Drifter enjoyed every minute of the challenge, strengthening his muscles while building his form to become the strongest and wisest of his entire breed. Being part wolf and husky made him special.

The last time Drifter saw John, he was lying in the frigid snow after carrying a load of supplies to the Eskimo tribe. His heart problems in the past few years led to his demise. Drifter thought of John's last efforts as he threw some scraps to the team. He spoke to them in his gentle but firm way. Drifter could not have known that his master, John, was dying and could no longer care for the team. Having observed slowness of breath and an inability to move, Drifter stayed on the alert close to his master's side. The inbred loyalty served him well as he watched with a protective eye. His master was dead. He never suspected the break-up of his team, never to be seen together again.

The team lingered by their master's side. They remained until hunger and thirst called them away. Drifter was the last to leave. He continued to stay another day for John, waiting for a command or movement. After the third day of no response from John, Drifter sadly began his journey, eventually leading him to Amos' cabin.

Wandering through the cold, drizzling freeze, Drifter hung his head low. John had been a good master and friend, one Drifter would never forget. His strength was beyond any other on the team, yet each step brought misery to tired aching bones. He would never see John again. Survival was all his instinct could tell him now. He had to reach safety and warmth; the sooner, the better.

The sky above was thick with fog. The cold wind brushed against Drifter's thick fur, and he longed for an end to this restless journey. He traveled for two weeks, and his stamina weakened, but the survival instinct continued. The weather was not relieving him as a fierce blizzard was approaching, prevalent in this Canadian territory. Winds were gusting up to forty miles per hour. He could not see more than one hundred yards. As the storm hit him head-on, his only hope of survival was to find shelter.

He was not looking forward to the increasing travel days, for a storm like this could last three days or more. Time was of the essence. He continued with his head down, the wind blowing his fur into gnarled knots. His nostrils were bleeding from the biting cold, and his paws became raw with each step.

Finally, he came upon a mountain cliff surrounded by deep crevices. He managed to crawl inside one, fitting very snugly. The fissure would keep him from the hazardous conditions that remained ahead. His thick fur, growing these past few months, gave him some extra warmth. No beast could survive in these conditions for very long.

Drifter longed for the tasty morsels of meat that John would so graciously give to him and the other dogs on the team. What would a fresh food supply need to strengthen his weary body taste like right now? His stomach lacked food since he left his master's side two weeks earlier. If only a tiny creature would also jump from the snow banks for a meal.

His mind was dizzy with thoughts of hunger. He was unable to concentrate on anything else. But he could not find any food. He would have to wait a little longer. Drifter was missing the special treats his beloved master often gave. Finally, after his strength was all gone, his eyes became heavy, and his weary body, exhausted from starvation, laid down to rest.

The morning was soon upon him, the brisk wind beating against his contorted face. He continued his trek to somewhere, anywhere that would keep him alive. He moved slowly and determined. Longing for some tasty morsels of meat was all he could think about now. All the creatures were in their hiding, secure from the blowing storm. When suddenly, hope arose as his keen eyes alerted him. The sounds of a beast scurrying under a rock, searching for air, would provide him with the food he desperately needed. So, he waited. The beast would soon surface, and he could catch his supper.

The sensation of hunting brought vigor to his weakened state as he stalked the unsuspecting creature. The lure. The excitement. The frightened animal cautiously peeked around the bristly pine to examine the surface while Drifter secured himself behind a nearby tree.

The creature made his way across the snowy mass of white like a coin sliding across a shiny tabletop. He slipped. Drifter pounced. Then he conquered.

Once satisfied, he continued his journey. The night air was growing colder by the moment. His weary body finally began to strengthen, but the harsh blizzard winds kept pushing him back. His face became distorted with every movement. The dinner he ate earlier was wearing off quickly, having to fight against such a storm. He trudged on. Each step became more of a struggle. The day's sunlight was lowering down behind the distant hills. The night was closing in on him, leading to yet another day of harsh weather.

The constant loneliness and cold, weary days made him wonder about the possibility of survival. His long journeys took him through a vast Canadian country, losing track of all sense of home and belonging. His travels lingered for a month, with only a few small animals to keep his body alive. He traveled on to what seemed like nowhere until, off in the distance, a faint, familiar smell brought him hope. He could smell smoke. He knew safety was near, whether from a blazing campfire or a chimney. He stalked carefully toward the cabin and nestled against the sturdy door.

The following day brought new hope when he awoke to the sound of a creaking door and noticed a tall man standing in front of the cabin. Raising his head to investigate, he inched forward. As he knelt on one knee, the man analyzed the dog's weak body. Still exhausted from his journey and nearly frozen from the chilling night wind, the dog let out a soft whimper, beckoning the man's help.

The kind man walked over and gently picked up the dog. Amos laid the massive dog on the soft rug before the fireplace and questioned his whereabouts. Never had he seen a breed of such incredible size and beauty, yet frail and piqued just the same. This dog's life was worth saving, and Amos needed a companion. Since the death of his parents, he had no one. After finding the dog half buried in the snow- drift, Amos recognized a similarity of being forlorn. He knew what he needed to do.

Amos patted the dog's head and felt the thick-matted fur as the dog gave a soft moan. He rested his head on the braided rug and fell asleep again beside the crackling fire's warmth. The husky and wolf breed would be a new companion Amos could cherish, one that would bring his sense of longing to closure and to a beginning at the opportune time.

"We will become good friends, Drifter. When you wake up, you'll see." Drifter awakened to his new master's soft voice and responded immediately to the sound of his name. It was a logical name, having found the dog in a snowdrift after wandering through the countryside. Amos could use his name to remember the beginning of a life together. Drifter made a new friend that would help him recover from losing his first master.

11

He loved the sound of Amos' calming voice. There was strength in this man he would consider a trusted master. Amos showed him great kindness. Now safe and secure in his new home, Drifter began his new life.

Amos longed for more companionship. Drifter and Amos were to become good friends. He looked longingly at Drifter and thought what a handsome dog he was. "He looks healthy, although somewhat ragged and dirty, but well trained," Amos rubbed behind Drifter's ears. He perked, responding well to his every command. They would get along fine.

As Drifter approached Amos, laying his head on his lap, Amos knew his perceptions were accurate. God brought him a companion.

One of Amos' dreams was to have a dog of his own. When he was a boy, his father said the idea was foolish. Canadian territory was harsh and unforgiving. There were too many other things to learn about survival in these vast mountains. It would be too hard a life for any domesticated pet. Times were hard enough for the family. They did not need the added burden of a pet. So, Amos put the idea out of his mind. He trusted his father and fully respected his judgment.

Although his father was a seasoned woodsman and an excellent hunter and trapper, the winters were hard to bear, and the food was sometimes scarce. Amos took advantage of gaining knowledge from his wise father at every chance. Amos watched his father for countless days, admiring the strength and agility of his steady hands as he skinned a buck or aimed his rifle to make a shot. He taught him to stalk prey quietly through the meadow and watch and wait. His father was the most patient man Amos had ever known, and it came in handy numerous times when they needed a meal on the table. Setting a trap was one of his father's specialties. Amos places every trap gingerly in the correct area. His father checked them often as Amos watched to learn firsthand.

Amos' first experience trapping was for muskrat. His father had taken him to a river bank where they roamed freely. Amos began to dig a channel about two inches below the waterline and five feet wide, leading to a tunnel covered with twigs, branches, and mud. Amos used a crisp apple to lure the muskrat. Amos' father set the spring trap and hid it well. The hardest part was waiting, but the reward was worth it when Amos skinned his first muskrat and sewed it into a warm hat for the winter months.

Amos adored his father, who was always by his side. He longed to be like him and follow his example like he guessed every boy wanted to be. His father had been an excellent teacher. He regarded life in the highest esteem, allowing no room for irresponsibility. He was strict but kind. His father put into practice lessons about life and spirituality. This training earned Amos the reputation of being wise and fair.

At a very young age, Amos learned to chop wood, handle tools, set traps, skin the hide of small animals, and aim for a rifle. His father had a particular one he was saving for Amos to use when he showed himself capable of handling it. He named it "Trusty." It always served him well. It was Amos' goal to fire that gun before he turned the age of twelve. He was only six when he longed to have it, his eyes beaming with delight at the prospect. It seemed so long, but he would be ready for another six years. He was sure of it! He would also have a pet someday and wait for God's proper timing.

But somehow, this other lesson was different. Amos' father was a spiritual leader and knew more Scripture than any preacher. He could quote verses suited for any occasion. He exemplified the Godly example through his daily reading and study of the Bible. Amos became familiar with Scripture when he and his parents sat together and read the stories to him at birth. Whenever Amos cried, his mother read the Bible, which soothed as a great lullaby. He learned to show reverence and respect for the Word of God. Amos also learned the importance of a servant's heart. He often watched his parents on their knees praying while enjoying the wonder of the night in all its splendor. The sweet smell of pine and wild sunflowers delighted their senses.

Amos longed to learn all he could about helping others and sharing about Christ, but he needed to figure out his capabilities. Amos trusted that someday he would overcome his shyness and be the man God wanted him to be. His goal was to be like Christ through his father's example with his desire to know the Scripture. *But it is going to be so hard. I am shy around people. I never know what to say. I can be bold when I need to be, though.* Amos spoke silently to himself as his father continued to encourage him.

He also strived to achieve his mother's sympathetic character. She was a woman of infinite beauty. No wonder his father fell for her and married so suddenly. Theirs had been a courtship like no other.

To imitate his parents in every way was his goal. Amos would often kneel beside his father and listen to his calming words from the Bible. They had no particular meaning at first but soon the words changed his life. God would give Amos many opportunities to have his prayers answered and increase his abilities.

A Prosperous Fall

It was Autumn in the early 1900s. The land Amos and Drifter roamed was wild and free, full of life. The majestic Canadian mountains were in perfect order, according to Amos. The crisp air, the rugged western peaks, the peaceful sound of ripples in the nearby lake, and tranquility stood vividly in his mind. This way of life suited Amos well. He respected Canada for its bold beauty.

His life could be treacherous, but Amos had a purpose in this vast country. Amos ventured far and wide, trapping with his father as a young child. They sketched every area they roamed on paper. Amos would draw the mountain banks behind their cabin. Each hill and valley with its unique characteristics was laid out and monitored for future use. The rivers and streams surrounded by sagebrush, the golden paintbrush, the turquoise splendor of the camas with their long delicate petals, and the unique-sized trees and shapes would make it to their hall of fame as he mapped the details.

Amos loved every minute of spending time outdoors, breathing in the crispness of the air. With each sound, the wind and small animals would make Amos alert. He learned to recognize the sound of the wild turkey and the ruffed grouse, the snowy owl, and Canadian goose call and to avoid milky or discolored sap, the dill, and parsley-like foliage, or three-leafed growth patterns because of their poison. He knew he could eat the chicory, dandelions, burdock, and cattails.

But his favorite of all things to do was trap as many creatures as he could with his father. He and his father were setting their spring-formed traps when they came across a small opening in the mountainside. Thinking nothing of it, they continued to explore until they discovered a grizzly bear eating the fresh berries with her cub. Thank goodness they ate so intently that they failed to notice them.

Amos and his father skulked away in their usual unobtrusive style. They moved up the hill close enough to watch yet far enough away to alleviate anxiety for the protective mother. Amos was always amazed at their size, strength, and calming mothering effects. His respect for these creatures reminded him of God's power.

Thinking of these memories with his father would comfort Amos in times of single yet peaceful moments. He respected the knowledge he gained from him and the methods of trapping he had learned.

Amos made a living using his understanding of trapping. Every winter, Amos would clean and check over for any defects in the traps he inherited after his father's passing. Amos learned to study the movements and habits of animals, from the tiny squirrel to the cunning fox and predatory wolf. He also analyzed their footprints and scat markings. Amos used this knowledge to stake out the best areas near the river edge or marshlands for setting his traps while strategically placing them.

He found the small animal prints and their pathways by searching the nooks and crannies of the woods. He would place traps by the rivers and then move to the lakes and other water sources where larger animals often came.

Amos also learned to look for tiny shrubs that were misplaced or bent that helped mark his path for a safe return. He looked for hoof and claw marks in the soil and antler scratches in trees. Then he would wait for the wolf, marten, fisher, or fox. It was not often a quick success, sometimes waiting several days or weeks for a catch. But if his father had shown him nothing else, he had taught him patience. Strong character and determination kept him from discouragement in times of light trappings.

When Amos retrieved all the traps, he used the animal's brains to skin and tan the hides. His father had taught him this skill from the old hunters' methods. He would then sell his furs to Sam at the nearby Trading Post.

Sam learned the tanning trade many years earlier when Amos was just a boy. He continued the training after Amos' father passed away. He had loved and respected his friend like a close brother. Sam promised to care for Amos and teach him all he knew about the trade.

Amos soon realized his mind was far away when the sound of traps clamping shut brought him back to the present. This trip was successful. It was one of the best he could remember in a long time.

He listened carefully to the instructions on assembling a travois to carry the meat and other supplies. He trimmed a harness with a poplar wood stick yoke shaped to fit on Drifter's broad shoulders. Two more giant sticks were attached, dragging on the ground. Amos placed smaller branches horizontally across Drifter's back and strapped them with twine or leather straps. Drifter could carry the load with ease.

Significant for his breed, Drifter could pull one hundred or more pounds of cargo. Before Drifter came, Amos would have to make several trips transporting his load, often losing much to other varmints inspecting his catch. With Drifter pulling the travois, they could haul his furs in one trip. Drifter was a quick learner, and his experience as a sled dog came in handy more than once.

"You are such a help to me, boy. God has blessed me," Amos said in hushed tones. Giving Drifter a welcoming hug, they set on their way. He had no idea where this mighty beast came from or his heritage. All he knew now was that God had brought him a faithful friend. One he longed for as a young boy.

The regular trip to the Trading Post had always been an enjoyable one for Amos. With Drifter along, it became even more special. Three to four times a year, Amos would make this trip. It was a day walk, so Amos stayed overnight at Sam's place. Sam, the owner of the Trading Post, enjoyed visiting with him every time he came. And for Sam, it was a very successful event with many furs Amos hauled.

"How did you manage such a load?" inquired Sam.

"Meet my new partner," Amos introduced Sam to Drifter. "Drifter was a great help to me, Sam. He showed tremendous strength and agility, pulling that load like a leader. I am blessed to have found him."

Sam intently listened as he began his story and soon became very fond of Drifter. He understood Amos' fascination with him. He was an energetic dog to be admired and trusted by all.

"It has been a long day's travel." Sam held the brewed coffee in his steady hand. "The sun will be setting soon."

The colorful sky sent glistening speckles of rays over the mountains, causing a luminous glow. "We better get you and Drifter rested up for your long journey home." Sam made the goose-down bedding with fluffy goose pillows to match, as he had always done whenever Amos came. Drifter was most comfortable beside Amos, where he could feel his heartbeat and heavy breathing. He became accustomed to this pattern, and Sam could see this close bond.

"You are a loyal friend, Drifter," Sam wished for a companion like this.

Before we bed down for the night," added Amos, I would like to read out of the book of John. Sam was agreeable as this was also one of his favorite books of Scripture. Drifter perked up to listen to his new master's calming voice. He soon fell asleep near Amos' feet, becoming a nightly ritual.

Their journey home was pleasant as the sun shone brightly through the trees, casting dancing shadows on the forest floor. Amos had beautiful memories of the autumn trapping season with his father. Their journeys brought them to a place of closeness that he treasured, a longing he felt at this very moment. His father left a legacy reminding him of God's presence; he could rely on that now.

Amos looked up into the sky. Even though it was crystal clear now, the weather patterns could change quickly, as was common in the Canadian Mountains. Amos decided the winter was going to be a hard one. The air was brisk and harsh. The wind whistled through the thick forest. Their breath was like a thick fog. Sunlight was not showing through the vast mountains. The leaves changed from delicate green to gold and brown earlier than usual, and the rabbit's fur was thick. Amos enjoyed this change of season in all its array of colors. He remembered how hard the winters could be.

As a young boy, the harsh weather frightened Amos until his mother calmed him and his father read from the Bible. Those were treasured times he would never forget.

He didn't rush their final trapping expedition because Drifter enjoyed chasing rabbits and squirrels to their caves and homes in the trees. He embellished the moment as revealed in his delight. He looked up at the sky once more and determined they must be on the move. A fresh snowflake fell upon his nose, sending a tingling feeling up his spine. The journey continued until the cabin finally came into view. What a welcome sight!

Amos lit several lanterns to welcome them home as they entered the doorway. A rugged blend of Douglas Fir outlined the house—a bench made from a solid oak trunk set inside the stable front door. Amos meticulously carved bold curves and gnarls, giving the legs a masculine and rugged look. Even though the cabin was robust, it had a beautiful structure with artistic carvings of rosebuds and large mountain scenes along the sides. Above the trunk, Amos laid the memorable treasures on a carved shelf with wooden pegs for hanging coats and hats. The window sill displayed a collection of handmade pottery carved crocks and earthenware vessels.

The cabin included a crafted table with a carved rosebud in the center, large enough to fit eight guests. He set the table against a solid framed wall. Amos set a chair with a bowed back in the corner. They used a sizeable pot-bellied stove and kettle for cooking meats, fruits, and vegetables. Many spice varieties of cardamom, garlic, rosemary, thyme, dill, and basil lined a shelf. Above the stove hung a variety of wooden spoons, spatulas, whisks, and an egg beater. Some crock canisters contained sifted flour, and next to those set a coffee grinder.

The living area, spaced across a finely structured wooden frame, was warm and cozy, with soft cushions made of Canadian goose down. The fireplace warmed and filled the house with love. Above the fireplace was Amos' "Trusty" rifle with a smaller black powder pistol on the shelf near the entrance. One large and one small bedroom filled the east and west corners of the cabin. A utility and storage space were behind those rooms. In the back was a house for bathing and daily necessities.

Amos' specialty was his smokehouse, used for making elk and deer jerky. The fixed structure provided him with his primary source of food, acquired from his hunting trips. The deep well his family dug when he was a boy still gave him plenty of fresh spring water.

His father did an excellent job of surveying the well precisely and carefully. He remembered the old "soddy" they once lived in before they could afford the luxury of the solid wood cabin. Amos made many improvements to the place as a teenager. His father taught him to use his resources and where to find spring water. The entrance into the house sent a warm feeling as they thought of resting beside a crackling fire.

Once warm and content by the glowing fire, Amos thought of making this hunting trip many times alone yet praised God daily for help from his friend. It had been nearly two weeks since Drifter came to live with him. Making the trip with Drifter allowed him to explore and gaze upon God's creation of beauty and wonder. He was glad he had a companion he could trust to make the journey.

Amos relished his special relationship with God as he sat alone in the woods praying and reading Scripture. God blessed his faithfulness, allowing him to share Christ's death and resurrection. Although it was still hard for him, he knew it was what God wanted. The natural shyness crept up now and then. He was working on completely surrendering his fears and overcoming them.

His mother had faith in Christ, praying daily. Amos always admired her courage, strength, and beauty. She had no brothers and sisters growing up. Anna was the only one to provide for her ailing father, who became sick after her mother died. Even though there were many opportunities to venture out and enjoy nature alone, she stayed by her father's side, nurturing him the best she could. There weren't many doctors or hardly any medicine available in the rugged mountains where they lived, so Anna felt it necessary to show her love by being a steady presence. Her father told her many stories from the Old Testament, and she learned them well. Not only did she know of them, but they also became a part of her daily walk in relationships with people.

It wasn't until her father passed away that she met Amos' father. He was a kind, rugged man with a pleasant voice, much like Amos's. He always admired Anna for the loyalty she showed her father. He thought she would make an excellent wife.

One day, while she was out in the field planting the crops of barley and corn, he came calling. Anna always admired him from a distance as well. It was a pleasant call. They spent many days together after that. She would prepare meals for him, and he would help plant when needed. After losing his parents to cholera, he was alone for many years, and her meals were welcome. They grew deeply in love and married after one month of courtship. Fourteen years after their marriage, Anna died. Amos' father, now grieving and alone, was left to raise their only child, Amos.

Amos thought of his vibrant mother, her strong faith in Christ, and how she taught him to always be there for others. As a child, he was obedient and longed to please those around him.

Awakened from his thoughts, Amos spotted someone ahead while traveling to the Trading Post for more supplies. A rugged-looking man was lying across a mud hole covered in mud and blood. He had tarnished features with scrapes and bruises. Drifter barked triumphantly and ran ahead as Amos followed. "We must help him. Here Drifter! Help me move him." Drifter nudged the man, and Amos tested his arm for a pulse. He was still alive.

Amos placed the travois next to the beaten man as Drifter helped guide him onto it. Amos had some natural cleansing solvents he used to clean the man's wounds and a cloth to dress his deep cuts.

Drifter took his place before the travois and moved swiftly to shelter. Once inside Amos' cabin, the man lay on a woven mat made from reeds picked by the nearby creek bed. Drifter never took his eyes off his new master.

Amos went to his supply room filled with natural herbs combed from the mountain valleys and open fields. Echinacea, calendula, and St. John's Wort grew abundantly, and he learned how to use them in healing. Amos also secured willow bark tea from a trade with an Eskimo long ago. Amos carefully applied the ointment on the wounds and wrapped them to protect against the spread of bacteria. The man dozed off in a relaxed sleep.

The night ended as Amos listened to the man's heartbeat become more regular. The swelling in his leg was starting to subside. He sat up all night, having dozed off a few times to see that the man was stable while waiting for his fever to subside. The fever lasted most of the night. He moaned and spoke uncomprehending words as Amos prayed for his complete healing.

When the man awoke the following day, he found himself in strange surroundings, unsure of how he came to be there. All he knew was a man had shown him kindness. "It has been a long time since anyone has shown me compassion," spoke the weary man. *They would not be helping me now if they knew of my past.* The man struggled to sit up when Amos coaxed him to lie still.

"You have suffered some terrible cuts. My dog and I carried you to safety. You are well cared for here."

"Thank you for your help, but I must go. I have other plans. If I stay here, they will not happen," said Jack in agitation.

"There is no sense trying to move now. There is a severe cut on your leg, and your fever just broke early this morning. No, it would be best to stay here until further healing occurs."

There was no reason to resist. The man knew his leg was seriously damaged and couldn't reach where he needed to go anyway. He would accept this man's help and move along quickly. There was no sense to burden this man with a kind heart. Jack knew his heart was not the same. He wondered if he had any convictions.

The guilt of his past lingered upon him like the smell of skunk spray. This kind man did not need to know about his history, and he would never tell him. He wanted to forget his past, but thoughts of his actions were lingering memories. The two men were still out there and would not stop until they found him. He would be safe now in this secluded site, but it would not last. They had ways of tracking and tracking they would. He feared he would never be free of them.

Winter Arrival

Jack was secure in bed. His wounds had been healing for nearly a week. When he awoke, he thanked Amos and headed toward his homestead nearby. Amos was sad to see him go but knew Jack needed to move forward.

With Drifter's help, Amos could now complete his quarterly task of unloading the supplies he purchased from the Trading Post. The winter months would soon be upon them, and securing the meat, vegetables, canned goods, candles, and a new warm blanket was utmost in his mind. After unloading the supplies, Amos and Drifter made their usual fire. Drifter curled up at Amos' feet while listening to his soothing voice as he read. Soon, Drifter fell into a deep sleep.

The morning came. It had been a peaceful night. The glistening stars covered the midnight sky while Amos and Drifter slept soundly. Only too soon, that quiet morning ended when a gust of wind whirled through the woods, sending its haunting sound throughout the Canadian woods. Amos knew this sound, having heard it many times before. It was going to be a hard winter. This sound in times past indicated a blizzard, and now one was approaching.

He thanked the Lord for bringing them home safely from the Trading Post before the storm hit. The furs and pelts he traded for supplies provided their needs through the long winter.

Drifter and Amos began preparing their home to withstand the coming brutal winter months. They gathered wood from Amos's chopped supply, yet Amos knew this would not be enough to last. "We must go out and cut down some more trees for firewood." Amos talked to Drifter, rubbing behind his ears. The touch calmed him so he could express his thoughts to the dog. Drifter could see the disturbed look on Amos' face, so he obediently tilted his head and barked in compliance. "Good Boy," Amos said. "Now, let's go!"

The day's work was challenging, showing Amos' sweat dripping from his brow. It might be his last chance before the big storm showed them no mercy. Amos harnessed Drifter onto the travois to help carry the extra load of wood. The wind was unmercifully blowing, producing a gale force as Drifter trudged through the two feet of snow. He plodded through, using his strength to endure more heavy snowfall and harsh winds.

It wasn't long before Amos felt a fever coming on as his cold hands cooled his warm forehead. He had to get to the cabin, and soon. Only one more load, he thought to himself. That will be enough to get us through. Drifter learned well to understand his masters' mannerisms. He could tell Amos needed help.

The firewood was nearly loaded when suddenly Amos fell into a heap of glistening snow. Bitterly cold. Frigid. Drifter nudged at Amos while licking his chilled face. Soon, Amos was aware of Drifter's presence and put his arms around his broad neck. His arms and hands were feeling numb. "Take me home, boy. Please take me home!" Drifter immediately obeyed. He managed to drag Amos by tugging at his thick leather jacket, pulling him nearly a quarter mile back to the cabin.

Amos had been unconscious for some time now. The door had been left ajar and opened from the gusts of wind. Drifter pulled Amos through the cabin door, scraping at it with his paws to close it. Drifter kept licking his face until he became aware of his presence inside his cabin. It was only momentarily when he closed his eyes again from the icy chill. The pain surged through his body. His head lifted, yet for just a moment. Then Amos' heavy head finally toppled into a soft chest of fur.

Several hours later, Amos awoke. He was unsure of what had happened. How had he managed his way back to the cabin? Looking up into Drifter's big eyes, Amos momentarily lifted his head, which had been resting on Drifter's chest. Thanking God for sending him this massive dog as a friend, he rested his head again upon the fur coat.

Drifter responded with pleasure as he continued to lick Amos' face and neck, showing his delight in his now conscious state. Nearly twenty-four hours passed since the incident, and his home never looked so good. Drifter's immense presence reassured him, but he knew this would be a long winter. Last winter had also been long and arduous. Amos understood what loneliness meant. He suffered through many brutal winters, and this was just the beginning. He was thankful for Drifter.

The haunting sound of the wind, the freezing nights, and the inability to leave the cabin for fear of more fever sent a cold chill through Amos. He had always been a loner with much experience in the wilderness and learned to respect the elements, using caution when necessary.

Amos managed to keep himself busy reading and studying God's Word. It comforted him in lonely moments. Amos acquired plenty of wood, water, canned foods, and smoked meat from previous hunting expeditions. Amos often came up with various tasty concoctions, which were quite satisfying.

Drifter was an excellent companion, leaving the cabin for short periods and returning quickly. They developed a special relationship between them—a bond like no other. Drifter placed his foot on Amos' leg, waiting for the pat.

The blizzard lasted two days, one of the harshest events Amos experienced. The blazing fire hardly flickered when Drifter barked and tilted his head to one side to warn Amos. Amos fell into a deep sleep only to be awakened by Drifter's signal. "Oh, good boy, Drifter!" Amos replied. "You are the best friend a man could have."

Amos moved over to the flame. He placed more wood on the fire and rested his cast iron pot of ground coffee on the cinder block of ashes. Amos poured himself a cup. Then he reached down and opened his Bible to the book of Galatians. He had been studying how our faith can make us sons of God, and with this faith, God will handle anything according to his will. All we must do is trust, and that is what Amos did. He closed in prayer, and Drifter gazed into his eyes as if he understood every word. It was a peaceful and restful night.

The clear showed promise in the weeks to come. The cold hung in the clouds all morning, yet by noon, the majestic beauty of God's creation surrounded the Canadian skies. The temperatures were frigid, and clouds drifted as if in a mist, allowing a glimmer of light. It was going to be a good day. "Let's get out today, Drifter," Amos beckoned.

The warm coat Amos received in a trade from an Eskimo long ago had served him well. His gloves were starting to wear thin, and his hat just slightly covered his ears, yet Amos appreciated these items and knew they provided the needed warmth. He would require them to work their way into the deep snow drifts surrounding his modest cabin. Getting the door ajar enough to dig his way out would be a chore. Forceful winds pounded snow against the lone cabin for nearly two full days.

His shovel was in hand as he approached the height of the snow drift blocking his exit path. He was now ready to tackle the piles. Amos opened the door slightly and then realized there was no way out. He checked the window to see how successful that would be. The snow drifts covered most of the opening, yet there was hope. He could see the snow just beyond the clearing. He could dig a tunnel from under the window to more shallow areas. Amos attempted to dig his way out. It was a slow process, but he persistently continued.

"I think I'm going to need more help," Amos called to Drifter. He used his mighty paws to dig, scratching away each clump of hard snow. After clawing with all his strength, Drifter successfully dug the tunnel. He reached the other side, and Amos could see him leaping about like a frog on a fresh lily pad. Amos looked on with delight.

Amos gathered his snowshoes, ice pick, dried fruit, and warm clothing. He crawled through the tunnel and finally reached the other side. They were excited to begin their adventure. After being cooped up in the tiny cabin longer than Amos had desired, an outing in the incredible outdoors was a welcome relief.

Drifter and Amos explored the valley below the mountain shelf near the meadow on which Amos' cabin lay. They found a clearing under some pine trees that served as a solemn, serene place where he could converse with God. He carried his Bible everywhere he went. Amos sat enjoying the beauty with Drifter by his side. At a young age, he developed a tenderness toward God. His faith was present everywhere. Now, he only needed the courage to share what he knew with others. God had given him the heart to share, but he needed to work on his shyness and confidence. Sharing with Jack had been an exceptional case. God helped him by boosting his frail confidence. He could do it again. Amos was sure there would be other opportunities.

He had been out nearly two hours when he realized home needed to be his next destination. The sun was fast descending the mountain, causing a severe coldness upon his face and hands. The warning signs were there. The brisk cold could easily cause frostbite if one were not careful. So, Amos and Drifter gathered their items and trudged through the deep snow toward home.

The twilight hours were here, and Amos and Drifter continued walking toward the cabin now in sight. It had been a day filled with peace and tranquility, resting in one of his favorite areas. A perfect ending to the day stood vivid before them. The colors of the sky opened a window to see God.

For the next few days, he continued peacefully. Amos and Drifter became each other's company. Plenty of dried fruit and venison hung from the rafter in the corner of his modest cabin. Amos began to think of the courage he possessed when he shared his faith with Jack. He knew there was something mysterious yet friendly about Jack. Amos wished he could have spent more time with him, yet he seemed hurried to get to his land. Amos couldn't blame him; he loved this land more than anything. Maybe that had been their bonding, yet there was something about Jack, some underlying story that Jack was unwilling to share.

As a child, he wished he could talk to people like his father did. Amos inherited his love for the land and instinct to survive in harsh conditions, but not the ability to speak freely with others. He did remember talking to Sam about Christ with his father. His father and Sam, who owned the trading post, had been friends since childhood, but it wasn't easy for Amos, even though they were close family friends. But after many years of prayer, Sam finally recognized the truth. His father's consistent prayers and encouraging spirit made Sam realize God's love for him.

Amos and his father bid Sam goodbye and rode home on his father's trusty stallion when a rock slide began sending massive clumps of stone and logs. The horse was spooked when a heavy rock came tumbling toward his side. The horse reared up, sending Amos falling; then, he began rolling toward the cliff's edge. His father held on, yet Buster broke his leg and crumbled, sailing over the cliff below. It happened so fast, no time for his father to react. Amos almost let go of the ledge while reaching out to grab his father, but it was too late. The wailing and mourning began sending a chilling scream throughout the land as wolves joined in with the chorus.

His father and he lived without his mother for several years. He did not know how he would survive without him. The grief continued to linger, but he had the will to survive. His father taught him well. *He would no longer have his father to guide him. He would have to rely on God more than ever now.*

Amos was just about to sit down for his daily prayer when a panicked series of knocks came at the door. Drifter's keen senses warned Amos of the intruders before they arrived at the hewn-carved door. Amos anxiously opened it. As the door opened, two Eskimos fell through, landing on the rustic floor. He helped these two men in a trade many years ago. They became familiar with the surroundings and knew of Amos' cabin. Amos picked up the men and noticed their fingers and toes had frostbite. These Eskimos traveled for many days and were very weary. He wondered why they had been so far from home, many days north of his cabin. Amos used the ointment of seal fat and the tree root antiseptic from wolf willows to help with infections. He applied it on their hands and feet. He warmed them by the fire, protecting the frostbitten hands.

After a time of warmth and relief from the outside elements, the Eskimos told how bandits loosed the chains of the sled dogs. Then they stole their prized dogs."There were two of them. We went to Sam's Trading Post carrying the beaver furs from our trappings. The successful hunt turned into night, slipping behind the western sky. We approached his post when two men came from behind and jumped us. We were not moving very fast. Our load was hefty. They were large, burly men with rough faces. They began to shoot with their long rifles at our lead dog. The shots rang like fire in our ears. The two men came from behind, knocking us with the butts of their rifles. The stinging blow brought us a wary feeling of death. We fell into unconsciousness.

When we awoke, we were alone. Nothing was left but the clothes on our backs and our sled. The bandits took our gloves. Why our gloves and no other piece of clothing? That will always remain a mystery to us. If they had intended to kill us, why not take everything?"

"I remember," Keomi said. "A spirit had been there to guide us. He allowed us to live. He drove them away before any more harm could come."

Amos could not comprehend what the Eskimos meant about the "spirit." He knew their superstitious ways. He believed that whatever they saw was enough to sustain their life.

The bandits took all of their supplies and food. All they had were the clothes on their backs and, luckily, some jerky, a hunting knife hidden in their buckskin coat pockets, intuition, and their sense of direction. Amos humbly offered Drifter and his services in tracking down the bandits. The Eskimos could be trusted and were free to stay in the cabin until Amos and Drifter returned.

Drifter sat close to the sled, ready for Amos to put on his harness. Amos attached Drifter's harness to the tow line, gathered his supplies, and set off. Amos was a skilled tracker with keen intuition and agility using his long rifle.

Others often relied on him when danger was near. Amos had followed the Eskimos' directions, leading them to the damaged sled. Broken runners and a cracked base indicated severe damage beyond what Amos could repair. There were no signs of any supplies left behind by the robbers, so he gathered his supplies and headed home.

Skillfully, Drifter guided the sled through the dense snow. Traveling through the night with the wind biting his face, Amos could detect a distant familiarity as he anticipated the warmth of his cabin. With the cabin in clear view, Drifter quickened his stride, racing forward like a ravenous mountain lion. The home became a welcome sight of warmth and long-deserved comfort. Now that he was home, he was responsible for warning the sheriff of the bandits' deeds and where he determined they were heading. Tracking them down and bringing them to justice would be his job now.

The Eskimos, Keomi, and Ketami, safe in Amos' hospitality, gave him yet another opportunity to share God's love. God gave him the words to speak as Keomi and Ketami listened as they shared about love and forgiveness. He learned much about their way of life and their healing remedies. Now, Amos could share a different form of healing through the blood of Jesus Christ. God was using Amos by building him into a bold disciple. He now knew God placed these men in his life for a purpose.

Jack

Christmas was almost here. Jack invited Amos and Drifter to spend the holiday with him. Amos stored some freshly killed venison in his smokehouse. He knew Jack would be delighted to have some. They set on their journey to Jack's home full of holiday cheer.

Amos knew the true meaning of Christmas and thought of how much joy it brought. He wished to share this joy with Jack.

His confidence was increasing with each opportunity. After his experience of sharing Christ with the Eskimos, Amos felt ready. He still did not know if the Eskimos were genuinely prepared to move away from their superstitious beliefs, but they now had heard the truth, and it was up to the Holy Spirit to guide them.

The journey was cold, yet well worth the anticipation of seeing Jack again. They arrived Christmas morning only to find Jack nowhere in sight, yet the front door was ajar. Drifter pushed his cold nose through the door, forcing it open. On the fireplace hung three stockings with the names Jack, Drifter, and Amos written on them. Amos could hear the scrunching of boots as Jack turned to greet him while carrying a load of firewood.

"It's so good to see you two." Jack set down a load of wood near the stone fireplace. "The stockings you brought were lovely, truly a generous idea."

Amos and Drifter looked at each other in puzzlement. "But I thought you made them, Jack."

"This certainly is a delightful mystery," Jack's smile beamed wide. "I wonder who could have brought them?" The two friends brought their hands to their chins and sighed.

"No matter, we'll soon find out. How about some homemade eggnog?"

Amos couldn't remember the last time he had a drink of eggnog. "This is delicious. It reminds me of my mother's recipe. She had a special talent for blending spices the same way you managed to do. Who would have thought a scruffy guy like you could emulate my late mother's recipe."

"Well, I had a mother once, too, and she won ribbons for her recipe," Jack spoke of his mother and her talent for cooking and how he inherited that talent. "After all, it was just the two of us." Amos was curious to hear the story but sensed a hurt on Jack's face when he spoke of her, so he didn't press. "She left me all of her favorite recipes."

The evening was coming to an end. Jack and Amos were relaxing in front of the blazing fire. Jack told Amos that his mother was nearly heartbroken when he talked about venturing up North to claim his land and build his homestead. But she couldn't stop her independent, strong-willed son from pursuing his long-life dream. She could never understand his desire to live in a cold, foreboding, and lonely land to build his place.

"But it was more than that," Jack openly shared. "She worried there was too much of my father in me." Jack paused for a moment, contemplating what he would say next. Amos patiently waited.

"He was a cruel taskmaster and only cared about the money he could make. He barely acknowledged me growing up or appreciated my mother's kindness and beauty. She was just a showpiece for him in his high society. He was a banker and a successful one at that. He knew the ins and outs of finance and where to place the best bet, which was his downfall. He was so intent on making money that he fell into a deceptive scheme and gambled our savings away. He left us penniless and alone. He moved to pursue another dream in another land. When his plans failed, he became even more bitter and turned to a life of crime.

Mother was crushed and depressed for a long time, sitting alone, staring at the glazed window. She hardly spoke of the incident and waited for my father to return someday. He never did, and after twelve years, Mother's health failed, with loneliness and grief. I tried to help ease her pain, and she loved me with all her heart, but the town gossip and her grief slowly caused her painful death.

Finally, I could take it no more and decided to leave my Massachusetts home and head north to this Canadian land. I found a deed to this place from a gambling debt my father won, but that was not enough for him. He always needed more. I haven't seen him in twenty years. I don't even know if he is still alive."

Amos empathized with his new friend and promised to be there for him. Amos used this moment of truthfulness to share about the death of his father and the wonderful years he had grown up with his mother. She, too, was a beauty and a treasure to behold. Anna was kind, giving, talented, and an active follower of the Lord. A day never went by that she didn't offer words of wisdom to Amos. She passed away before his father, a trying time for them both. It was their solid faith in the Lord that pulled them through.

Their days together were filled with mystery and delight as Amos shared with Jack about his family and the true meaning of Christmas. He intently listened as he told about the birth of Jesus. Amos silently prayed as he began: The angel went to her and said, "Greetings, you who are highly favored! The Lord is with you."

The night ended, and the sun rose over the Canadian mountains, filling the sky with wonder and delight. The mysterious stockings hung so precisely from the mantel were still a mystery to them both. *Inside the socks, there could be some clue of who sent them and placed them carefully above the fire.* Jack was the first to pull out one item. It was something he needed for the cold winter months: a woolen hat with side ear muffs. Amos was delighted. He also pulled out some leather gloves and a hunting knife. It was now Amos' turn. His earmuffs, leather gloves, and hunting knife were identical to Jack's. Someone knew what they needed. Amos continued to contemplate.

It was Drifter's turn."Here, boy," exclaimed Amos. Drifter showed his manners by gently pulling out an enormous bone. One that size would last Drifter a month. He also received a collar with an extraordinary name tag. It read Drifter, a loyal friend.

Amos and Jack were amazed at their gifts, yet they still didn't know who gave them. Jack noticed a house down from his, but he never met anyone from there. Eskimos often journeyed this way, yet he knew many could not afford such lavish gifts. They conversed back and forth when suddenly a knock came at the front door.

They peered out the window to notice a sleigh filled with supplies. These people had a gift for sharing with others. They looked like Mr. and Mrs. Claus, equipped with red coats and stocking caps, and Mr. Claus with a long white beard. In amazement, Jack opened the door and greeted his guests.

"Hello, my name is Harold, and this is my wife Cora, Harold, and Cora Wilson. May we please come in?"

"Guests are always welcome here." Jack needed a respite from his lonely life.

We have traveled this way often. Your cabin seemed so quaint and homey, yet somewhat alone. Living out here in this country can get lonesome at times. That's why we came to show brotherly love and generosity to our fellow neighbors. We hope you enjoyed the gifts. Amos, Jack, and Drifter looked even more puzzled than before. How did these people learn about them? The Wilsons sensed their puzzlement and proceeded to clarify.

"We had been traveling for a long time. Our original home is in Pennsylvania. Many people inherited this land years ago. We were never sure what we were going to do with the property. We were never folks accustomed to this challenging way of life. Our way of living was quaint and straightforward, with every rule and custom of etiquette in place. We knew we needed to see the land at least before deciding.

Our children turned away from us as soon as we expressed our new-found faith in the Lord. We tried to share our faith with them often, yet to no avail. They did not want to accept our beliefs. We knew the Holy Spirit would have to work in their lives. And until he began to work, we stepped away for a while before we lost them for good.

That's when we decided to travel and look at the land we planned to homestead. We fell in love with the country when we saw its rugged beauty. We explored more of the area when we found a lone cabin: your home, Amos. We knew there would be love and friendship once we saw this cabin. The sign "God Blesses this Home" was a sure clue. We continued wandering until we approached another cabin closer to our own."

Amos and Jack were still puzzled. "Yes, but how did you know our names?"

"Oh, that was easy." Harold showed a glint in his eye. "You see, the town knows you very well, Amos. All we had to do was ask about a lone cabin west of here, and people knew who we were talking about. They also knew of Jack because of your acquaintance with him. So, when we saw the liveliness of this place, we made our best guess that here is where the fellowship would be this season."

Now Jack finally had more people he could depend on who lived just down the mountain in the nearby meadow. He knew of the cabin and its vacancy and always seemed puzzled. Jack was glad they had come. He longed for friendship, having entangled with the wrong kind of people in his past. God could not have blessed him with better friends, first with Amos and now with Harold and Cora. These people were kind, generous, and very genuine.

The evening was one they would always cherish as the new-found friends shared their lives. The Wilsons were fascinated by the miraculous way Jack and Amos met and how they stayed connected. Harold and Cora's story was intriguing, but little did they know how much they had in common with the others or how their stories would intertwine.

They were enjoying their time when Sam came calling. Jack ordered some supplies from his trading post, so Sam decided to deliver them himself in hopes of finding him at home.

"Sam, what are you doing on this fine day?" Jack recently met Sam and admired his mannerism and trustworthy professionalism.

"I decided to deliver your supplies as a goodwill gesture and take advantage of your great coffee!"

"I am so glad you came. Too much time passes between us. Let me introduce you to my close neighbors,

Harold and Cora Wilson. They have a small parcel of land and a quaint cabin in the meadow below."

"It is so lovely to meet you. I saw a sleigh near town and wondered who the new community members were. We so rarely see new faces here."

Up until now, Sam had been Amos' only Christian friend. He was eager to learn more about the Wilsons, who shared their faith in Christ. The Wilsons often brought gifts to them, but the greatest gift was the fellowship he could now have with more Christians who shared the same ideas and principles. These people courageously left their homeland to venture into the untamed wilds. They were not afraid of adventure. They would make a great addition to their little community.

The following day provided a comfortable temperature for the few friends to enjoy the leisure of ice skating. Amos noticed that the lake between Jack's and his property was frozen. It had been a long time since he skated. He glanced over at Jack, who graciously let them stay the night, and asked him if he would be interested.

"That's a splendid idea! I'm up for any challenge," Jack said energetically. "Let me go and find mine. I boxed them years ago. I used to skate all the time; it will be a fun activity." They headed toward Jack's cabin and then the Wilsons and invited them along.

The Wilsons agreed that they had never been skating before. It was considered improper in their elegant upbringing, but after seeing that Jack was willing to try, they decided it was time to join in the fun. Drifter was also excited as he anticipated something new. The walk brought pleasant conversation as they reminisced when they gathered the warmth around the blazing fire.

The lake was soon in sight. The sun was shimmering on the ice. Drifter had never seen such a view before. Sometimes, he had to lead a team of sled dogs over a rough frozen portion of water, but never over a smooth frozen lake. Drifter's excitement overcame him as he bounded toward the lake, only to meet the ice face-to-face. It was most unexpected as he never anticipated losing his footing on the slippery yet smooth surface. He propelled across the lake, swirling like a whirlpool.

All the friends laughed until their hearts were content. Amos and Jack glanced at each other as they knew each would give a show of their own. Amos was the first one to have his skates fastened tightly. It was like he had been skating every day. "Well, like they say, once you learn, you always remember." It was thrilling. Jack now ventured out. He was somewhat more cautious than Amos had been and was succeeding until he started to fall again and again. Everyone laughed once again as he tumbled and groaned with every step. "Oh, go ahead and laugh, but I don't see you out there yet, Harold and Cora," Jack said in an upbeat tone. He felt more confident as he glided across the ice like a veteran.

After that first run of events, Drifter mellowed out until he spotted a snowshoe hare blazing across the distant ice. The temptation was too high. He had to take a chance on the ice. His speed nearly overcame him as he approached the creature. The rabbit seemed to be enjoying himself; either that or he was fidgety and flighty, as instinct would prove. The agility and speed of the hare proved to be a challenge for Drifter. The hare playfully teased Drifter, but he did not get discouraged. He gave him an actual chase. If Drifter's paws had not slipped so precariously on the ice, he would have indeed caught that ol' hare. The entertainment sent the friends rolling with unbearable laughter. He became the day's highlight as their laughter nearly took their breath away.

The sun was starting to rest as it headed toward the horizon in brilliant color. His day was a joyful time of sharing, laughter, and peace. God had unequivocally blessed their friendship.

The Race

After Jack and his new friends went their separate ways, Amos and Drifter made their plans. Amos remembered wanting to enter a dog sled race. The town was bustling with activity. Everyone was eager for the upcoming race. It was an anticipated event every year as dog sled teams came from all over Alaska, Canada, and the Dakota Territory.

The sled racers chose excellent gear while sporting quality dogs of stature and strength. They were ruffians, but everyone expected sportsmanship. Most were experienced racers, having practiced with their dogs for months already. Having bonded with Drifter would be in his favor. Now that he had a dog that could pull abundant furs and supplies, he could count on Drifter as his lead dog. He would now have to rent a team and hope to gain their respect in time for the upcoming race.

Amos went into town and scouted dogs for rent from owners who couldn't race. Many were too old to continue the pace, or some other circumstance prevented them from racing. But most of the men still enjoyed the thrill of participating by cheering on the others.

Mike Angora, a sled team owner, approached Amos. "Hello, my name is Mike Angora, and I noticed your dog. He is quite impressive." He heard of Amos from Sam and knew of his reputation. He was missing his lead dog, who had recently died. He was excited when he saw Drifter, so he approached Amos about renting his dog team. Amos was delighted to see the team. They were beautiful specimens of breeding. He prayed the bonding would take place quickly with the team and Drifter.

The next four weeks were a challenge for Amos to bond with the dogs and gain their respect. Drifter proved to be natural at leading the team. That immensely helped as Amos mushed the group through several trial runs. Amos knew the land well, which was to his advantage.

It was time for Amos to again harness the dogs onto the sled that the town blacksmith molded and shaped to Amos' specifications. He learned about dog sledding as a young boy with his father. His father also entered a race as a young man, and Amos always wanted to participate but was too young at the time; now Amos had his chance to race.

The day of the race was soon upon him. He gathered his ropes, his father's harness, matches, flint, steel, and various dried types of meat cured in his smokehouse. He also carried nuts and dried berries in his leather sack and a supply of dried meat to outfit a team of sled dogs. Amos finished the final preparations on the sled, checking each molded shape to meet the race's specifications and polished perfection.

As he prepared for the last moment, his mind wandered to the past of a woman he had known and loved since childhood. Maggie was his childhood sweetheart, but time and circumstances beyond his control had separated them.

Maggie and Amos loved watching Amos' father while he was racing. His skill was unmatched in the valley. Everyone knew about his speed and thoughtful approach to surviving any strenuous race. They enjoyed the adventure and thrill of it all.

Amos dreamed he would see Maggie again soon. Amos collected his thoughts, focusing on the present and his purpose for coming to town. He was ready. His body was in perfect condition. Drifter would avidly lead the supporting team. His lifelong dream was about to become a reality.

The trip to town usually took Amos a full two days of walking. The walk was his time to enjoy nature and contemplate God. Amos had been reluctant to purchase a horse since his father's death. He developed his strength and endurance through walking. But now, with Drifter as the lead dog anticipating the race, he could use that strength while mushing with the team.

Mike Angora was still amazed at Drifter's size, energy, and stamina. He knew he had seen this dog somewhere before. He tried to remember where until it came to him. John Severs had a team of sled dogs and had mysteriously disappeared. He was sure this was the same massive dog he owned. He remembered the bond they had with each other and wondered about the circumstances of how he came to be here. Something tragic must have happened to John.

"Yes, he has been my loyal friend for over a year."

"May I inquire how he came to be with you?" Mike said in a mysterious tone. Amos was unsure how to take this and was concerned with his question. He lifted a short prayer to his heavenly Father.

"I found him nearly starved, alone in a snow drift outside my cabin. I brought him in and nursed him back to health. He has been my loyal companion ever since."

"Amazing," Mike said in a curious tone. "I am sorry to alarm you, but I recognized this dog from a friend named John Severs. He had been a friend for several years when he ventured out alone. He had a rough home life and needed to get away. He loved his dog team. I never knew what became of him, but now I know he must be dead. He would have never left Choda alone."

"So, tell me, Mike! Did Choda used to lead a dog sled team?"

"Yes, he was splendid. I saw him pull a sled filled with bricks across a finish line with energy to spare."

"That makes perfect sense. Drifter is a natural. I am sorry about your friend, John. I am sure he was an exceptional man."

I am glad to see that Choda is with a new master. He loves and respects you as much as his previous master."

"I have named him Drifter because he came to me from a snowdrift. And yes, he is the most loyal friend I have."

Amos answered Mike's questions about Drifter's agility. He was also at peace, at least learning more about his friend's fate.

After almost four weeks of nonstop training, Drifter had two days to rest before the race. Amos used these two days to make final preparations. Mike and Amos worked together to secure the sleds for the race. They double-checked for any missing bolts and tightness of the lashings to hold them together correctly while still allowing the desired flexibility of the sled. Ensuring each harness was securely fastened to the tow line and tied to the proper length enabled each dog to reach the required space between them.

The final day was here after weeks of preparation. After thoroughly checking the gear, the tow line connected each harness across the dog sled team's shoulders. Drifter took his place in front. He knew that was the proper place. He felt at home there.

Many memories came rushing back into his mind, thinking of his first master. He had been a kind man and cared for him and the other dogs on the team. He served his master well and was determined to do the same for Amos.

Amos and Mike woke up early, ready for the event. Amos gathered his new earmuffs, leather gloves, and the hunting knife he received for Christmas. As he put them on, he said a quick prayer of thanks for his new friends and safety in the race.

The contestants came to the starting line. Drifter proudly led his team. The race was a fifty-mile-long venture — a reasonable distance for a first race. The contestants expected many hills, valleys, thin ice patches, overflowing rivers, and cold conditions. Any man and dog brave enough to withstand such circumstances was a winner already.

After Amos looked over at Mike and winked, Mike knew all was well. Amos had the opportunity over the past few weeks to gain respect for Mike and all the sled dogs he was allowed to rent for the race. Mike was a hard worker with goals and dreams of his own. With that respect, the dogs would work well and hard for their master.

"Contestants prepare to race!" the starter of the sled race shouted. The gunshot blasted, and the race was on. Amos held back his team from the rush of mad racers. He knew being first to begin would cut the trail for everyone else. Drifter was a wise lead dog with an incredible instinct. Amos left Drifter to use his ability to lead the way.

The first hill to cross was a steep grade, yet light and smooth. The sled was able to flow freely upon the hard-packed snow. The downhill side was exhilarating, taking Amos' breath away with every waking thought of God's brilliant and mountainous beauty.

Amos traveled twelve miles, nearly half the distance for the first day when Amos noticed one sled team broke down, the driver nowhere to be seen. Amos stopped to investigate. Down below a cliff lay a man unconscious. Drifter barked to let Amos know he was ready to help. Amos unstrapped Drifter and led him to the wounded man. With all the strength Drifter could muster, he and Amos pulled the man up the cliff. The self-made carrier, consisting of blankets and branches, was quickly constructed, serving its purpose as Drifter continued to tug successfully, reaching the top. The man was placed on Amos' sled and brought safely to the checkpoint not more than one mile ahead.

Many men passed them up to this point, yet Amos knew what he needed to do. God would honor his sacrifice. Not with prizes or money, for this was not Amos' goal. His only purpose was to help a hurting soul. He trusted God would be glorified. The Lord's honor is what Amos always had in mind in every adventure.

God prompted his heart as a young child. At times, if life became hard for Amos, he would gather his courage and meet the challenge instead of complaining. Amos gained more and more strength each day while trusting God. Enduring his childhood hardships gave him the strength of character he now possessed.

After a grueling twenty-five miles, the first day of the race was complete. Many broken sleds needed repairing. The weather had been intense. Several men already suffered from frozen faces and numb legs due to the constant harsh winds blowing the entire day. Amos lifted his hands toward his face, unsure if he had one left. His fingers were so numb. He didn't think they were frostbitten. All he could think of now was warmth. The harsh weather could take any man by surprise, even the most experienced of racers.

Drifter and Amos found the check station a comfort as they and the rest of the team warmed themselves by the blazing fire. A kindly woman had prepared a hot meal, determining what each racer would need. Some warm meats and delicacies of fruits and vegetables topped off with homemade baked goods served them well. The conversation around the table opened a variety of interests and opinions about what happened during the race.

Many congratulated Amos for his heroic feat of saving a young man's life. Other racers felt he had been foolish to risk his own life for someone as inexperienced as that young man who had made a costly error in judgment. Amos enjoyed the conversation with each one. They had a right to an opinion if tempers didn't fly or fisticuffs started.

Bright and early, the racers began their plight to finish the next twenty-five miles of some of the most challenging country left to cross. Amos was familiar with this country. He recognized the harsh conditions and was familiar with the rugged mountain passes, but he still respected how the weather could change instantly. With this knowledge, Amos had an advantage over those who came from far-off lands.

Amos enjoyed the tough competition, and he was ready for the challenge. With Drifter as his lead dog and being familiar with the country, he felt winning was a real possibility.

After going over highlands and around substantial canyon walls, a frozen lake in their path that was not completely solid became a hindrance. Many racers unfamiliar with the Canadian countryside would not know the hazard, so Amos led his team around the lake, through a valley, and up a small mountain range. Traveling this way would take extra time, but he could save their lives if the rest of the teams followed his cut path.

One man who had been boisterous at the first checkpoint knew that he could beat Amos. He boasted about it to everyone. He chose the path near the lake, providing a shorter route. He came around the corner, sliding across the narrow ridge, and suffered the consequences of his folly as he tried to race over the lake. His sled and dog team crushed through the weakened ice; he sank to the bottom. Only through God's grace did the man escape and climb to safety. It was a sad day for the lonely man who now had to find some way to reach the checkpoint without a sled where food and warmth awaited.

The rest of the racers were fast approaching the finish line with just a few short yards left to cross. Amos and Drifter had managed to sustain the lead, even though he paused for a moment, allowing Drifter the long-deserved rest he needed. Many of the other teams did the same. Those who chose not to came against peril as the dogs gave up determination and stamina. The rest gave Drifter strength and courage to charge forth with the will to win. His team followed with an obedient howl.

Drifter and his crew crossed the finish line just seconds before the second-place team. All the women who graciously provided food for them the first night were there to greet them again with food and warm drinks.

The man whom Amos saved the first day was there to greet him. He was incredibly thankful as his family approached with tears and warm hugs. "If only we could repay you." The man's wife showered Amos with hugs.

"You already have," Amos winked and waved goodbye.

Drifter served his master well. He tilted his head to one side as he often did and looked up at Amos with appreciation.

Mike Angora was glad to be reunited with his dog team. Amos and Drifter made one last trip to visit the man he saved and his family before they headed toward their home in the Dakota Territory. They greeted him with joy and wished their time together had been longer. Their goodbyes brought joy and sadness, but Amos knew he made another friend and thanked God for another opportunity to make a lasting difference.

Amos spoke with few words, but every word came from his heart. To Drifter, he was very transparent, showing respect for his new master. Walking beside each other toward home, they always cherished the love between man and dog. Drifter would be by his side as his protector.

The trip home was quicker than anticipated as the sky opened to an iridescent color. Drifter, too, stopped for a moment to enjoy the beauty with his master. Their enthusiasm made the trip appear less strenuous and more joyful. Amos loved nothing more than venturing into this Canadian wilderness he called home.

That next evening, Amos built his fire as usual after the long, cold journey. His flint and steel and char cloth were made from an old worn cotton shirt and were used to start his fire. After blowing softly on the spark, he could add the small pieces of kindling, then more substantial amounts of dried bark, working up to twigs and finally logs. Amos learned as a young boy to form his fire to perfection. Drifter and he were now ready to enjoy its warmth. Amos curled up peacefully and snuggled against his soft fur.

Drifter listened to Amos' calm, soothing voice as he read from the book of Psalms. It was comfortable for Drifter to sleep listening to him speak. Amos placed his Bible on the hand-carved wooden stool next to his cotton-filled mattress with metal bed springs attached to the inside of his metal frame for support. They both fell into a restful sleep.

Remembrances

The sheen of the sunrise lit the Canadian sky. The splendid orange and dusty red rays shot through the sky as though looking through a kaleidoscope. The air was cool and crisp, the perfect spring morning. The crocuses began showing their faces in the rolling meadow, opening to a feeling of serenity. The freshness spread through the valley. All these perfect creations were a good sign spring was near. After the long and brutal winter of freezing temperatures and bitterly cold winds, the colors and sounds of the season were a welcome change.

For Amos, spring was his favorite time of year, with the crocus budding and fresh scents after an afternoon rain. It reminded him of the many outings with his father, especially fishing at the nearby stream just north of the meadow behind his cabin. His rod was in hand, waiting for that first bite.

The moment's intensity sprang upon him as he reeled in a beautiful rainbow trout fighting for its life. The sturdy rod never failed to deliver him a delightful lunch to share. As he thought of those memories with his father, he knew it would be a good morning.

Amos handcrafted his fishing rod from an old poplar tree branch. He acquired the fishing line from Sam's Trading Post and attached it to the end. There was just enough pull and spring to provide a good catch. He organized and created a variety of flies, from streamers to nymphs and black flies. Amos learned the art of fly tying as a young boy. His father taught him how to pass a leader of the line through the fly's eye, keeping it out of the way. He then could attach the slip knot at the end. Then he made a loop into a double-hand knot and tightened. Then he wrapped around the back end of the hook's eye and stretched tightly. He was careful to trim any excess string to avoid knotting.

His father often took him to the stream behind their old soddy home. It was his first home. He remembered it as being cold, damp, and musty. Eventually, he got used to the smell but preferred the log cabin home where he now lived. He carved and framed each log with his own hands.

His father also shared the wonders of fishing with him. He often looked down in the fresh spring water below the cabin and wondered how fish got their name. He remembered touching their shiny, slimy scales. He laughed when he tried to hold onto his first catch, only to watch it swim away in the eddy below.

"Whatcha laughing about?" His father's grin showed perfect teeth. "Now I know God has a "magnatin." He could never get that word "imagination" quite right. His father would join in with his contagious, robust laughter. He would never forget those times of fishing with his father.

Another favorite activity Amos participated in was entomology. His father guided him in finding and naming as many insects as possible. He particularly loved the colorful dragonflies that frequented the spring. Many mosquitoes, tree bugs, and water striders were used as examples to form fishing fly designs. His Dad had a way of matching them with extreme care. Amos' knack and instinct for outdoor activities made him an excellent learner.

Amos remembered times of joy and sadness associated with his father's death. He left many memories as a legacy for him to share.

He was only twelve when his father died. They all came rushing back to his mind like a flood, as did the tears, showing Amos' quiet humility.

There was no shame in crying now, even for a rugged individual like himself. His tender side to that masculine frame allowed him to serve others.

Amos knew Drifter would enjoy his first lesson at catching trout, so the adventure began. Amos loaded his gear while Drifter watched with his tail wagging and jumping like a froghopper catching his meal. Drifter was always polite and patient, minding his master's every command. He was born to please.

The time was now at hand for the fishing trip to begin. Drifter learned the trade of dog sledding; now, he was ready for a new adventure. He tried catching fish before when he separated from his first master, John, but failed. Drifter was just a young pup when he first attempted fishing. He considered it a game and splashed about in the water, looking like a fish struggling to escape. Drifter experienced the lure—the excitement. The enticement of the silvery creature pushed him to make a second attempt without success.

The adventure began with Drifter gazing at the glistening cool and crisp spring water flowing into a nearby lake. They followed the flow of the spring with intense anticipation as it led them closer to the glistening lake below. They were nearly there when Drifter darted ahead, ready to explore.

Once they arrived at the lake, Drifter glanced to observe a silver-colored creature that eluded him through the glistening water. He plunged into the lake in a rare attempt to catch it. He swatted at the beast with his front paws, twisting and turning only to discover the fish had long left his presence. Drifter looked up at Amos' amused face for guidance and sympathy. Amos had too much fun watching Drifter's antics to offer much sympathy. But Drifter showed tenacity as he did not give up easily. He was bound and determined to conquer this ridiculous feat.

The fish was more challenging to catch than Amos made it look with his hand-carved pole. Reeling in another fish, Drifter once again gazed up at Amos with a questioning look as to how he was to accomplish his goal. Drifter became determined to catch one as he plunged in again with a yelp of victory when another rainbow trout darted before him. Without a move, Drifter cautiously gazed at the fish, took one quick swipe with his firm paw, and finally found success.

Amos watched his friend play with simple amusement. Drifter discovered a new and hidden talent now outlined in full bloom. Drifter's newly improved skill sent each fish sailing through the air. Amos could catch a few with his bent willow pole and mesh net, but not at the speed of Drifter.

The day ended abruptly, for neither Amos nor Drifter had kept track of time. They were having too much fun to worry about the day's end. Too often, Amos would allow time to upset a tranquil moment of quiet peace, but this would not be one of those times. He was going to rest and enjoy this interval of time in play.

There was a fantastic day of sunshine with just a slight breeze for them to enjoy, and they planned to take every advantage of it. But soon enough, time was no longer on their side. The sun was now resting slowly behind the nearby mountain. It was time to pack up their gear and head toward home.

It was a peaceful journey as the sunset in the deep western sky filled the sky with vivid colors of orange, pink, purple, and deep red, sending him a message of beauty and wonder. It reminded him of a beautiful childhood friend he had in Maggie, she being his lifelong friend and love. She always enjoyed these sunsets as they talked for hours about everything. It was one of her favorite times of the day. The two of them had often sat together under the stars after an array of colors left their presence. As Amos walked on the smooth stone steps to his front door, the thought of Maggie comforted him. The day ended, but never his thoughts of her.

Maggie

The morning was bright and crisp. The supplies Amos gathered in the fall carried him through winter, but they were slowly dwindling. He began examining his travois, preparing it for a journey into town. The winter had been a long one, and spring was approaching. There was no better time to make his two-day journey into town.

Drifter knew what the gathering of the finely constructed travois and supplies meant. It was time for another trip. Drifter twirled around, knowing he could help his master once again. Amos packed his lunch of jerky, dried fruits and nuts, and berry juice squeezed from the wild berries near his house. He brought a survival kit with warm blankets and rain covers. Amos packed a hearty steak bone for Drifter.

Survival preparation was something Amos learned well, and he did not take it for granted. Even though the weather was spectacular, it could change at any moment in these rugged mountain ranges. He placed all the necessary supplies in the travois. Amos then attached the harness around Drifter's broad shoulders so he could pull the travois. Drifter always looked forward to the trip. He was gregarious for his master's companionship. Amos suspected Drifter would have a long, arduous trek coming home because they would need many supplies, and the load would be complete. He thought of making a trip to the Trading Post but planned on making the long journey to the town first. He would have time later to visit his old friend, Sam.

Sam's Trading Post was one walking day's distance in the opposite direction of town. Since lumbering was not Sam's delight, nor did he share it with the loggers in the West. No one built a city around his home. Sam had always liked the openness of the valley. The bulk of his business came from Native Canadians and the Inuits. Many trappers were also aware of his land and enjoyed working with him. They appreciated Sam's peaceful, friendly, and honest business. It had always been a novelty to remain the same. Amos let go of his thoughts and continued toward town.

He made this trip many times alone, yet was so thankful for the help from Drifter and another opportunity to visit Sam, who usually arrived to get supplies himself at this time.

Amos enjoyed the journey while admiring all the beauty around him. Since the morning was so gorgeous, Amos decided to relish the time. They were nearly halfway there when Amos found a sweet resting spot under a poplar tree. He laid out an old blanket perfect for this outing. It had been a tradition when he was growing up with his mother. She loved to picnic, and the memories were fresh in his mind. Many days passed, but this place's serenity and memorable moments never ceased. Drifter gazed into Amos' face and could see contentment there.

"Well, Drifter, I guess it's time to continue." Amos packed his belongings and continued the trek toward his destination. The day was perfect. The crispness of Spring filled the air. The wild grasses displayed a picture before them.

His mother loved this view. Her favorite was the wild sagebrush and scent of daisies, Black-eyed Susans, and purple coneflowers blooming in all their glory. The memories of her were more enjoyable with each breath.

His continued jaunt brought back even more memories of the beautiful woman he had fallen in love with years earlier. Each vivid memory made his steps come with ease. Her long, flowing honey-blonde hair and deep-set opal-blue eyes remained in his mind. Her gentleness and delicate walk always delighted him as he thought of those excellent feminine features.

Amos and Drifter were nearing the small town. As they entered the outskirts, off in the distance, he saw a familiar face glance at him. She stood on the front patio of an old country schoolhouse. It was her. He would always remember her straight posture and beautiful hair. She glanced his way, looking at him as if they had never parted. He stopped to catch his breath and stepped outside the town general store, mesmerized by her youthful appearance as she walked toward him.

"Hello, Amos. It has been a long time."

Amos was tongue-tied, just like when he realized he was in love with Maggie. Now she was here. What would he say to her? Time passed, yet his feelings for her were still aflame.

"Hello, Maggie; it sure is good to see you."

Amos thought back to when he first met Maggie. It had been on a chilly spring morning, much like today's. He thought she was the most beautiful lady he had ever seen. Her cheeks were rosy. Her eyes were blue like the clear morning sky. The long golden hair that showed in the morning light accentuated her beauty. Her whole face lit up when she smiled. Her countenance was that of an angel, the brightness of an evening star.

They grew up together; their parents had been good friends. She was only ten when he had first noticed her more intimately. She was running across the meadow chasing a butterfly. She moved with such grace; he couldn't help but see her. Her thick golden hair in one long braid was near her waist. When she looked in his direction with a smile, he turned away, too shy to show his true feelings. He thought his heart would melt at the sight of her. It was evident today as it was nearly fifteen years ago. His feelings for her never changed.

She now stood on the front porch watching over her brothers and sisters, and his heart took another leap. *Where had the time gone?* All the memories came rushing past to remind him of the emptiness he now felt without her. But she was here. She had come home.

As they looked at each other, love filled their hearts once again. "It has been so long." Amos looked at her in quietness. "It was like a distant memory when I saw you standing there. How have you been?"

"I know it has been a long time," Maggie said. She felt Amos gazing up at her with all the love he had shown her before. She thought he needed an explanation, although Amos never asked for one. Many times, he thought of her and knew. Amos understood her devotion to her family. He appreciated the kindness she always showed everyone. She touched many lives, especially his.

Amos asked Maggie to marry him under a starry sky when she was eighteen. She loved Amos with all her heart. Maggie knew she loved him more than any man. He demonstrated tenderness unlike any other, including from her father, who himself was a man honored by all he knew. Her place was with her family. They needed her care and help. But she was young, and growing up had been a hard life. Her mother and father struggled through many hardships. Before they came to Canadian country, they lived in Ireland, controlled by the British. They were young and knew they wanted to be together. The landowners of her Irish parents were cruel. They struggled for every ounce of food. The taxes and rent were beyond what they could bear. The hard work was inevitable, and for what, but to pay the landowners more money in taxes. Because people couldn't pay their taxes, the landowners burned their homes. The government left them no choice but to emigrate to a new land, and they chose Canada.

They were married in the new country but also found many hard times pressing them there. Not only was their rebellion in Great Britain but also Southern Canada. They wondered if coming to this immense land had been a mistake, yet the beauty and the dream of freedom kept them hopeful.

Once there was an established government, they could homestead land, which they almost lost because of her father's illness. It was too much for her mother to bear when her father died, becoming silent for weeks and frightened to the point of exhaustion. There was too much in this land to overcome: the weather, long distances to travel for food and supplies, and the scary sounds of cries in the wild. She knew it best to move her mother, younger brothers, and sister and head toward the tame and more civilized eastern colonies. They would put behind the life before them and leave for another land that was not so harsh and lonely. So, Maggie packed up her belongings and made arrangements to travel, and her family agreed. It would be the best thing for the family. They left the next day.

Their destination was Pennsylvania. Maggie had an aunt and uncle that lived there. She knew they would help her family get settled. The family members on her father's side always cared for each other. When life in Ireland became unbearable, her uncle and his young bride decided to leave, and they landed in Pennsylvania. She knew they would help them get settled. Maggie sold all their provisions and a portion of the land to make the journey. The house her father built remained. They decided a fraction of the property near her aunt and uncle would stay the same.

They would have a good life there. Pennsylvania was more modern, with high expectations of decorum and observing proper etiquette. Maggie loved the wilderness and the thrill of adventure the Canadian land provided. She loved romping with her best friend, Amos, but she needed to think of her mother, brothers, and sister. Eventually, she would return, but quickly leaving was the best option, less heartache in goodbyes.

Amos asked Maggie to marry him the night before the planned journey. It had been a perfect Sunday afternoon. They walked up the canyon and looked at the vast mountain expanse below. It was one of Maggie's favorite places to go. The mountain's crest, with its jagged peaks, was a wondrous sight to behold. Both he and Maggie stood transfixed by the view. They momentarily lingered as they looked at the delicate yet rugged canyon walls. Amos had taken a deep breath, preparing himself for the question he wanted to ask Maggie. She had just closed her eyes, taking in all the beauty, for she knew this was to be her last view. Amos did not know of Maggie's plans to leave, this being the last time he would see her.

He leaned over to give her a gentle kiss. He tipped her chin to see her sparkling blue eyes and asked with all the courage he could muster, "Maggie, I love you with all my heart. Would you do me the honor of becoming my bride?" Maggie, filled with tears, answered contrary to how she felt. She knew her response had to be no. Her family was dependent on her. Her brothers and sister were too young to handle her mother alone, and her mother was too weak to travel without her. Amos knew of her mother's illness and was ready to take on caring for her family. Maggie knew Amos would be willing. She did not want to burden him with all the care necessary for her family.

"Amos, you know I love you with all my heart, but. . ." He wouldn't let her finish the words. It would be too hard to hear them. His love for this outstanding woman went beyond his desire. The respect he had for her was incomprehensible. "I know you must go. God has other plans for us right now." He spoke in hushed tones as his heart broke. This moment would be their last goodbye as she walked away from his life. He didn't know for how long, but his love for her would never die.

And now she was here, hoping she was here to fulfill his dreams for their lives, but he knew he had to give her time. Maybe her feelings for him had changed in the past fifteen years, yet his feelings for her were still the same. Her brothers would be twenty and twenty-one now, and her sister eighteen, so the timing was right for her to return. He gazed upon her, looking as if she was still fifteen. There was a radiant glow about her that shone brighter than the sun, accentuating her beauty.

Although feeling as comfortable as always in their conversation, Amos knew they needed more time to get to know each other again. *Was Maggie planning to stay or return to Pennsylvania?* He would give her time to explain. So, Amos asked Maggie to lunch at the newly built hotel in town, and Maggie graciously accepted.

"Everything has changed. It doesn't seem as lonely as it did when our family was here fifteen years ago," replied Maggie in her calm, soothing voice. She expected to change, yet she wasn't sure how that difference would affect her. One thing she did know, Amos had stayed the same. He was still the rugged, handsome man of courage and determination. His shyness had somewhat dissipated, but she liked the new confidence she saw in him. After only one afternoon with one longing look at Amos, she knew this would be her home.

Here she was with the man she loved all these years. There had never been anyone else. The old, rugged log cabin was the same as before she left. Animals came to roost in the living quarters, yet she could make repairs. It was dusty and dirty, but she looked forward to making it her home again.

There was so much for them to talk about. Maggie shared with Amos about her life in the past fifteen years. Amos intently listened, admiring every word with compassion and yearning in her voice.

"My two brothers and sister have married. They now have families of their own. My responsibilities to my family are complete. I have left them in good hands. Ronny has his wood carving and furniture business, and Roger works at the local bank. He always did have a way with numbers. Mary is married to a fine young man of wealth. His parents own the mercantile and the post office, and he is learning much about the businesses. He particularly loves working in the mercantile. Ronny is organized and confident and loves talking with the local people. They all respect him and his family. Mary works with him at the post office and works hard to get the orders to arrive promptly. She hopes to have children someday, and I am sure we will be the first to hear when it happens!"

"It is so good to see you, Amos. Would you like to take a walk? It is a glorious day." He took Maggie's arm and led her down the sidewalk to the open meadow in the distant field. Her favorite daisies and purple cornflowers were in full bloom. Her long, silky hair was flowing as usual down her back with just a hint of curl running through it. She was still as lively and contented as the day she left.

Amos wore the cotton shirt she designed for him and his leather leggings sewn from a deer kill last fall.

Amos appeared more solid in masculine form, and his beard was coming in as a patch of wild new whiskers lined his cheekbones, chin, and lip.

"You didn't share about your mother. How is she?"

Telling about her mother was harder for Maggie to share, but Amos patiently waited for her reply. "My mother, as you know, firmly believed in the Lord. Her faith was strong even until the end. The pain of losing our father was too much to bear, the loneliness causing her heart to fail. Each year, she became weaker but held on for her children's sake the best she could.

This past year took a turn for the worse as she contracted pneumonia. She no longer had the will to live, and the Lord took her home to be with him." It was a sad, solemn time, yet Maggie's contentment guarded her through intense grief of loss. "My mother will no longer suffer; she will be with her Savior and live with her father forever."

Amos watched as the pain showed on Maggie's face. It had only been a few months, but Maggie's vitality would flourish, and the pain would lessen with each passing day. "I will always be here for you, Maggie. You can count on me."

"I love that about you. You are more loyal than anyone I know." Maggie, too, shared a deep faith. Amos had always admired this quality about her above many others. Amos and Maggie's relationship was pure as they shared their hopes and dreams of earlier times.

He felt sure he and Maggie would be man and wife someday. When the time was right, Amos would ask Maggie, once again, to be his wife.

"Would you tell me about your adventures and life in the past fifteen years?" Maggie sat with an intent ear, listening to Amos' every word.

"Please allow me to introduce you to Drifter. He has been a good companion these past few years. He helped me win the race of a lifetime."

"You did it, didn't you!" Maggie knew of his desire to enter a dog sled race, but he only had a travois when she left. She was bewildered when she saw him walking without a sled or team.

"Yes, the dog sled race. I met Mike Angora, who wanted to enter his team in one last race but didn't think he could conquer it, so I rented his team. He needed a lead dog after he lost his own. Drifter was a perfect choice. He was amazing."

Maggie was proud as he spoke of the details, having saved a man's life and winning the race.

Amos mentioned his new neighbor, Jack, and the bond they quickly shared.

The day passed quickly, and his time with Maggie ended. Amos looked forward to the rising sun, dreaming of seeing her again.

After seeing Maggie for a leisurely breakfast, Amos reminded himself why he walked to town. He used his travois with Drifter's help to carry all the fresh fruit, vegetables, and seeds to grow in his newly plowed field and daily needs that would last him again through the brutal winter.

A trip to town, being the two-day walk, was a luxury Amos could only afford every three months until now. Maggie lived in town. To see her, he would make the journey as often as possible. He felt good knowing they reconnected and their friendship would continue. Her presence meant everything to him, and the sacrifice of extra trips was well worth his time.

After Amos bought his supplies, sleep was on his mind, so he bedded in the hotel as always when he came to town.

Drifter was allowed in the room with him. The manager of the hotel respected and trusted Drifter. He was a clean, well-kept dog, so no one worried about fleas or disease. He knew Amos's love for the dog and admired Amos's integrity and authentic character. Not many dogs were allowed in the hotel, but Drifter was different. He became the town's treasure and trusted companion.

Joshua, who managed the Inn, felt a little safer with him around, like his private guard dog, and everyone nearby loved seeing Drifter.

A delightful array of colors filled the valley. The air smelled of freshly fallen dew. The crisp coolness brushed against Amos' skin. Amos walked a short distance to the nearby schoolhouse.

Maggie tended to her children at the school where she acquired a teaching position. She looked so content and happy as she guided their hearts and minds. Teaching school was the perfect place for her. Her gift was hospitality to other people. She had a gentle way about her, especially with children.

He repeatedly saw how she cared for her younger siblings. They had plenty of good food and clothes for each occasion. Working with children was her special gift. She fits perfectly at home here.

Amos thought she would make the perfect mother, not to mention a wife. The life she always wanted was just around the corner. Her countenance now was more angelic than he could have ever remembered. She greeted him and said their goodbyes before he returned home. They longingly looked at each other, realizing that a momentous occasion was about to begin.

"I love you more than I can express," Amos replied, caressing her arms and looking into her deep blue eyes.

"You have always been the love I dreamed about." Maggie was fulfilled on this day and would remain with Amos always.

Fever Scare

Amos gathered his things and draped some supply packs across Drifter's back. Amos made a leather pouch from deer skins that he had tanned years earlier. He knew this leather would come in handy someday. The bag was perfect for easing Amos's load, and Drifter was pleased knowing he was helping Amos.

The trip to his cabin was a pleasant one. The song of blackbirds, robins, meadowlarks, and lark bunting carried their melodious tunes. There was no hurry to reach home. The weather provided an opportunity for a leisurely walk through the glorious valley of lavender, sage, and lilies.

They were nearing one of the quietest spots near an old poplar tree that grew away from other trees of its kind. Amos lifted the pouch from Drifter's back and then his own. He placed them on the ground to provide a pillow for his weary head. The two-day journey turned into three as he and Drifter enjoyed each other's company. Drifter was ready for a restful sleep. Amos gently closed his eyes and dreamed of days in the past.

When they awoke, the twilight hours had fallen upon them. They were more tired than they thought, for the one-hour nap became several more. They knew at this moment in time they would be spending the night here. That didn't seem to bother either one of them. Gazing upon the bright sky would be a delight—a perfect way to sleep some more. The nights could get very cold in the Canadian mountains, but Amos had ample warm items to get him through the night. Amos tied a piece of canvas to a branch of the poplar tree as a cover in case of rain and dew. His flint, steel, and char-cloth had come in handy more than once. The hunger swelled inside him as he realized he had not eaten since early that afternoon with Maggie. Amos prepared a fire and heated some beans. He threw in a few pieces of venison jerky and dug in. The taste of beans was always one of Amos' favorites under an open pit fire. Drifter looked up at Amos longingly as Amos replied with a gentle voice. "You didn't think I would forget about you, ol' boy?" Drifter's slight whimper and perky ears told Amos he understood.

The night had been restful, waking to a clear blue sky again. They would reach the cabin by noon. It would be a welcome sight. Amos' legs and muscles were tired, but he needed to put the supplies away before spoilage and mildew began.

They were nearly approaching the cabin when they noticed the opened door and smoke rising into the sky from his fireplace. "What could it be, Drifter? Let's make our way cautiously to the front. We don't want to alert anyone that might harm us. Quiet now, boy."

Drifter obeyed as Amos stealthily walked toward the front door. He peered through the crack and spied two men rummaging through his things. He promptly set his fingers on the long rifle, ready to shoot, when one man turned around. Amos quickly set his rifle near the front entrance and welcomed his guests. "Hello, dear friend," spoke Keomi while his brother Ketami continued looking for a unique blend of healing herbs.

"What has happened here?"

"Jack is ill. We knew you had some herbal medicines we traded with you last time we were together and hoped they were still here." There wasn't time to explain how they knew of Jack's illness. All that mattered now was reaching Jack in time.

Amos gathered the herbs from his wooden supply box and quickly attached the harness pockets to Drifter, with the herbs sending him on his way to Jack's place. Amos and Keomi promptly followed, with Ketami in a close trek behind them.

At an average pace, reaching the cabin would take two hours, and Jack's life was in danger. Amos' adrenaline was pushing him along with Keomi by his side. After traveling for two days from town, his lungs weakened, but Jack needed his help. Running unusually fast became a necessary but temporary moment of discomfort. He prayed as he ran through the vast forest that he would reach Jack in time for a quick recovery.

When Drifter arrived at Jack's house with the medicinal herbs, the Wilsons had already been there for some time. They recognized Drifter and welcomed him. The Wilsons placed a note around his neck with the willow bark herbs and quinine to bring down the fever. They quickly administered them, hoping to bring down Jack's temperature quicker than their cold rags and English tea. He received them well and could slowly swallow, unaware of the situation. Only time would tell what his condition would be. The evening rolled on, and still, there was no improvement. They gave him another dose of the potent purple coneflower and honey concoction.

Cora's face lit up when she saw Amos appear through the door. His face was exhibiting whiteness, and he was short of breath. But he was here now. Amos and Keomi, and now Ketami, were intently watching on while Amos lifted a prayer to his Lord. "Please, give Jack the strength to survive, and bring his fever down quickly. Thank you, Lord, for your mercy and promises. Amen."

It had been a long, exhausting journey from the two full days. God gave him the strength to conquer it with overwhelming power, but not without consequence. Amos needed rest as well. So, Cora brought him a warm blanket to avoid a chill or fever from setting in. They knew of his strong faith and how it always pulled him through in the toughest of times, and this was no exception.

The Wilsons exemplified compassion and showed skillful expertise to Jack, never having left his side. They had become especially fond of Jack, who reminded them of someone but unsure of whom. Their cabin is just a few hundred yards from Jack's, and they often visited. "We were going for our daily walk and thought we would stop in and say hello to Jack when we knocked on his front door. No one answered, so we gently tipped the door to surprise him. Only we were shocked to find him slumped over on the floor. He looked so pale and felt hot. We carried him over to his bed and quickly applied cold rags to cool down his feverish body. He had some tea leaves given to him when we first met from Ireland. We hoped the herbs would help, but they weren't working. You will never know how pleased we were to see Drifter enter the door." Drifter felt pleased receiving hugs and gentle pats upon his broad shoulders.

The night dragged on for hours. Jack was going in and out of consciousness while the Wilsons applied the unique blend of herbs and honey as often as Jack could handle their contents. They also spread crushed herbs on a damp cloth and rubbed them all over his face, chest, arms, and back, working hard to save his life.

Finally, morning came, and the fever seemed to be breaking, but Jack was weak. Amos held his hand while fervently praying for Jack's life as he dozed peacefully.

Days before Jack awoke, Cora told Amos that Jack asked for him. He repeatedly said, "I'm sorry; I'm so sorry for what I have done. Please don't take my child away." Neither of them knew what he was talking about nor of any child. He was delirious, the only explanation.

Amos approached his bedside, relief showing at the sight of his friend. "Jack, it is so good to see you smiling. You are quite the trooper!" Jack had no idea what all the fuss was about, nor why all these people gathered around him. Nonetheless, he gave a bright smile to all. Jack recalled Amos' voice and knew something was wrong. He always loved hearing him read from the Bible. Amos's deep, soothing voice reminded him of his estranged father.

Even though Jack had not accepted the Lord as his personal Savior, God tugged on his heart. So, Amos read one of his favorite chapters from the book of John. Jack cheerfully accepted as his face shone with peace.

Jack had been sleeping for eighteen hours straight since his illness struck two days earlier.

"I've seen this kind of sickness before. In the city, many died from it," Cora said discontentedly. "It was rare that anyone recovered quickly from it, if at all." The Scarlet Fever was a severe and deadly disease. She paused for just a moment, thinking about her words. She had no desire to upset or worry anyone, but he needed to tell the facts. They had no idea where Jack contracted the disease but hoped it would not spread — many hours had passed again.

Jack awoke for a short period of dozing off into a more restful sleep the second time. The medicine had taken effect, and his breathing patterns were regular. Jack had made it through the most robust portion of his illness but needed more time to regain his strength.

After a few weeks, Jack was ready to sit up and eat a healthy meal. Amos and Drifter had been by his side daily. Jack didn't remember what happened to him. When they told him about his delirium, he hoped he hadn't given any indication about his past. He trusted Amos but was not ready to reveal his mistakes or the poor decisions that ruined his life.

The Eskimos, Keomi and Ketami, and the Wilsons went to their separate homes shortly after Jack's fever broke. There was no need for them to stay. He was in good hands. And the Wilsons were never very far away. Drifter rested his head on Jack's lap and looked up at him with ears pricked forward and eyes that gazed into his. Jack gently patted and rubbed behind Drifter's ears in thankful admiration. "Thank you, Drifter, for being here." He wagged his tail in total satisfaction as Jack patted his thick neck.

Amos shared about the Lord during these past few weeks. Jack was close to accepting Christ's forgiveness. He knew how the Wilsons and Amos had that in common. He longed to have what they had but did not feel worthy of the Lord's love. Jack appeared to understand God's love and impartiality, but there was a reluctance that Amos did not understand. It needed to be in the Lord's timing. He prayed one last prayer with him before making his journey home.

Amos returned home to tidy up and put away his supplies. He hoped they were okay and had not spoiled. The coolness of the night air would have helped. When he left to help Jack, all his supplies were scattered about the room, but when he returned home, they were neatly arranged. The rough-hewn wooden floor looked swept, and someone cleaned the soot from the grate. *It had to be Keomi and Ketami.* His thoughts were confirmed when he saw a hand-carved sculpture of Drifter lying on the fireplace mound. It was the handiwork of the Eskimos, with its detailed look and smooth, sleek appearance. They had touched his life; he now knew they reciprocated the same feeling.

When he entered the other room, a fresh floral scent with a familiar aroma awaited him. He knew this couldn't be the Eskimos. He glanced around to find her standing there, looking at him longingly. "Maggie, you are a pleasant sight to see."

Surprise filled Amos' heart with wonder and question, "I have something to share with you, Amos."

"Come look outside. I think you will be pleased."

Amos walked from his door and saw a beautifully enhanced open carriage, "This is wonderful. How did you manage to get it here?"

My family had it sent over by ship from Pennsylvania. She hoped her presence would be a welcome surprise. She wanted to see Amos, and this long two-day trek would not allow much of that. The finely crafted carriage capable of traveling through rough terrain would cut the trip in half.

She was on her way to Amos when she passed Mrs. Wilson. She kept her secret, allowing Maggie to store the carriage at their house until the proper moment to surprise Amos. The road they both traveled was rough but passable. The other direction is how Amos always went: a shorter distance traveling by foot.

Maggie dealt with the Scarlet Fever before. She had volunteered at the small hospital near her aunt Caroline's home in Pennsylvania. Her aunt had often scolded her and felt she was foolish to expose herself to indigents and their diseases. But Maggie had insisted, so her aunt reluctantly agreed. One time, Maggie nearly escaped exposure to the Fever, but God spared her to help others.

75

She could reach the cabin in a day using the horse-drawn carriage. Some old friends living in a nearby town in Pennsylvania had neatly preserved her carriage and had it shipped when they heard of her destination to Canada. Of course, they thought she was foolish, but what could they do? Maggie was kind and determined, and they treasured the friendship between her and her mother. So they gathered a donation and had it sent to her. When the medicine arrived, Maggie knew what to do, sharing it with Amos.

"Harold told me about Jack's sickness, and I immediately offered assistance. I guided them with herb remedies, and they obliged," Maggie said.

"The two Eskimos arrived at the cabin soon after Maggie when they saw us racing toward the cabin. They had been setting traps nearby and longed to greet their long-time friends."

Maggie watched over Jack for one day now. The Eskimos had no idea who or why she was there, but she appeared to them as a glowing angel spirit sent to help. They believed in magical and mysterious things happening and thought the gods sent her. They diligently obeyed when she asked them to help.

They knew Amos' cabin and thought to go there. The thick brush covered the place about a hundred yards beyond Jack's. But, as it turned out, Harold had been sent to retrieve the wild herbs while the Eskimos headed toward Amos' cabin. He was a natural at finding the exact remedy. Cora was left behind and arrived at the cabin just before Maggie.

"Hello, my name is Maggie," looking toward Harold while gathering herbs. "I am a friend of Amos. I can help. Take me to the sick man." Cora was amazed at how Maggie took charge with authority, determination, and kindness. She was a remarkable woman.

God placed Harold and Maggie in the right place and time. "Isn't it so like God to work out this miracle," Maggie confidently said. When Cora responded with the same sentiment, she knew she found a true spiritual friend. She longed for a mentor and someone to fellowship with, and God had brought them together.

"Yes, God's timing is impeccable. He often uses the strangest situations to do his work." Maggie's gregarious laugh sent chills up Cora's spine as she chimed in with the same sentiment.

Their conversation continued for hours until Maggie realized she needed to reach her destination and deliver the carriage. Jack was in good hands, and the medicine from Amos' cabin would work as it had for many in Pennsylvania.

When she arrived at Amos' home, she hid the carriage behind his smokehouse directly north and behind the cabin. She hoped Amos would be too tired to notice it. And tired he was. God used them both on that precarious day.

The Hike

Amos visited Jack several more times after hearing of his recovery. He was still somewhat weak but could work slowly and care for himself. Jack often asked about the angelic face that guarded him so soothingly. He explained to Jack about Maggie and told him they would meet again.

After visiting with Jack for some time, Amos felt comfortable leaving him. God was watching over him, and the Wilsons were close by to help if he needed it. Amos joyfully anticipated his hike up the cliff to the canyon wall northwest of his cabin, approximately five miles from the trailhead. He longed for a hike to the hillside after his recovery from his town's journey and caring for Jack. Amos made a similar trek last summer memorable. It was a breathtaking view with its spectacular waterfall and granite cliff. He looked forward to taking it all in once again.

They began their hike with much anticipation. The contrasting meadows blended delicately with rugged mountain ledges. Pure babbling stream beds set off by a powerful gush of water fell from the cliffside. As he and Drifter enjoyed the spectacular sights, Amos never forgot once to thank the Creator who had set it all in place.

Their journey led them to a dark cave nearing the edge of a cliff wall. Amos did not notice any danger signs, so he cautiously investigated the surroundings, a wondrous sight. He had not been sure of its appearance from the outside, but once inside, he knew. It was a bear cave. The smell and claw markings on the wall were signs of a bear claiming its territory. Drifter was by his side when a frantic bark came from him. Amos knew what his fate would be if he stayed. He lunged out from the cave and around the cliffside, only to come face to face with a she-cub. The mother would not be far behind. He scampered down before his presence was known. A full-grown bear sensing danger to her cubs could be a dangerous and deadly fate. Amos dashed around the bend and headed for the waterfall ledge. Once he reached this point, the grizzly would most likely stray from this precarious ledge.

Amos safely arrived on the other side and saw that Drifter was nowhere in sight. He heard a yelp from a distance. Then he saw him. Drifter was on the other side of the waterfall, defending himself from the terrified mother. Amos' instinct had been wrong. This mother was ready to protect her cubs at any cost. She was not about to let a narrow ledge barely big enough for Amos to stop her. Never had he seen such a tenacious black bear before. He encountered the trail of a Grizzly known for its unpredictable behavior, but never a big black.

One swift strike from her powerful claws would send Drifter to his death, sailing over the cliff. Drifter was up against a terrible fight. Amos called to Drifter, assuring him of his safety. Once he knew that Amos was safe, he planned his escape.

Drifter had given the mother bear a run, but the grizzly was very agile. He turned around and noticed a protruding log reaching across the ledge that would lead him to the other side. When the grizzly turned for a moment to check on her young, Drifter took advantage and leaped away from her lethal claws and powerful jaw, approaching his neck as she turned ready to strike a deadly blow.

Drifter made it safely under the waterfall near the log, which fell right where he needed to cross. The she-bear accomplished her feat. Now that the danger was gone, it was safe for her to return to her family.

If it had not been for Drifter and his courage, he would have been fighting the bear himself under a narrow waterfall ledge, which was not a pleasant thought to Amos. It was a downright terrifying thought. The pleasantness did come when he hugged Drifter mightily. Drifter could sense his anxiety and gave him a reassuring lick on the cheek. The danger had escaped them once again.

Now that Amos was relaxed, they looked forward to a delicious lunch. Amos had prepared smoked venison meat with fresh garden lettuce and a touch of chive. Some wild berries were growing near the peaceful creek bed. Amos joyously picked a handful for himself and another for Drifter.

Before they could approach the creek bed, Amos had to conquer a hazardous cliff. One Amos dreaded for many years. Every time he was here, it brought back memories of his father's death and a horse he decided not to ride ever since. The climb down the cliff was not one Amos would have naturally chosen, yet the alternative of facing an angry bear that was still lurking about was even less appealing.

Amos climbed many rocky ledges but purposely avoided this canyon wall. Even when he was a teen, this was one challenge that Amos avoided. The cliff was one he left to conquer. Amos reluctantly accepted the challenge. He now had no choice. Face an angry bear or face the cliff he always feared. Each step had to be a sure one. He thought of Drifter yet couldn't let himself lose his concentration. He trusted Drifter's resourcefulness and expected to see him at the river bed below.

The memories haunted Amos with each step. He had to focus on something else, concentrate on his footing. He thought of Maggie and his friend Jack and how God used them to help restore him to health. His fear subsided when he sang a tune his mother taught him as a young boy. Descending this cliff was a challenge that would make him a stronger person. He needed to conquer it. "Well, God, you put me here, now please help me through it," he recited as he continued to sing his tune.

The nervous tension was all he could bear until he realized he had not seen Drifter for some time. Without looking down, Amos took one more sure-footed step. He could hear many small stones crumble below him with every step. Amos was thankful that only rocks were hitting the surface below. He laughed at his ridiculous thoughts, helping him relax.

It was almost more than he could muster as he scanned for a foothold to place his next step. His hands began slipping, and the old fears came rushing back. "A mighty fortress is my God, a bulwark never failing," he hummed the beloved hymn as his hands continued to slip. Having to think quickly, he pulled his sturdy belt from the hoops around his leather hide and attached the end to a secure stump, catching his fall. It could not hold his weight for long. A small ledge large enough to keep his weight rested not ten feet below. He had to reach that ledge. His fear was building up with each thought. He had to do it. He had to jump. It was the only way. As he was ready to plunge, the belt slipped from its position, sending Amos to the ledge below. He fell with a thud. He had reached the landing, a rough landing, but he was thankful he was still alive.

He noticed he was now sitting somewhat precariously on the edge of the ledge. Positioning his footing again, he pulled himself close to the ledge wall, hugging it with all his might. His heart was almost in his throat. He closed his eyes and meditated for a moment. He achieved the challenge he dreaded for so long. He made it past the point of the deadly feat that took his father's life.

His body felt sore and tired, but there were no broken bones. He could make it the rest of the way. He dared to try. God helped him this far. He couldn't doubt it now. The challenge must be complete. He took a bold step.

With each step, he cautiously neared the bottom toward the soft meadow and gurgling stream below. He thought of how his mother had taught him to overcome his fears and how his father taught him to come prepared. That wisdom had not failed him yet.

Once reaching the bottom, Drifter came rushing to his side. He wondered which path Drifter chose and thought his way might have been more natural. Yet he was thankful for the opportunity to face the challenge he avoided all these years.

His fear of that mountainside now subsided. He could conquer about any outdoor challenge now. He never dreamed how tackling that wall would open doors for more adventures and, unfortunately, danger.

As Amos contemplated the challenge, he felt a burden lifted. There was so much bountiful land there for him to enjoy and conquer. He relished his time and sat by the river while listening to the birds chirping and squirrels rustling about building their leafy nests. The river had been one of Amos' favorite and most serene places in all the valley. He often would go with his father and spend the night under the starry sky - a memory he wanted to hold onto for a little longer.

After the escape from the bear, Amos was ready to relax with his fishing rod made from poplar. It was exciting to watch Drifter perform his new talent. He watched Drifter leap and bound like a young pup in the freshwater. It would be interesting to see who would be the first to catch their meal for the day. Amos carefully baited his line while Drifter began his skillful attempt. His first strike was a loss, but that did not deter him from his mission.

Amos' poplar fishing rod was in the water for only a few minutes when Drifter succeeded with his second attempt. "Well, you did it, boy!" Amos looked at Drifter with a simple grin.

Appetizing delicacies reached Amos' taste buds as he prepared to cook Drifter's catch. Amos prepared his flint, steel, char-cloth, and cast-iron pan to fry the fish. He also brought along a hearty meat bone for Drifter. His pack, filled with dried jerky and fruit, provided a tasty morsel to enjoy along with the fish. He was famished. The wait for the catch was deemed worth it.

The meal would not be complete without the tasty wild berries growing on the hillside. The unique blend of spices Amos brought along provided more flavor. Man and beast enjoyed the well-prepared meal together. Stomachs that once ached from hunger now hurt from a generous portion of food.

Success had been the theme for the day. A nap was what Amos and Drifter needed now. The peaceful meadow supplied just the place to rest. Amos loved this place. It was where he could open his heart to God, lifting every request to him.

Amos remembered as a child how the mountain beauty completely satisfied his hunger for the outdoors. His adoration for the wilderness taught him to respect the power of nature. Amos' father was a rugged, robust man with a gentle heart. He always wanted to be a combination of his mother and father.

His nap was peaceful, dreaming of his past until he remembered the tragic day that had changed their lives forever. He awoke to memories that almost destroyed him.

Amos' father searched for gold in his mine claim. It had been a beautiful morning filled with sweet smells of freshly bloomed wildflowers. His mother had been preparing an afternoon meal for his return. Amos remembered her singing. Her voice was so melodic. He enjoyed listening to her tone singing praises to God. His father loved the Lord, but the mine was all on his mind these days. It seemed to be taking him away more and more often.

The deed to the mine was all his. He deserved it. He searched out and found the exact point of an abundant supply. No one before him had dared the challenge of it. From his research and determination, he found his gold. He fulfilled his dream.

His parents had few possessions, but his father wanted more for Anna. He wanted her to have everything he couldn't have growing up. Anna never complained. She was content to have her husband, Amos, and God in her life. They were born and bred in this country. They knew how to live with hardships growing up. Anna never dreamed of being anywhere else. Until the day she was not coming home. After that day, life would not be the same for Amos or his father.

Time passed when Amos fell back into a deep sleep. As he dreamed again, pain filled his heart. His mother was sinking deep into the pit. His nightmares were starting to reoccur. These dreams had been gone for a long time now. He used to have them every night since the tragedy. He prayed for God's comfort and relief from the pain. He finished his prayer and looked to see his loyal friend beside him.

The one pet he had longed for as a child was here with him now. It was a welcome change to have such a loyal friend. God works in many ways, and only his timing is perfect. Amos' mother needed him to be responsible and courageous as a child. He always tried to live up to her expectations. It was not often when he failed her. One time, he thought playing outside in the weather, just appropriate for romping in the forest, was one of Amos' favorite activities. He could not resist exploring and venturing out. He usually kept an accurate track of time, but now, as an eleven-year-old, all sense of time overcame him.

He was unsure of the animal tracks he was following. It puzzled him, becoming determined to track and find this creature. After studying the tracking guide he always brought on his adventures, he decided the animal had to be a raccoon. But this raccoon seemed like a ghost. Every time he found his tracks, they disappeared again. He was not going to be defeated. Not realizing his mother was at home worrying about where her usually faithful and prompt son was, Amos continued trying to solve the mystery. Did he have this animal trapped in a tree? He began to climb the tree and capture the helpless victim, seeing the raccoon just above him one moment, then losing him again. "How could this have happened," thought the curious young Amos. Determined again, he found the beast looking up at him from the bottom of the tree. His eyes glared at him with a sly sense of accomplishment. He was now sure this raccoon had him on the run.

The raccoon and his cunning skill played an awful joke on him, a wonderful yet horrendous joke. He became more and more intrigued as time went on. How could he let an animal get the best of him? But somehow, he had. The night quickly surrounded him with darkness, and he knew his mother would be home worrying. As much as he hated to, he had to quit. He knew he must get home. It was a very humbling experience, one he would never forget.

His mother was waiting at home, worrying, just like he thought. She only scolded him for a short time and let it rest. He knew her disappointment, and that made his heart heavy. She needed him more now than ever, with his father often gone at the mine. He would try harder next time. He did not want to disappoint her again.

"Amos, I have been waiting for you. I am going to the mine to bring your father his lunch. It is long overdue. You stay here and rest. I'll be home shortly."

So, Amos obeyed. The day ended as he rested his head on the soft pillow. "I wonder what is taking Mom so long. It never takes her this long to bring Father his lunch. He continued waiting when, off in the distance, he heard a terrible wail that curled his hair on ends.

His father was coming down from the hillside carrying his mother, tears streaming down his face.

"Father, what happened?" Amos screeched.

His father did not say a word as he lay Anna on the soft feather bed. She was limp with no movement. There were terrible bruises on her face, arms, and legs. His mother was dead. Father left the house, walked to the nearby hill, and let out a terrifying cry he never heard before as it echoed through the valley below.

His mother entered the mine to surprise his father when the beam came crashing down, crushing his mother beneath. Now she was gone, and his father would never be the same again.

New Treasures

As Amos finished thinking about that terrible day. He tried to regain his focus on the present. Amos thought of checking in on Jack, taking the cut path to his place. Amos approached his door in the evening and gently knocked. Jack came to the door looking quite chipper. Jack welcomed them in. He was thinking about them, grateful for their presence in his home.

Jack looked like he completely recovered. His pink-colored cheeks returned, and his temperament was back to normal. He was happy-go-lucky once again. The doctor told Jack to take it easy, so Amos helped in every way he could. Jack looked well stocked with fresh meat and other supplies, the house looked in order, and he looked content. "There is just one thing I might ask of you?"

"Anything," Amos said.

" Tell me how you are doing. How are things with you and Maggie?"

Amos was surprised that Jack knew of her. He didn't tell him about her or their plans to marry when they were much younger.

Jack explained how the Wilsons went to town and met an old friend of Amos. He gave a wink in Amos' direction and nodded his head.

"You rascal, you!" They both laughed.

"They could tell that Maggie has extraordinary feelings for you," continued Jack. "And, now, by the look in your eye, I can tell you feel the same about her. She is indeed an amazing woman. She didn't even know me yet, came from town, and offered to help a stranger."

"She's exactly the way I remember her. Loving

unconditionally, putting others first, sacrificing her needs for others."

Jack and Amos talked for hours about their pasts, lifting Amos' spirits as they consoled each other's lives. Amos and Jack became even closer than before.

Amos prayed that the Holy Spirit would prompt Jack to accept the Lord. Sharing his adventures on the ledge and how God had protected him helped Jack see there was something different about Amos. He told of his fears and how he was able to overcome them. Jack, too, talked of the concerns he used to have and ones he still had, only he was unsure how to overcome them—the days of his past repeatedly haunted him.

"You sure do think a lot of your God, don't you?" Jack wondered about this God Amos knew.

"He is more important to me than anything," Amos said.

Jack asked many questions about a God that could love that much to sacrifice his only son. Amos knew the time was right for him to ask Jack if he was ready to accept the Lord as his personal Savior.

He looked at Amos for guidance with a repentant heart. "I am ready, Amos. I want what you and the Wilsons have. You have so much life to share and love in your hearts. I want that, too. But I didn't share something with you about my past." Amos compassionately spoke and assured forgiveness for Jack. "But you don't know what I've done or where I've been," Jack said, shaking his head. "There will be time for us to share more," now, let's pray and ask God to relieve you of this guilt.

Amos humbly prayed before the Lord God with Jack and guided his words: "Dear Lord, I know I am a sinner, and I know that you love me. Please accept me now as I give my heart to you. I want to have what Amos has. I want to serve you. Forgive me for my past wrongs. Guide my footsteps as I serve you always. Amen."

Tears welled up in both eyes as they hugged each other, sharing the Love of the Lord. "We are truly brothers now," said Amos with a genuine love toward his new fellow believer.

That was just the beginning of their new friendship of faith in God. Many tests and challenges would pave the way for Jack to serve Him. Jack's heart was sincere. Jack also knew that the Lord and Amos would be there to guide him in his new faith. Experience and time would be his teacher.

Jack was eager for the challenges ahead. He was no longer afraid to face the many trials that may come upon him. Jack had Amos' friendship and God to guide him. The time would be suitable for him to tell more about where he came from and why he was here, but now was time for rejoicing.

Drifter was outside chasing squirrels as usual for this time of day. He chased one up a tree, thinking he was frightening the animal, only to find the squirrel was playing tricks on him. The squirrel pounced from behind Drifter, catching him off guard. He then spun himself in a frenzy only to find Drifter doing the same thing, trying not to let the squirrel escape his keen eye. At this point, Drifter was so dizzy he didn't know when to stop. The squirrel outwitted Drifter again as he looked to the tree, finding him in the same spot. Drifter was not one to easily give up, but this creature had the best of Drifter for one day.

Drifter headed to the door of Jack's cabin, tuckered out. "What happened, boy? Did that squirrel get the best of you?" they laughingly teased. Drifter was a good sport. He reached his paw up into Jack's and then Amos' lap and lay his head down as if to say he was glad it was over.

The conversations he and Jack were partaking in while Drifter romped in the woods brought Jack new peace and knowledge. They were Christian brothers now.

The day ended abruptly, and Amos knew he needed to head home before the harsh weather arrived. His cabin required some attention itself. He needed to do a thorough cleaning and organize his supplies. He said goodbye to Jack and quickly stopped at the Wilson's home before returning to his own. Amos asked them to continue keeping an eye out for Jack. He also told them Jack had something significant to share with them. He knew Jack would want to say to them himself. The Wilsons looked at each other, anticipating the moment. They both hoped he accepted the Lord. They would be delighted and content when they found out.

It was an ominous clear blue sky, a vision of splendor. The color reminded Amos of the glow he saw in Maggie's eyes after seeing her earlier. He could think of nothing else but to see her again. He told Drifter he was going to make an unexpected trip into town. Drifter was always eager to go anywhere with Amos. He looked forward to the attention he still received from him.

Just as they were about to leave the door, a loud burst of sound came from the other side of the cabin. Drifter tore around the cabin to see a large moose swaying back and forth. Amos came running beside Drifter and saw the moose collapse near his feet. He was still breathing. His right hind leg looked as if some sharp object had mangled it. How it became entangled frazzled his comprehension. He asked Drifter to stay, knowing the moose was in terrible fright. He waited for the opportune moment after the moose lost consciousness. Then Amos used some of the purple coneflower ointment and dressed the wound. The chance of infection was great for this kind of injury, yet Amos knew he needed to help. The sick animal, which was enormous, regained his normal breathing movement. All Amos and Drifter could do now was wait.

A few hours passed by with no movement from the animal. Finally, unknown to Amos, he pulled himself up and ran off limping. Amos and Drifter followed his tracks far enough to know he reached the waterhole where many animals would go to finish their last days. He glanced at Drifter with a tear in his eye. He knew God had a plan for everything.

That evening, as the twilight sunset in the western skies, Amos called to Drifter. He longed to be near him. Drifter obligingly came close as Amos patted him with a firm yet gentle touch behind his ears. Drifter could sense some loneliness in his master. After quiet moments, he perked up his ears and headed toward the door. Drifter's keen senses knew someone approached. He longed for it to be someone who could brighten up Amos' spirits. Drifter's wish came true as Maggie knocked on the door.

Amos alerted to the knock, anticipating who it might be. He hoped for Maggie. His heart skipped a beat when he opened the door to find her. "Maggie, I was just thinking about you." His voice quivered a bit when he spoke. She remembered the tenderness in his speech. She would never forget his deep, sultry tone. He remembered the golden glow upon her silky blonde hair, her face radiantly filled with heavenly joy. He always knew she was a strong woman. She had the capability of brightening up any day. He always admired her devotion to her family and, above all, to her God.

"Please come and join me," Amos asked them in for some home-brewed lavender tea. I am glad you came. I longed for some companionship.

Amos went on to share what happened earlier that

morning. Maggie knew that Amos showed appreciation for God's creatures. She understood him fully. She adored his kind ruggedness and desire to serve. There were many challenges in his past. Someday, she would hear all about them. She hoped, eventually, she would become an exceptional part of his life. But for now, she was content to be with him; God would work out the rest.

As they talked about the days gone by, it seemed Maggie had always been here. Like she never left. They appeared like children once again, touching each other's lives. He understood her reasons for going. He knew her gifts were to reach out to others, never thinking of her desires. God allowed their separation to make the necessary changes to strengthen and mature their service. God came first. Amos thought of when they were falling in love, God was not first. Amos' only desire was to serve Maggie. In that case, marriage would never be successful. He understood more of why she had to go. God was developing his character, molding him to be his servant.

Amos awoke from his daydream. Maggie sat with complete quiet and serenity. She was indeed a sight to behold, not only in her outward appearance but an inward beauty that captured his heart many years earlier, as it did today.

They sat down at the rugged table Amos chopped and then carved from an old conifer tree. They began sipping tea as they looked into each other's eyes. Amos glanced up for a moment and looked outside. He noticed the carriage Maggie had shipped from Pennsylvania. "I took the carriage to a blacksmith and had it converted into a sleigh for snow travel," Maggie said. Amos liked the idea. Amos could easily change the runners back to a carriage. "I thought it would be much easier for us to see each other, Amos."

"It could be very romantic!" Amos reached out and touched her hand.

"Shall we go for a ride?" Amos persuaded.

Drifter hummed a low whine as they started toward the door.

"Of course, you can come!" Amos tipped Maggie's chin and gently brushed his fingers against her lips.

The ride in the sleigh brought back so many memories. They hadn't seen each other for years, yet it seemed like yesterday with the same tingly feeling.

The pond appeared around the corner. Amos stepped down, ready to guide Maggie, as Drifter leaped into the cool, glimmering water. "Spring is just as I remembered," Maggie said, "with its gentle breeze and serene wonder. I love this place; I love the vastness of it all. God is always so real and near here. Don't you think so, Amos?" Maggie asked in a tone that was as fresh as the Canadian spring air.

Amos replied in a robust and collected manner. "This place is where I met God. My mother and Father taught me of God and all His splendor. But this is where I came to realize His presence truly." Maggie intently listened as he shared his experiences. Maggie grew to respect him even more than ever. His humility was not a weakness but a quality she admired.

They sat quietly near the clear pond's edge, watching Drifter splash playfully in the water. "He has been a real friend for you, hasn't he." Maggie sat near the spring, giggling at Drifter's antics.

"He has been my best friend." Amos had no reservations.

Maggie said no more words but rested her head on Amos' broad, firm shoulders. The crispness in the air told them their day ended. They gathered the blanket Maggie provided thoughtfully and slowly walked toward the carriage. Drifter was resting, his head on Amos' lap, as he knew the day was ending. The ride back to the cabin was a blessed time of quiet contentment—the shared moments had brought them closer than ever before.

Maggie said goodbye and led her horse back to the destination of her home in the town. The cabin and the land Amos lived on were just as she remembered. Maggie often thought about what it would have been like to live there. She knew it wouldn't have been easy, with its harsh winters. But to Maggie, spring and summer made up for the cold temperatures of winter. She thought no other place in the world was as grand. She thought of Amos and knew he was a humble man. He was also a tremendous man of strength and honor. Thinking of the day brought her home to a peaceful slumber.

Trials, Preparations, Memories

Amos awoke bright and early that morning with a song in his heart. The morning song of the blue jay and white-throated sparrow lifted his spirits even more. The brisk spring morning gave him a thought like no other. He had been in the presence of God this morning. He could feel Him all around. He opened his Bible to the twenty-third Psalm. "The Lord is my Shepherd; I shall not want...." He continued to read when, from nowhere, came a dizzy spell. He felt very nauseous. Amos remembered this feeling once before as a child. Amos had not been sick like this since he was a child.

As Amos read some more, Amos finally set his Bible near the wooden stool, only to find himself doubled over in pain and sweat. His throat was sore for a few days, but he thought nothing of it. Amos called for Drifter, who was out on his daily squirrel chase when he heard his master's call. He bolted through the door to find Amos on the mat near the hearth. Drifter licked his face over and over again, but Amos was unconscious. Drifter bolted out the door as suddenly as he had come in and headed straight for Jack's place.

Jack was the nearest neighbor, and Drifter was anxious. "What's the matter, boy?" cautiously asked Jack. Knowing something was wrong. He grabbed his coat and some ipecac near the door as he raced toward Amos' cabin. Drifter had never behaved this way before. He only hoped Amos still had some of the special medicinals he used on him when he came down with the Scarlet Fever. He didn't know if that was the problem, but he prayed it wasn't. Drifter darted ahead, looking back occasionally to ensure Jack was still following.

It was a few hour's journey from Jack's place to Amos'. Jack knew he had to keep up an incredible pace to reach Amos in time. He heard a rumor about Scarlet Fever and how quickly symptoms came on. Continuing his trek with all his strength, he realized the situation's urgency. Even with all his anxiety, he knew God was in control. Being just a young babe in Christ, it was sometimes hard for him to remember this. He tried to continue concentrating on the faith Amos had so generously shown him. Now, God would guide him.

It was nearly noon when Jack came bursting through Amos' sturdy door. He saw him lying pale-faced on the mat. He had not moved an inch since Drifter left him early this morning. Jack carefully examined his heartbeat, which seemed to be beating even. He carried Amos to his bed and found an old, torn cloth in the wash area. Jack also found some of the same medicinals he had taken from the Eskimos when he had Scarlet Fever just weeks earlier. The dampness of the cloth on his head was starting to break the fever, yet not enough for Jack's contentment.

Drifter stared up at Jack with fear in his eyes. He grew to love Amos more than any master. John had been the only other master Drifter knew. He treated him well. He had been loyal to him, yet he had a different relationship with Amos. Amos had a quality about him Drifter could understand and love.

Jack again checked Amos' pulse, and it was racing. So, he placed more saturated cold rags upon Amos' fevered head. He remained still and limp. His face was the whiteness of snow. He continued with the cold compresses on his head, chest, arms, and legs. The mattress soaked with moisture provided a moist environment for his body to cool down.

Jack did not remember much about his treatment when he was ill. He knew the Eskimos and the Wilsons had been there. He knew an exceptional woman was there, who he now knew was close to Amos. Amos sacrificed much of his precious time to be with him. Amos was a dear and beloved friend. Whatever it took, Jack would be there for him.

As Jack thought about the weeks in solitude in his bed, he mourned for Amos. Jack knew of Amos' faith in God and how that faith had brought him to realize how mighty God was. Kneeling by Amos' side, he said a short prayer and lifted his requests humbly to God. Trusting in God was still new to Jack, but he did know God would be there to watch over Amos.

Soon after Jack finished his prayer, Amos opened his eyes. He needed to be more coherent, wondering where he was. His fever was still high. Jack made sure he gave Amos plenty of liquids. The medicine had helped him, and now it would help Amos. He mixed up a portion of the syrup and spoon-fed him. Amos slowly moved his weak head toward the spoon. He felt confident in Jack's ability to care for him. Amos looked for Drifter also, to find him right by his side. His smile of satisfaction made Jack understand the love he and his dog had for each other.

After three days, Amos' fever was still high. Jack noticed a rash on Amos' neck and face. He was sure he had Scarlet Fever. Jack knelt before his God and lifted his heart and soul in hope for his friend.

Long anticipation made it almost unbearable to Jack and Drifter. He feared for Amos' life. He had never been in such a challenging situation before. It would be a long wait. He had to think of something else while waiting for the fever to break. It could take up to two weeks. He walked toward Amos' bookshelf and found his Bible. He began to read and slowly drifted off to sleep.

Jack abruptly awoke. He heard a noise. A faint moan.

Drifter was letting out a yelp in a threatening tone. Jack stood frightened. He walked cautiously toward Amos, anticipating the worst. Listening for a regular heartbeat and hearing one, he rested easier. But something was still terribly wrong. He had never seen Drifter in such unrest. He felt Amos' head. His fever was getting worse. He quickly gathered cold cloth rags to cover his entire body. "The fever must come down, and it must. Oh, Lord, please."

There was no time to lose. Jack must get more help. He sent Drifter to the Wilsons. They would know what to do.

They gathered the needed supplies and swiftly moved toward Amos' home in their sleigh. They arrived in enough time to ease Jack's mind, making sure to give Amos plenty of liquids, willow bark tea, and quinine to lower his fever. "He needs to rest. In good time, God will handle the rest." Cora made sure Amos had the remainder of the medicine.

Jack's faith was still so new. It was hard for him to wait. But, he did wait. They all waited.

Finally, around midnight, Amos asked, "Maggie, Drifter, where are you?" Drifter perked up at once and went to his side. Amos knew everything would be fine. He could feel God's presence all around him. Knowing people who cared had been praying for him gave Amos comfort. Before saying another word, he drifted off into silence once again.

Amos awoke to find Jack and Drifter faithfully by his side. There was no worry as he rested his head again on the soft pillow. It was a calm, peaceful slumber. The fever finally broke. Now, it was just a matter of time.

The next morning brought promise as Amos sat up and spoke in his sure and steady voice. The last thing he could remember was reading the Bible. The twenty-third Psalm, "The Lord is my shepherd; I shall not want. ." He continued to read. "Yea, though I walk through the valley of the shadow of death . . ." Amos thought of these words and knew God had spoken to Him personally. God had used Amos to reach Jack, and now Jack had the opportunity to see the power of God and have his faith tested.

Amos thanked God for teaching this lesson of faith to Jack. His trust could now continue to grow. The fruit of the Spirit could blossom into Jack, producing a mighty man for God. Amos shared these thoughts with Jack as he continued to pray. He thanked God for his new Christian friend, someone he could mentor.

That morning, Amos was considerably better. Jack felt good knowing Amos could be there for him. He thanked Harold and Cora for their help and vote of confidence as they went home. They knew Jack could handle things. Jack continued nursing him back to health, providing him with what he needed.

Drifter never left Amos' side throughout the entire ordeal. Jack could see his loyalty and true nature. Drifter looked up at Jack longingly. He barked to thank him for his guidance in coming to Amos' rescue.

It had been three weeks since Amos' scare with Scarlet Fever. He now felt rested enough to continue his chores and daily activities. These activities were a pleasure for Amos. He enjoyed working, using his talents to make a living. Now that he had Drifter to help, they seemed even more enjoyable.

The summer months were approaching, and Amos needed to gather water from the nearby stream. Amos made some jugs of rawhide to carry his supply of fresh water. Amos called for Drifter and gently placed the harness across his broad shoulders. Then he brought the water, storing it in the tank behind the cabin. Amos always looked forward to drinking water from the fresh spring discovered one day on his daily walk. The refreshing crispness of the water upon his body was exhilarating as he waded at the foot of the spring. The mouth of the spring came from a slanted mountain edge that veered off past a solemn poplar tree that spread its broad limbs for all to see. Not many people traveled near that spring. There were no houses for miles around. Very few people ventured this far north.

After Amos gathered the water and carried it to the holding tank, he went to the stream again. Finally, he filled the last pouch of water.

After completing their chores, they sat near the cool, refreshing stream. Soon after, Drifter decided to take advantage of cooling himself there. The first splash seemed like ice, yet it was well worth the long-anticipated wait. Amos sat near the brink, enjoying the excitement shown by Drifter. It pleased Amos to watch him play.

Amos continued to grow fonder of Drifter with every passing day. He looked forward to his company on long mountain hikes and backpacking excursions. With Drifter along, the days passed by even quicker than before. He could always find something to amuse Amos. Amos would always smile, whether it was chasing squirrels or merely how he looked at him, with those calm, soothing eyes.

Amos usually went on these trips alone. It never bothered him, yet he still made a friend whenever he met someone. His acquaintances were usually with other trappers. They all respected Amos and his ethical way of living. He would not often meet with them in this vast country, but when he did, he was cordial.

Even though Amos enjoyed being alone, he desired to be with others. He was becoming so close to Jack and the

Wilsons. Amos thought of Maggie at this moment and wondered if God brought her here to complete his healing process after losing her before.

Although Amos dearly enjoyed thinking of Maggie, he couldn't imagine them together. She had only been back for a few months. It had been fifteen years since he last saw her. He had to give her time to settle back into this country. He wasn't sure she would want to live out here, away from town and the school, quite a different pace from what she lived in Pennsylvania. She lived in the village near her brothers and sisters and became accustomed to their ways. *Could she adapt once again to his way of life?* These thoughts of Maggie passed the time quickly. Before he knew it, the sun was setting, with its beautiful colors of orange and deep red with a hint of purple radiating through the translucent sky. A few more minutes would not matter. He sat back and absorbed all of its beauty and tranquility.

Now that Amos had plenty of water stored. He had an idea of filling the old smokehouse. A hunting trip was now in order. Even though the Scarlett Fever set him back for a time, he felt perky. His energy was back to normal. He was ready for hunting, a necessity and an opportunity that filled his days with joy.

He gathered "Trusty" and his other supplies back to the cabin and headed toward the meadow beyond. Not long after his mother passed away, he built the smokehouse. This old building had served his father and him well. He felt confident that fresh venison would soon appear in its hollow space.

Amos carefully watched his steps as he approached a bull elk grazing in the meadow. A small herd of doe was not far off. Quietly and cautiously, he prepared his rifle for a precise shot. While waiting for the exact moment, he looked at his black powder rifle. He anticipated always wanting this gun. He remembered as a six-year-old telling himself he would have it someday. After his father discovered the mine, he bought Amos the rifle and gave it to Amos shortly afterward. He would need it on the long days when he was away. His mother knew he was capable of handling it. She told him, "Papa will be very proud of you. Listen to your father, and he will teach you well." He remembered those words, and sadness filled his heart, but he would not forget their teaching.

It seemed very little time passed when another bull elk appeared around the meadow bend. This elk was even more massive than the first. Seeing two bull elk of this size near the same herd was scarce. When Amos saw the larger elk charge toward the other, he knew why. A dominant fight was soon to begin. Rising on their hind legs, the smaller one began to defend himself. The sound of cracking antlers and high whistling tones came from the beasts, filling the meadow with booming sounds. The battle continued with the younger, recognizing defeat. Lying down on the ground, the weakened elk gave up his herd. He was severely bruised and injured. The torn flesh was left open for the vultures to prey upon. Amos knew this to be a fact of survival, but still, it was hard for Amos to watch an animal suffer. With the elk in sight, he aimed carefully and took the shot.

Killing the elk did not take long, but loading him up, skinning him, and cutting the meat would. Drifter took his position in the front of the travois, ready to carry the buck to the smokehouse soon after Amos had gutted the elk. "Good-boy, Drifter. That sure was quick thinking," Amos said proudly. The beast was ready for skinning and then brought into the smokehouse. His solid hunting knife, which he received from the Wilsons this past Christmas, would serve him well in this tedious job. He learned from Sam while helping him at the Trading Post. Sam was an excellent teacher, and Amos was an eager learner.

While preparing the meat for the smokehouse, he thought of Sam. It had been a while since he last saw him. He would need to make a trip to visit him. Sam would look forward to a visit and welcome him with open arms.

The smokehouse needed some preparations before it would be ready to smoke the meat. Amos did not anticipate a kill so quickly. The animal's size would provide enough meat for the rest of the summer and then some. Amos stoked up the fire in the adequately sized smokehouse. The beef had been skillfully cut, packed, and placed in the warmth of the smoking fire. Amos wanted the meat to cure for at least ten days to get its flavor and tenderness. Some of the meat would dry into a spicy, flavorful jerky. He could almost taste the juiciness of it now. This jerky served Amos well when he was away from home for trapping, hiking, or traveling to town. While the meat was smoking, this would be just the occasion to visit Sam.

He made the preparations for his visit. The trip to the Trading Post was a day walk in the opposite direction of town. The summer months were approaching him, and Spring was becoming the past. Sam would be very busy with hunters and trappers coming to him for supplies, trading, and selling goods. He might appreciate Amos' help right now. He remembered Sam mentioning how much he would welcome his help whenever he could find the time from his busy schedule.

Drifter and Amos were rounding the last bend when they could see many trappers outside his door. Many of them were smoking and being their somewhat crude selves. They had long winter months almost behind them and were ready for storytelling and companionship.

Amos was well known in this part of the country and respected. Most of them also knew Sam would not provide them with liquor. So, when they saw Amos rounding the bend, they quickly put away the whiskey they provided for themselves and welcomed him.

Sam and Amos had seen these men many times and tried to share the Lord with them. Even though they respected them as men, they could not see to their religious ways. Their beliefs were too unpredictable for them. They were content with their way of life. It would be too hard to change now, replied many of them, although Amos never gave up praying for them and talking to them when he could.

Amos had an eventful day, more than he anticipated. The warmth emanated in the clear blue sky. Its animated show of sparkling light brought a feeling of sweet contentment. He and Drifter sat down to a relaxing break of iced tea and crumpets. Amos loved his mother's recipe. He recalled how his mother combined rich, unsweetened batter into just the right texture as she made the small round cake into curled-up wafers. Amos used her same griddle. She had just the right touch as she toasted them to a golden brown, always a tasty treat for Amos after a hard day.

He had appreciated his mother's work in that tiny kitchen, made of an old cast iron stove and pantry shelves that lined the south wall. She used an old washtub to scrub the dishes. Amos would gather water from the water storage tank every evening, then heat it on the wood-burning stove.

His mother had been a strong woman. Her faith in God excelled above all others, loving his father to the fullest. He always prayed the Lord would bring a woman he could love as much as his father loved his mother. He thought of Maggie again, then drifted off into a delightful dream of days gone by and days he was sure would come.

Festivities

The fourth of July approached. The town Amos traveled to for supplies held a yearly carnival for families throughout the territory. People from the town brought hand-made cannons forged to perfection to help increase the festive mood. Men from all around prepared their black powder rifles for the occasion. Bonfires were carefully formed and used to warm the guests. The men held the women close as they sat in the blazing warmth. Children of all ages took part in shaping booths for the carnival as Drifter wagged his tail while following Amos. There were races of all kinds and candy prizes supplied by the General Store. The ladies always brought their freshly baked goods to be bought for a fair price. Some of the single women prepared food baskets for the auction. The man who bid on the basket could enjoy a relaxing afternoon picnic with the lady who prepared the food. Adults and children could participate in square dancing.

"Amos, would you like to join me in the next dance?" Maggie looked beautiful. Amos couldn't take his eyes off her.

"I haven't danced since we were teenagers, but I can try it." Amos was shy about dancing, but he would do anything for Maggie.

As the celebration began, everyone found their place and started tapping their toes to the rhythm of the music, with each dancer taking one step for each beat. Then the dancing resumed with swinging partners to and fro. Family members, young and old, looked forward to the event. The Virginia Reel was Amos' favorite.

"Amos, you did well. I am surprised how each step flowed so nicely for you."

"Well, I couldn't have done it without an excellent

partner." Maggie swooned in Amos' arms, gliding across the dance floor.

After the enjoyable evening of dancing, Amos awoke smelling the fragrant scent of flowers in the summer breeze. He spoke to Drifter in his smooth, calming voice. "Are you ready for the celebration? Everyone will be there; Jack, the Wilsons, Sam, Mike from the sled dog race, Maggie, and the Eskimos."

Drifter looked up at Amos with a familiar look about him, almost like he sensed something, yet Amos was not quite sure what. "I'm going out to clean and prepare my black powder rifle, and cannon, Drifter," Amos questioned the look about him. "You know something, don't you ol' boy?"

Drifter continued wagging his tail and following Amos into the blossoming meadow. He looked about while sitting contently, eyeing Amos' every move. He knew Amos was excited about an event, and that was enough for Drifter to be equally excited. Whenever Amos was happy, so was Drifter.

Amos thoroughly cleaned his gun when Jack approached from around the bend. He had a pack and several bags of supplies carried on his back. Across his shoulder, he brought "Black Bullet," Jack's trusty rifle.

"Ready for the big celebration?" Jack tugged at his belt, adjusting the strap holding his rifle.

Amos reached out his hand for a big shake. "I'm so happy you decided to go along with us," Amos said.

"I wouldn't miss this celebration for the world," Jack gregariously replied. "I hear this is one of the best shows in this part of the country."

"It sure is. People from all around come to participate. I once knew of an old widow who lived alone for many years. She traveled one hundred miles for the event to find a husband." Jack and Amos roared in laughter as Drifter continued to sit contently, wondering about all the commotion.

The bright and early morning was slowly turning into mid-afternoon. "We better head out," suggested Amos, "if we don't want to miss out on the events." Jack agreed.

Drifter had quite a load in the packs across his back, but he didn't mind. He would do anything to help.

The journey into town was always an enjoyable walk. The time flew by quickly as Amos and Drifter stopped for the night. Jack brought along some of his specialty bread and jams his mother taught him how to make as a child. She showed him where to find the plumpest, juiciest berries and how to can them, turning them into delicious tangy flavors.

Amos supplied some smokehouse-cured meat from his last hunting expedition. He saved this meat for this special occasion. Of course, Amos, Jack, and Drifter decided it was worth the wait.

The conversation and food were delightful. The friends built a fire, and then Jack, Amos, and Drifter dozed off into a restful sleep under the sizeable coniferous tree.

Dawn soon arrived, and the men were packed, ready for the day's travel. The pace picked up considerably. Everyone could hear the sounds of excitement and laughter. The festivities were already underway. They arrived much later than he remembered from last year. They hoped they got all the information.

The town was just a few short steps away, and Amos could see familiar faces. The Wilsons, who had driven their wagon several days earlier to help with decorations, greeted them with a warm welcome. They embraced with warm hugs and headed toward the food buffet. Amos arranged Many homemade biscuits, muffins, jams, and other home-baked pastries on a long row of wooden tables.

They all looked so appealing; it was hard for Amos to choose one. He eventually came to where he saw some pies with a familiar look. He picked one of them and shared it with the Wilsons and Jack. It was one of the best pies Amos had eaten in a long time. He was sure he remembered the taste of the rare succulent apple and spices blended and formed to perfection. The sauces were a superb blend of nutmeg, cinnamon, sugar, and tarragon - just a touch for that bold taste of licorice. The crust was so flaky it melted in his mouth.

This pie could only come from one person. He turned slowly and gently after feeling a soft tap on his shoulder using her delicate, soft hands. It was Maggie, the one he had longed to see. Drifter wandered off shortly before and returned with Maggie by his side. "I was looking for you." Maggie batted her eyes teasingly and spoke delicately, "I sure am glad Drifter recognized me. When I saw him, I knew you weren't far off."

"I enjoyed a wonderful breakfast thanks to your pie. I recognized the special care. And after tasting it, I knew it could only come from you."

"Thank you for your compliment, kind sir."

"Would you like to lead me to the dance floor? The Virginia Reel is about to start, one of your favorites. I hope you still remember how to do it?"

Amos nodded, walking toward Maggie, "How could I forget our dance."

The dance was about to begin as they stepped into their places in the line. The music started to play, filled with joy. Hands began to clap as each partner took their turn swinging around the others down the line. People also participated in many other dances that night, yet this dance held an extraordinary memory. It was the first dance for Amos and Maggie when they were very young. He remembered those days and never dreamed how that love would blossom.

The next event involved Drifter in a sled pull. People from all over came to see this event alone. Drifter was excited as he twirled and spun, jumping all around Amos. Amos had to calm him down several times. He knew Drifter was a powerful animal with tenacity like a wolverine. The race would be challenging, but his faith in Drifter stood above the others.

This pull was to last one mile with an accurate load of rocks packed onto each sled. The sleds were marked and measured carefully. Each dog would have the same advantage. Whoever crossed the finish line first with the sled, dog, and rider would be declared the winner. Each winner received a one-year supply of staples at the General Store. Considering the distance he traveled to receive the goods, these supplies would be helpful for Amos.

Amos looked at the other teams of man and dog and thought to himself. "There sure are many fine-looking animals here. Many of them are going to be hard to beat. No matter what happens, I know God will supply all our needs. We'll do our best, won't we, Drifter!" He doubted for a moment, then looked at Drifter's keen anticipation of the event. The doubt was lifted from his mind immediately.

After an hour of planning the route and harnessing the dogs, Drifter was ready. The preparation was always the hardest because of the long wait and anticipation of the outcome. Drifter was eager, and the masters arranged the dogs against a long row of tables.

The mid-morning sun began to glare down upon the sleds and dogs. The grassy area used for the summer race appeared in fair condition. It would provide quite a different feel for Drifter being used to the brisk, cold snow.

It turned out to be a slightly warm day, indeed. Amos looked up for the support of all his friends as the black-powder gunshot was like a cannon into the sunny sky.

The race began in all its flurry. Drifter charged out ahead of the others. The strength he showed was tremendous. He knew Drifter was strong, yet never dreamed he would bypass every contestant so soon.

A steep hill was just ahead, and Drifter escalated to the top. Just beyond the ridge came a sharp turn, which Drifter handled with excellent skill and determination. A large willow tree with low-hanging branches stood in the middle of the path. Drifter's training and keen sense anticipated the move. Amos watched Drifter and followed his lead while riding on the back of the sled. His weight shifted at the right time as Drifter lunged and turned to avoid the obstacle. It was a success. Amos was thrilled at the way Drifter handled himself.

When Amos first found Drifter, he was unsure where the dog had come from. Someone must have trained him very well. Amos admired how the man trained Drifter. Amos only knew now that he was proud to be his new owner.

Drifter crossed the finish line leaps and bounds before all the other teams. The race came to an end.

Amos graciously accepted the prize certificate and held it up for Drifter to sniff. "After all, boy, you are the one that did all the work. We'll have to ensure many large steak bones are brought home with the rest of the goods." Drifter proudly looked at his master as he handed him a steak bone. "I came prepared with high hopes and faith in your abilities." Amos passed the bone to Drifter, which he accepted with an appreciative look.

Amos glanced over to see Maggie, the Wilsons, Jack,

and many other friends congratulating him and Drifter. He was excited about their joy!

They began their walk to the rest of the festivities when the loudspeaker blared, "Everyone, prepare for the bidding of the lunch baskets. Come everyone, make your choice, and get your wallets ready."

Amos sauntered over, looking for one basket. He knew there would be many bids on this basket; everyone knew what an excellent cook Maggie was. But to him, it was priceless, and he came prepared.

The widow Snead's basket began the bid. She was known for her excellent taste in bread and candies. The bids started—one dollar, two, three dollars, then four. The bidding continued until it reached ten dollars. That was quite a high price for one basket. A new man in town made the bid. The two looked like a good match. They intended to spend the day together.

He knew Lila Snead and thought her to be an elegant woman. Her husband had passed away only two years earlier. It had been tough for her to participate in any events up until now. Many of the women in town encouraged her to come. They knew the fellowship would be suitable for her. It turned out to be very eventful indeed. The two looked like they were getting along tremendously. He wished only the best for her.

The bidding continued for nearly an hour before Maggie's basket was issued. There were some delicate and incredibly assembled baskets. They each had their unique quality and personalized touch about them. He was tempted to start bidding, for some baskets looked mighty fine. But Amos held out for the one he had been waiting for since he knew Maggie was back in town.

Amos anxiously stepped forward as the bidding began.

The arena was quiet as the auctioneer started. One dollar - two dollars - three - then four. Amos heard the auctioneer say, "Ten dollars. Will anyone make it eleven?" Just as Amos was about to bid, someone jumped in before him - twelve dollars. Amos had precisely twelve dollars, and someone outbid him. He understood when he looked up and noticed who was bidding against him.

Maggie's brother came into town unexpectedly and wanted to surprise her. Amos walked over and cordially welcomed Ronny. Maggie came running out of the crowd, jumping into Ronny's arms. "How did you manage all these miles from Pennsylvania?"

Ronny had been working on planting new churches, giving his woodworking business a break, and this was the perfect time for a visit. "I'm so glad to see you. Where are the children - my niece and nephew - and Sarai?

Ronny approached calmly, "Now, slow down, Maggie." She was so excited she could hardly stop to take a breath, nearly running in front of a swiftly moving wagon.

"Sarai and the children will be here shortly. They asked me to go on before I missed seeing you. They knew the bidding on the baskets would be soon and that Amos would most likely be bidding on yours, so I took a chance and bid on the basket Amos was bidding on, hoping my hunch was right."

"I see it was. I know you have much to talk about," Amos stood mystified, listening to Ronny.

"You're probably wondering why I had to bid on Maggie's basket, knowing you would want to share a quiet lunch with Maggie."

Maggie and Amos looked at each other, "Well, the thought crossed my mind."Amos and Maggie stared into her brother's eyes.

"I knew that was one sure way of seeing both of you simultaneously, and I wanted to help fund the new church. We have been prospering in Pennsylvania. The church is growing, with many new families coming in. A young, eager assistant pastor helped expand the ministry and is ready to become a head pastor. God's new church in Pennsylvania is strong. I loved my devoted congregation but listened to God calling me here. We missed seeing these magnificent mountains with all their wonder and glory. That is why we're here. Sarai and I heard of your town building a new church and that they were looking for a pastor.

Surprised and delighted looks appeared on Amos' and Maggie's faces. Ronny knew they received the message well, and they were pleased.

Maggie's brother continued with his story. He shared how much Sarai longed to live in this country and how she had a heart for God and wanted to serve Him wherever he placed her. God was calling them to a ministry, and they were faithful. They prayed about other opportunities, but it was time to move when they heard of a need for a pastor in the town where Maggie and Ronny grew up. Someday, they would return and visit their congregation in Pennsylvania, but this is where Ronny and Sarai belonged once again.

A tasty lunch basket turned out to be a pleasant event as brother and sister were reunited. It brought joy to Amos' heart as the love lit up Maggie's face at this very moment.

The turn of events was undoubtedly different than Amos anticipated. God would provide the funds to build the new parish that this little community desperately needed. Amos longed for a place of worship with other believers. Even though Amos could rarely attend services, he knew Ronny was preaching a powerful message. He thanked God for bringing

Ronny home.

Amos looked for Drifter as the fireworks display was about to begin. Drifter wandered off to find Mike and his team of dogs. The sled team bonded after the sled dog race last winter. Amos had an inkling that was where he would be. He was happy Drifter had an opportunity to be with others of his kind. The change of pace would be good for Drifter. As Amos approached, Drifter recognized his sound and came running. He was enjoying his little excursion, yet happy to be beside Amos.

Returning to Maggie's and Ronny's presence, Amos lay down a warm, soft blanket on the cool grassy area near the fireworks display. Everyone cheered and clapped after each show of color. The town mayor would shoot the black powder rifles and cannons in the grand finale, in which Amos was to participate.

After all the events, folks gathered their things and celebrated through the night, dancing around a bonfire that lit up the clear night skies.

Ronny approached Maggie to dance near the luminous light under the crescent moon. Amos followed his lead, ending the glorious evening.

The night ended with farewells and longing goodbyes. The peaceful rest and warmth of home were soon awaiting them. Everyone settled into their warm beds, bringing peace and tranquility throughout the town. Amos, Drifter, Jack, and Mike nestled around the small bonfire and discussed the day's events. Drifter laid his head in Amos' warm lap, and soon, they all drifted off into a restful slumber under the clear, starry sky.

The following day was thrilling. The friends gathered their things, packing them neatly and ready to load on the wagon, carrying many people to their homes far away. It had been a successful event for all the town merchants. The funds for building the church came in with some left to buy Bibles and songbooks. Ronny was excited beyond belief that the Lord provided so quickly.

The construction of the new parish would begin in the morning. The new pastor invited Amos, Jack, Mike, and Sam to participate in designing the building. Some were already starting to chop down trees, while others managed to shave the bark and branches from the timber. Because of the help and craftsmanship of so many townspeople, they would be able to start services the next month.

Sarai and Ronny prayed for many months about their move. They were certain the Lord had brought them here. The people were excited and hungry for the Word of God. Many were coming to know the Lord, yet others had not heard the Gospel. Ronny prepared his heart and was ready for the challenge. Amos and Jack expressed their full support for his work.

Amos and Jack began working on the building. It had been one month since they camped under the luminous sky, enjoying each other's company.

The sun's warmth with a few clouds for coolness allowed all the men the opportunity to look at their handiwork. They were delighted with the results. The townspeople were amazed at how fast it was built and excited about the first service.

Ronny's eyes cascaded tears of joy as he saw the Lord at work. He always dreamed of a church like this one to make his home. Now, his dream has become a reality.

"Services will begin next Sunday. Everyone, come prepared to receive a blessing from the Lord," Ronny announced as he stood on the front step of the church.

Amos and Jack stayed for one more week. They couldn't miss the first service. Drifter saw the excitement on Amos' face. He knew his master was pleased. Drifter often shared in Amos' moods. He could sense his desire for solitude and his desire to be comforted. He knew his anxious moments and the calm, restful times most familiar to Amos. Drifter's loyalty showed that his master was extraordinary and Drifter, as Amos thought, was no ordinary dog.

In the first service, Ronny gave an elaborate expository sermon on atonement. Christ's love shone in Ronny's face as he spoke of God's love, sending His son to shed blood for all.

Tears welled up in Maggie and Amos' eyes. The atmosphere was one of contentment and peace. He could sense the Holy Spirit at work as many people came forward after Ronny gave the altar call.

Amos did not know that his two Eskimo friends, Keomi and Ketami, were sitting in the back with tears flowing down their dark cheeks. Amos had no way of knowing whether they had accepted the Lord yet, but he would ensure the opportunity would come to talk with them.

As the pastor preached the first sermon in the new church building, the Fourth of July celebration ended, and his precious time with Maggie would soon be over. It was now time for his journey home to his cabin in the wilderness. The anticipation of reaching home more than a month away was a much-needed endeavor. Drifter shared this feeling as well. Amos said goodbyes to all his beloved friends, and he was on foot again, traveling home.

The journey was exquisite, as usual. Drifter began his typical chase of squirrels and rabbits - never intending to hurt them, of course - while Amos stood in awe of God's wonder.

Jack decided to travel home earlier than Amos. Jack

had to clean around his cabin and knew Amos and Maggie would want to spend time together without interruptions or feeling rushed by him. His journey was a peaceful rest, absorbing the message from Ronny's first sermon. It was the first time Jack heard the word "atonement," and he had many questions. He saved them all up for an opportunity to share with Amos. Ronny had a gift for helping people understand God's word and trusted Amos' knowledge of the Scriptures. Amos was a man of much wisdom and looked forward to gleaning from that understanding.

Amos neared his cabin as the sun began to shine a beautiful array of colors. Drifter sensed someone in the house but recognized the scent of familiarity. Amos knew who was there. The Eskimos greeted Amos with arms opened wide. Amos noticed something different about Keomi and Ketami's countenances. He was excited as they told them about their acceptance of the God Amos shared with them so often. Drifter sensed Amos' excitement and shared in his joy. He performed his dance routine to show his pleasure.

Hugs lasted unusually long this time. The Eskimos would now be together in God's kingdom with Amos, Jack, and the many other lives Amos so generously touched.

The Eskimo friends could stay the night. They had a long journey to their home and people. They committed to preaching the true gospel to the native people of their land. They committed to God and wanted Amos to hold them accountable in his prayers. Amos felt honored and promised to engage them in prayer daily. He knew the road would not be easy. Native Eskimo tribes held to their superstitious ways. But Amos learned through the years that love could conquer, and Keomi and Ketami had persuasive determination. They could reach those of their native tongue in a way Amos could not.

The men left without fear or doubt. God would guide their way.

Gold Mine of Blessings

The day was filled with wonder and surprise as Amos and Drifter headed toward the mountain range behind their home a few miles away. Amos often dug for gold in these hills and acquired a small amount, which he stored in a locked box hidden behind a loose brick in his fireplace structure. It was very obscure as Amos searched for its presence this last time. He anticipated his trip would be good if he found more gold. His departure predicted complete satisfaction.

His excursion began as he gathered his gold pan and other supplies and headed toward the mountain. Amos substantially placed his sluice-way. Everything looked in order, exactly how Amos left it. This particular canal served him well.

As he approached, he noticed the rain washed away the water's entrance. The residue of mineral deposits settled in the sluice box. Drifter was by Amos' side when he spied a large chunk of rock at the entrance of the sluiceway. Amos looked with anticipation by carefully examining the contents. Amos gathered the pebbles and rinsed them in the flowing stream below. He swished the water around, allowing the gold to find its place in the bottom of the pan. As Amos eagerly anticipated, there was abundant gold throughout the area. The excitement soared. Amos never in his life saw such a wealth of beauty.

Amos safely stored the contents in his pack. The water freely flowed while Amos used his gold pan for more gold. The water swished in the pan as he moved it in a circular motion. Some more specks of gold ore were at the bottom of the pan. Amos continued the adventure while Drifter waited with hopeful expectation.

Time flew by, and neither noticed how late it had become. Nighttime's golden glow approached. Amos calmly spoke to Drifter. " It's time to place the contents in the pack." Amos draped them over Drifter's strong shoulders as he proudly served his master.

Amos came prepared. The small lantern Jack gave him was perfect for carrying in a pack. The light would provide them with a safe night's journey home.

The cabin would soon be near, and they would be safe inside; what seemed like out of nowhere, Amos noticed smoke rising above the nearby mountain ledge, and Amos' cabin was just below. Once they neared the edge of the distant meadow, there was a blaze of flames.

There had been some frightening lightning streaks earlier the previous morning; the land was arid for this time of year. That's when it must have happened. The flames swiftly moved across the meadow. The destruction occurred across many acres of land. Amos' cabin would be right in the direct line of traveling flames. Hopefully, the lake and stream near his cabin would quench many flames. He hoped they could not go any further once they reached the water. The extensive stream ran east and west just opposite the direction of the fire.

As Amos and Drifter came to the mountain's edge and looked below, they saw the overflowing lake and stream quench most of the fire. However, some flames managed to jump the river, heading straight toward his smokehouse and cabin.

Drifter dashed ahead, running toward Jack and the Wilson's place. They would be able to help. But even with their quick arrival, more help would need to arrive soon before the flames reached the cabin a few miles from where Amos was walking.

Drifter charged with all the force he could muster to reach Jack in time. Jack saw the smoke before Drifter arrived. He was on a small hunting trip and just returned to smell the acrid scent. As soon as Jack was aware of the disaster, he gathered what he would need to help. Jack came running when he met Drifter close to the burning flames. He knew at once Drifter's bark, and Drifter was never happier to see Jack than now. He was quickly ready, dashing toward the home with buckets in hand.

The Wilsons gathered buckets and charged forth in their wagon. The journey was quick as the powerful horses raced to the danger. Luckily, the flames were leading toward the stream, yet a few flickers escaped the path heading toward the cabin.

Amos ran with all his might, for he was still some distance away to help. He could see the flames and felt helpless as there was no way around them. Amos stood back while looking down upon all the burning land and his smokehouse going up in flames. At this moment, he knew he had to rely on God's prevention of the fire spreading any further. He prayed for His mercy in protecting this beautiful land and keeping all the generous people who came to help safe.

Soon, more help arrived. The Wilsons were now in view as they peered around the bend where Amos could see them.

Amos saw buckets of water showering onto the blazing flames, but they couldn't contain the fire. His smokehouse burned to the ground, and the back side of his cabin was in flames. His homestead was quickly fading into the distance. He thought of Maggie, and he knew God's plan. The couple would need a larger home, and Amos' reluctance to move forward in their relationship needed a push from God.

"Thank you for pushing me along, Lord, but this will be a lot of work." Amos lost his year's meat supply from the previous hunting trip and most of the furniture he carefully handcrafted. Building a new home would now push Amos toward a fresh start.

Just as he lost all hope of saving his cabin, God graciously answered his prayer as lightning and thunder sent an array of mist, quickly turning into a heavy shower down to the surface of the flames. The rain saved the front half of the cabin. The steady flow of water from the sky seemed so gratifying at this very moment. Everyone stood out in the rain, absorbing the moisture without concern about how wet they were becoming. As the rain slowed to a soothing calm, the friends laughed at each other's appearance. It was quite a sight as water dripped from their hair and clothing. They rejoiced that much of the meadow was still there and everyone around was safe.

All the friends gathered around the warmth of Amos's glowing fire in his pit below the cabin. The sun peered from around the clouds, and a beam of light began to dry the soaking guests.

"What will you do now?" asked many of the helpers.

"I know God has a plan for all of this. I am so blessed to have such loyal friends and prompt help. I will need to rebuild soon," Amos spoke in hushed tones.

"You are welcome to stay with us." Jack and the Wilsons hunched over in exhaustion.

The next morning brought a fresh feeling of newness and anxiety. Most of Amos' possessions were gone, but his life would improve.

After all the friends returned to their separate homes,

Amos took Drifter and himself for another excursion to the hills. That would give Amos time to contemplate the previous few days and consider what he needed to do next.

Before Amos and Drifter began their ascent to the hills, some jerky, fruit, and water bottles given to Sam were placed in Amos' backpack. Amos closed his eyes, took a deep breath, and headed to his favorite mountain ledge. His eyes became transfixed at the beauty of the rolling hills that lie just below the rugged cliffs of the canyon. Much of the burnt meadow and trees would be evident for quite some time. The regrowth would happen soon, and the land would flourish once again.

He remembered his last climb, facing a fear he never could as a child. God helped him overcome this ledge with its impressive steepness and massive boulders connected in full view. Another challenge would soon be upon him.

After stopping at the lower waterfall, the two followed the stream bed to the narrow trail leading to the water's source, crashing down the cliff below. It was a good hike. The weather held up as the sun shone through a thunderhead cloud some distance away. Recent heavy rains had eroded part of the trail they would soon cross, but that didn't hinder their enthusiasm.

They stopped momentarily to admire the sights when a terrifying roar came from a rocky ledge above. Amos stood stunned. He had never seen a lion of this magnitude in these hills before. Drifter stayed close by his master's side; it could be disastrous for Amos. They stood perfectly still in silence while watching the creature's every move. He pranced back and forth, carefully overlooking the victims.

Amos slowly reached for his trusty rifle, which he carried whenever he left his cabin. The rifle was a beautiful artistry made by the J&S Hawken rifle company. The almost full-length stock structure of highly figured maple caught one's eye when looking at it. The octagonal barrel was a full thirty-four inches, making it more accurate than the common thirty-inch variety. He often browned the barrel, offering protection from the elements. The 54-caliber gun could easily take down an elk at one hundred yards, and it was more than sufficient for smaller animals.

Amos held the rifle in the sling over his shoulder. He slowly reached behind and placed the black powder in the barrel. Amos used the ramrod to push the patch and lead ball until it was seated down at the bottom. The percussion cap was now in Amos' hand, ready to be placed on the nipple; he had succeeded without drawing further suspicion.

Amos cocked his rifle when what seemed like a flash of light, Drifter charged toward the leaping lion. He nicked the lion's heel, sending the lion down with a jolt. The lion became stunned only momentarily when his ferocious speed charged again at Amos. Drifter caught his heel once again, and the fight was on. Drifter's tenacity took over as he lunged at the lion's throat, weakening the lion for only a moment. The lion was still too mighty for Drifter to hold him off much longer. He had fought for his master until his strength was no more. Suddenly, Drifter flew in a sudden jolt, landing him on the cliff's edge!

Amos aimed his gun to shoot with the lion in sight when the eroded ledge he was standing on gave way. The lion was already in full flight toward Amos when he lunged out of the way while watching the lion soar to the bottom of the canyon wall to its death. Amos went over the cliff with the lion but was able to grab onto a sturdy tree branch nearly ten yards below the surface of the eroded ledge. He knew his strength would not last as the tree was about to give way. Reaching behind his back, Amos grabbed the rope carefully placed inside his backpack for easy access. He swung the rope, hoping it would become attached to some point. His grip was on the line, securely tied and placed around his waist. He could feel it tighten as the tree gave way. Amos again went sailing a few more feet, interrupted by an abrupt slam into a massive rock against the canyon wall. The rope attached itself to a long, sharp boulder point extending near the surface where Amos hung unconscious.

Drifter was still lying where the lion threw him. He was deeply wounded and wrung out of energy. His left front shoulder blade had a deep gash from the lion's powerful claws and sharp teeth. He looked up long enough to see Amos tossed over the cliff's edge. Drifter's hurtful yelp could be heard throughout the canyon as he cried for his beloved master. Drifter tried to move but to no avail. He had fought deftly, risking his own life to save Amos'. His only thought at this moment was to search for his master. He knew Amos would need his help, so he put aside any feelings of pain and forced himself to his unsteady feet.

The second attempt sent him falling to the ground once again. Finally, in one last effort, he was successful. His two hind legs were healthy, with no apparent sign of wounds. His right front leg had some scrapes and slight bleeding, yet they were strong enough to carry his weight while he limped with the other. He peered over the edge to see Amos still fastened to the rope. There was no way he could reach Amos without falling himself. His only chance of saving Amos was to walk to the nearest home.

He knew Jack and Wilson's homes were far from these mountains. The closest friend's house was Sam at the Trading Post. He remembered the way and knew it was Amos' only chance. Still, it would be a day's walk, yet it would probably take longer in Drifter's condition. He had to try.

He managed to make his way down the other side, where a calm meadow with a fresh stream lay below. Wounded and in immense pain, he made his way to cold water. Lying in the pool would nurse and anesthetize his wounds. His front shoulder ached beyond belief, but Amos' life depended on him. The gash in his leg was still bleeding. His only instinct was to rest in the water until the pain lessened. After a half hour, Drifter felt like continuing his journey. He could not think of the pain. He had to walk steadily to reach Sam before they lost their lives.

Drifter was nearing the last curve that would take him to Sam's. The bleeding slowed down a bit but was still flowing steadily. He could feel himself weakening, unable to bear the pain. Only a little further and help would come. Slower and slower became his pace. He began to feel dizzy, losing his sense of direction. A few more steps kept filling his mind. Soon, he would be close enough for someone to see him. He was still in the thick brush where his presence would not be known. Ten more yards and he could be in the clearing, nearly one hundred yards from the Trading Post. He began to waver back and forth until total collapse was his fate. As he fell, he barked one dynamic sound heard through the Trading Post window.

Sam was sitting at his window when a very unusual-sounding yelp caught his attention. He set down some tools he was cleaning to investigate. Sam searched the premises, ready to return, when a bundle of silver-colored fur off in the distance caught his attention. His first notion was a wolf, but he had not seen wolves in nearly a year. He returned to the Trading Post's living quarters, prepared his black powder pistol, and headed toward the brush. As he neared Drifter, he recognized his stature. Even in Drifter's state, Sam knew it could only be him. He picked up his one hundred-twenty-pound stocky body and carried him to safety after nursing his wounds and stitching a deep cut.

Sam began to wonder what happened. Drifter and Amos always traveled together, never one without the other. Something was wrong. He wished Drifter was strong enough to guide him to Amos' presence.

It was nearing nightfall when Sam went in search of Amos. He thought of the path he usually took when coming to the Trading Post and retraced his route. But a wound like that of Drifter's could only come from one animal. He had not seen a mountain lion in these hills for a while, especially one that would do this kind of damage to a mighty beast like Drifter. Thinking of this wound, he headed for the high mountain cliff wall where he last saw an animal of this kind. There would be no chance of finding any trace of Amos without Drifter's guidance, especially now having to face the approaching darkness.

Sam found a soft bed of grass for the night. He wanted to start his search again after the first sign of light. He said a quiet prayer upholding his friend and Drifter's quick recovery.

Drifter lay content to rest soundly, sleeping while allowing his body to recuperate. It was nearly morning when Drifter felt like moving. Full strength did not come to him entirely, yet the wound began healing. Any quick movement from him could cause more damage and no chance of rescuing Amos. But the tenacity of Drifter drove him to try. He began lifting himself from the soft bed Sam provided. The first attempt was successful, but his head spun around, causing him to fall again upon the soft bed below. He rested his head once again.

Drifter needed to gain his strength back. He felt a surge of pain flow through his body with unbearable pain. He was anxious about Amos, his beloved master. He somehow felt useless, yet without even knowing it, Drifter succeeded in rescuing his master by reaching Sam in time.

Sam woke up at dawn with all his gear on his back. He continued his ascent toward the vast mountain wall. He used his keen sense of tracking to guide him. Drifter, sure enough, had been in the stream, and his tracks were apparent. Another set was also visible. Just as Sam predicted, a Mountain Lion. He continued to follow the prints that led him to the cliff. It was apparent that a fight had ensued. He directed himself away from the mess of tracks. Coming across a fresh impression of Drifter's paw led to the edge of a cliff. Sam looked over in hopes of finding his friend.

Amos had been dangling with no apparent sign of consciousness. His body had a rope attached to his waist secured around a boulder. Sam reached far enough to grasp the dangling line, but the weight of Amos was too much for Sam to handle.

Sam climbed back up the cliff while thinking of a plan. If only his trusty workhorse could make it up this rocky height. But he couldn't think of that right now. He had to come up with a plan to rescue his friend.

Amos last remembered being hung by a rope on the cliff's edge with one broken rib and a dislocated shoulder when he awoke to find himself in a soft feather bed. He was unsure where he was or what happened these past days. Amos did not realize his unconscious state lasted nearly a week. The people above him were familiar, yet he did not know who they were. He was only awake momentarily, then fell into a deep sleep.

Amos had been unconscious on the mountain's edge for nearly two days before being rescued. Jack, Maggie, the Wilsons, and the two Eskimos sat in the living room space of the Wilson's home, thinking over the past week's event.

Back at the Trading Post, Drifter was regaining some strength. He was a fighter, a dog with tremendous intensity and love. Amos was all he could think about at this moment. Drifter made one more attempt to stand. Even though the wounds were painfully unstable, his concentration became one of diligence toward his goal. He was successful and was able to walk at a steady pace. He headed toward where he last saw Amos. He finally approached the point of the cliffside. His bark rang out in full force, catching Sam's earnest attention. "You arrived just when I needed you, Drifter," Sam said excitedly.

Sam began to drape the rope, attached to a harness fitting snugly across Drifter's shoulders. Even with his wound, Drifter proved his love by pulling with all the force he could muster. Sam heaved along with him, making it possible for Amos to reach the surface successfully.

Drifter and Amos lay their heads back safe and sound in a comfortable bed at Sam's place. Quiet, content, and peaceful were their breathing signs. Sam kept a close watch on them. He admired their strength and loyalty.

Having had some recent first aid training, Sam knew Amos had a broken rib. He saw dislocated shoulders before and could pull them back in place. Because of Amos' unconscious state, Sam knew very little pain would be apparent to him now. It had been a lifeless two days since his rescue, yet all of Amos' vital signs were under control.

Drifter was recovering at a remarkable rate. His

courage remained firm even after he struggled to pull Amos to safety. After that event, several of Drifter's stitches tore loose, which Sam carefully sutured.

Nearly a week passed, and Drifter could now roam regularly, although he was growing eager for his master's recovery. Restless and uncertain, Drifter left the cabin to find Amos' other close friends. He arrived at the home of Jack but found no one around. His next stop was at the Wilson's house. Drifter found them and Jack together.

They were stunned to see Drifter alone without Amos. They noticed the stitches and patches of bare skin. Drifter had received some help and prayed Amos was also in the same care. They contemplated for just a short time before speculating where Amos was.

In a harmonious tone, the friends looked at each other and said, "Sam." They dashed toward the carriage at full speed and drove like the wind toward Sam's Trading Post. Wisely, Sam had harnessed the horses from the earlier excursion Mrs. Wilson had taken into town.

Reaching Sam's effortlessly, the friends entered the open front door. There on the feather bed lay Amos, still unconscious. Sam relayed the events of the past four days when Amos briefly awoke for a quick glimpse at faces he did not recognize. Sam was excited at this first sign of his friend's conscious state.

Nearly two weeks after Amos' and Drifter's complete recovery, Jack, Amos, the Wilsons, and Drifter celebrated God's faithfulness. The friends knew Amos could have easily lost his life without their prayers.

Bandit Hunt

It had been one month since his accident. Amos appreciated the warmth and comfort of his cabin. Drifter was a dog beyond compare, yet after the events of his accident had been relayed to him by Sam, did he realize just how much his loyalty meant? Amos and Drifter would remain best friends throughout their lifetimes.

After the fire, the townspeople pitched in and helped him rebuild his smokehouse and repair the damage to his cabin. The month went by quickly; before Amos knew it, it was time for his hunt to replenish items and food lost in the fire.

It was always an exciting time for Drifter and Amos. He had plenty of black powder supplies to make it a successful hunt. Amos went to his storage room, where he kept all his hunting supplies, and found his favorite hunting knife with the Elkhorn handle. He gathered his whetstone and began sharpening the blade to the particular vertex. Amos carefully packed his compass, lantern, cooking utensils, flint, steel, dried jerky, dried fruit, and canteens in their appropriate slots. Drifter carried an abundant supply of food and supplies on his back. Amos also set blankets and a rain tent in the harness packs.

Amos began gathering up old pieces of cotton for making char-cloth for more natural fire starting. He made one last perusal to be sure he had remembered all essential items and double-checked his first aid kit, finding it complete and in order.

He was on his way out when an unexpected visitor rode by on his mighty stallion. The Deputy Marshal approached Amos with a friendly greeting.

"Hello, Amos. My name is Jared, and I heard of your expert tracking experience. I need your help. Bandits are back in the area."

"I will do whatever I can."

Amos suspected they were the same bandits that ransacked the Eskimos' dog-sled and stolen their supplies. The Marshal described the two felons, and they matched what the Eskimos told him about their appearance.

"I have some friends that these men attacked."

"The Sheriff had been tracking the men for months when he turned ill and could not complete his mission," explained the Marshal.

"I have been helping catch these two harmful criminals. Many other innocent trappers - mainly Eskimos and Indians - had become the victims," the Marshal was sympathetic toward his friends. He had enough of the bandits' tyranny. Amos knew the area well, and with Drifter's help, they would apprehend the criminals.

"My two Eskimo friends told me how the two men had attacked them. They spoke of a third man running off in the distance." Amos shared the necessary details with the Marshal. "They had been too shocked at the time to think. They talked of a spirit that guided them and drove the men away."

"I am amazed at this new information, Amos. It will surely help to know we have a third man to look for from the gang."

"Drifter is the best tracker of any dog or man I have seen. He will be able to guide us." The Deputy Marshal loaded his rifle and saddled his horse. Finding these three men was essential to Amos. Although the hunting trip was necessary, he could delay it for a few days.

Their first stop was the site where they attacked

Keomi and Ketami. Drifter quickly recognized the area and began searching for any sign of a scent. Months passed since the attack, and any signs were unlikely, yet it was worth the effort. Suddenly, Drifter dug and found a red scarf. The Marshal was amazed! This scarf was significant evidence that would eventually trace them to the thieves.

The scent was undeniably one consequence as the trail continued to lead them South toward the border. Closing near the border country lay an old shack, looking very suspicious with freshly cut logs and various pieces of debris and rubbish. It seemed as if the occupied cabin had been there for some time. With the fall season in full swing and cold winter months not far off, Amos suspected these men would find a remote place - unknown to the commoner - to settle in and make their home. "These men have been on the run for nearly a year now. They probably thought it was safe to settle in without being detected." Amos covered the tracks near the cabin, but now they were in plain sight.

As Amos, Drifter, and the Marshal approached the place, signs of life were visible. The door was left ajar with scents of bacon and coffee. Amos was unaware this cabin existed here. The Marshal was equally surprised. Drifter came close to their home somewhat sheepishly. That was very unlike Drifter.

"What's up, boy?" Amos said in a soft, disturbed voice. Suddenly, Drifter found an old cracked board covering a window leading to the cellar floor. Amos was already loading his rifle, ready for action. They darted across the yard, approaching the cellar opening. With guns pointed, the Marshal spoke his words of surrender. The men didn't move or make a sound. He again said his words for the men to give up. The Marshal and Amos had surrounded the hideout with no way of escape, but the men would not budge.

Unknown to Amos and the Marshal, the two convicts escaped through an underground tunnel leading to the current border territory. Drifter valiantly charged toward the exit of the tunnel. His enormous size and vicious appearance at that moment would be enough to curb any man's idea of escape.

Drifter saw men quickly approaching and stood his ground. Two large bodies appeared at the small, narrow opening, ready to enter the new territory, when a sudden roar reached their ears. Drifter's ferocious bark sounded like a freight train running through the tunnel exit.

The startled men backed away from the sound, unknown of their fate.

Finally, they brought the men to justice. They stood before the county judge who fined them and gave them a strict penalty of ten years - labor included.

The Eskimo friends of Amos were pleased to know that the criminals were unable to hurt others again. Even though the Eskimos had not recovered their supplies, they were at peace, knowing these men would now serve time for their crimes.

When Jack heard of the arrest, he was alarmed and restful at the same time. As a young boy, Jack spent his life trying to please a father he hardly knew and helped his mother the best he could. He had a kind mother who wanted to please her husband, but he always had ideas for a different life. His father was a brutal man who only cared about himself. He wasn't always like that; he hid his true character until after they were married. After his mother took ill and passed away, his father went into a rage as he had never seen. He blamed Jack for not being the son he needed to be. Jack loved his mother deeply and always cared for her, but he hated his father. So, he ran as far as possible before fulfilling his dream of claiming land.

His way of survival was to steal bread and pickpocket. He was a desperate teenager who needed to learn how to survive the best way he could. No solid influence had been in his life to train him right. His mother was kind but weak. She loved Rupert, even with his cruel ways.

One day, when Jack was out near the river baiting his line, two men approached him. They were polite and appeared compassionate. They offered to help him and provide hot meat, preparing to cook over an open pit. A vulnerable Jack took them up on their offer. He grew to like these men. They were like brothers to him. He enjoyed their company.

A year passed, and the men told Jack he was now a man and could do a man's work. He enjoyed the praise and wanted to please. "May I go with you to your next job?" Jack begged Titus. "Sure lad, you can help us carry the goods," Titus sneered.

Jack was so excited to be with them finally. Titus asked him to wait as they gave him the lines to the horses.

Jack stood looking for his "brothers" behind rugged pine trees in the wooded area, not far from the city. It seemed like forever, but he was patient and proud to think he was chosen to oversee guarding the mares.

Titus and Jonas came running through the trees, carrying bags and firing their pistols in the air. "What took you so long?" scolded Jack.

"Shut up, you little . . .," blurted Titus in a roar that frightened Jack. His words had always been kind and comforting until now. "Get on this horse and ride or stay here and die," bellowed Jonas. Jack reluctantly obeyed. He did not know from where this was coming. From the sound of Titus' voice, he knew that he must be obedient.

And that was the beginning of his new life. Jack was a pleaser and had no other family. It was travel with them and their angry ways or be left alone to fend for himself. He lived that way long enough. He missed being with a family and the companionship of others. So, he submitted to their ideas. He followed them, becoming more vulnerable with each passing day. He did not find out until much later about the plan of Titus and Jonas.

Betrothal

When Amos arrived home, a surprise visit from Maggie became a welcome sight. He had not seen her for several months. Every moment he thought of her was pleasant, yet seeing her here was even more spectacular. She heard of his courageous plight to hunt down the two bandits. When she heard of their capture, she had to see him and share her excitement with everyone in town.

Many people gathered together and provided Amos and Drifter with a year's supply of elk jerky, homemade pastries, and freshly grown vegetables. Amos never dreamed he would receive such a generous reward.

"And just think," Amos said gratefully. "I was on my way to a hunting trip right before the change of events. God sure does have a way of providing."

Amos began thinking of the time alone in his cabin after his mother and father died before he found Drifter. He thought of how marvelous it would be to have Maggie here with him to be a helpmate. Amos always carried an abundant love for her. He was sure she felt the same. God used her in the past to take care of her own family; now, he was ready to listen to God's voice as he asked Him for guidance in asking Maggie to marry him.

It was a time of quiet peace and solitude as Amos spoke to his lovely maiden. She had a rare beauty about her. There was no one compared to her in all the land. Many men had come in and out of Maggie's life, but none courted as beautifully as Amos. He was tender, compassionate, and understanding. His love for her only grew through their parted years, and she became an exquisite woman of wisdom.

Alone in the beauty surrounding them, he gently took

Maggie's hand and spoke the words he dreamed about for many years. "Maggie, we have known each other our entire lives. We grew up as great friends. I have grown to love and respect you more deeply, and it would be my honor if you were to take my hand in marriage." Amos' heart overflowed with love as she gave her answer.

Maggie responded with an excited, "Yes!" She had been waiting since she returned from Pennsylvania for this moment to arrive. She thought of Amos often while taking care of her family. She never regretted a moment of coming back here to her own home. This land had always been her rightful home, and she was proud of her heritage. People here still showed her love. Now, she was going to be Amos' wife.

Her lifelong dream was coming true. God brought them together from the very beginning. They were best friends growing up. They played together in childhood, watched each other struggle through adolescence, and finally grew to maturity. They respected each other's feelings and desires about life. They knew their strengths and weaknesses and developed to show that love unconditionally. They would be together through all life's many trials. They shared the same belief in God and continually grew in the Lord. Now was the right time to accept his proposal.

They planned the wedding right before Thanksgiving. Maggie waited patiently for this day and had a dress set aside for the occasion. She had sewn her dress years before delicately placing embroidered rows of tiny rose petals upon the silky chiffon bodice. The dress showed her delicate, curvy features. Her veil flowed along her slender back, accentuating her blonde hair. Her brother, the new preacher in the town, would perform the ceremony. It would be a festive occasion as everyone in the surrounding area would be there.

Some of Maggie's close friends offered to help with the preparations using their talents. Four town women derived an old family recipe into an exquisite cake with a frosting bouquet arranged in the center. Other women gathered fresh wildflowers from the nearby fields and placed them in splendid bouquets around the churchyard and inside the building. The smells sent a pleasant aroma of lavender and sweet orange verbena. Mrs. McGregor provided Maggie with some old pearl earrings from her mother. Sarai shared her garter from her wedding. The plan was running smoothly and in order.

There was no doubt there would be enough food, for some of the finest cooks in town were participating. Everyone in the small town played a part in some way, and the word was spreading across the countryside of the blessed event. Everyone that heard the news in the territory would be welcome.

While Maggie and her friends gathered to share their blessings, Amos was in a different state of mind. He felt complete peace about marrying Maggie, yet slightly nervous contemplating this new change in his life.

The day was finally here; an incredible day. All the hustle and bustle of close friends made their final preparations a joyful feast, arranging the flower bouquet for Maggie and the Maid of Honor while sharing their thoughts of hope and joy for the loving couple. The men dug a pit for roasting the pig provided by the local butcher. The spices were delicately blended, ready to spread over the hearty beast, sending an aroma throughout the countryside.

Sam was Amos' best man, and Cora dressed in pastel colors as Maggie's maid of honor. The weather held splendidly, with sunshine and a slight breeze. It had been an unusually calm spring compared to the previous fall and winter. "Thank you, Lord, for this beautiful day!" Amos lifted his hands in praise.

Everything was set in place as Maggie and Amos looked themselves over one last time in the mirror. The wedding party assured them of their appearance. Maggie's walk down the aisle was now to begin. She immediately focused her eyes on Amos with lovely thoughts of this handsome, gentle, and Godly man.

Ronny approached the couple with a tone of blessing in his voice. "Blessed be this man and his lovely bride for now and eternity. I know God will richly bless their lives as they continue to serve the Lord together." These were the words that Amos longed to hear for so many years.

He was looking forward to serving his faithful bride for as long as they both would live. He saved himself for her and her alone, and God was richly blessing him for his trust and patience.

The festivities began as Maggie walked down the aisle in her silky chiffon dress with puffed sleeves, and Amos looked most exquisite in his black tailored suit. Maggie appeared radiant. Amos was quite proud of her, being the self-assured, prudent woman of God.

She would be an excellent helpmate for Amos. As Amos thought of how blessed he was to have Maggie, she also thought of the quiet, gentle, courageous man Amos had always been. Even though many years separated them, they were still part of each other in thought and heart; now, their lives would be complete.

Smells of roast pig, home-grown garden vegetables, a variety of fresh fruit salads, potatoes, corn-on-the-cob, and lemonade - made from Homer Gross's lemon trees in the southeastern territory - were served. There was an enormous crowd who helped in preparing the meal for Maggie and Amos. Everyone was honored to participate in this particular occasion, having looked forward to it for many years.

The crowd gathered around as Maggie and Amos prepared to cut the cake. It took only a few seconds when the guests were in tears with laughter as Maggie fed Amos an oversized piece of cake. Amos' cheeks looked like a chipmunk who overestimated his portion of nuts. Everyone formed a long line. Their mouths watered for the delicate blend of chocolate and spices covered with a creamy chocolate frosting.

While Amos and Maggie sat back, enjoying the laughter around them, they thanked the Lord for his rich blessing and guidance. They acknowledged and praised Him for His wondrous love and mercy he so graciously bestowed upon them. They looked around at all their friends enjoying themselves. That almost brought more joy to their hearts than their happiness.

The day ended as the last ray of light slipped behind the evening mountain. Now they looked upon the soft Milky Way stretched across the Northern sky. They took one last glance when a shooting star caught their eyes. It was as if God blessed them personally; they knew love and beauty would fill their marriage.

Amos and Maggie were planning to spend the night in the town hotel. The church women had lavishly showered their room with gifts. They looked very tempting to open at once, yet exhaustion overtook them. The newlyweds' warm baths soothed their weary bodies. The night would be restful and peaceful.

Their journey home followed the carved trail in the meadow, allowing the gifts to arrive safely. Maggie's handsome carriage stood solid and sturdy. It was a casual, slow trip. The newly married couple could use this time to reminisce as Sam drove the horse-drawn carriage. They could get to know each other all over again. They were delighted with the opportunity, bringing them closer together. They increasingly realized how pleased they were with each other's company.

Drifter, who had gotten lost in last night's crowd, was thankful to receive a feast of pork rib bones. It was Maggie and Amos' special day, and he knew he did not deserve much attention. But now he realized the wait had been worth it. Drifter feasted on his share of meat while riding like royalty with Sam.

It took several weeks to find a place for all the generous gifts they received. The couple received fresh fruit and vegetables, canned meats, jams and jellies, staples, and jerky. Amos enjoyed every moment with Maggie. Their faith and God's grace pulled them through the long wait.

Maggie received a handmade quilt from her sisters in Pennsylvania. The fabric was a woven cotton blend. Each square had a piece of her childhood delicately embroidered. One square had the verse." Delight yourself in the Lord, And He will give you the desires of your heart." Proverbs 37:4, written on it.

Maggie often repeated Proverbs as a child. Tears welled in her eyes as she wondered how accurate that verse was. Maggie sacrificed her desires for so many years. She cared for her family, and now God provided her heart's desire.

New Beginnings

The new morning of their lives together brought a rich blend of sweet-smelling herbs and spices. They filled the room as Maggie cooked up one of her recipes. Amos was sound asleep, with Drifter lying at the foot of the bed. The smell of aromatic flavors awoke him. He would never forget the smell of bacon sizzling on an open iron stove, with eggs basted from the taste of its grease. The biscuits, made from her recipe, were moist with a golden-brown crust. Amos gathered from the beehive down in the valley, covered in the honey, accented them well. Before his mother passed away, Maggie used to cook for them. He was eager to taste the delicacies once again.

Maggie had been in the kitchen several hours before Amos awoke, with Drifter by his side. As Amos approached the kitchen, a warm smile welcomed him. The aroma was tantalizing. Having a woman in the house again was delightful, especially Maggie.

"Good morning, my love."

"You are a delight to behold," Amos lovingly caressed Maggie's soft features.

"What would you like for breakfast?"

Amos was used to fending for himself, often without a morning meal. He looked forward to Maggie's home cooking. "I have some cured jerky in the smokehouse."

"Yes, and our chickens are not laying eggs." Maggie went to the chicken coup that Amos had constructed before he asked Maggie to marry him. He knew how she loved her fresh eggs.

Amos and Maggie delighted in every flavorful bite of their breakfast. The freshly cured jerky smoked perfectly, and they cooked the recently laid chicken eggs, adding them to the tangy squeezed oranges Alex had bought. When they finished, a mid-morning walk was next on the agenda. They opened the front door to feel a fresh wind touch their faces. Amos loved this feeling of a fall morning. But he also knew winter was soon upon them. Fall was always a short season in Canada. Winter seemed to slip around the corner at the first sign of cold, brisk air, but Amos did not think this would be a challenging season. The summer had lasted relatively long, and the fall was still extremely mild. Even with this in mind, he was in no hurry for the coming frigid weather.

"Oh, Amos, look. The black-eyed Susan is in full bloom. They are filling the meadow."

"Yes, they look like golden rays of sunshine."

"Thank you for taking me on this walk. Everything is so fresh, and the fresh smells fill the air."

"With you, everything is fresh and full of life."

"My life is now complete with you by my side." Maggie looked forward to her life with Amos and all the treasures of love he had to share.

The rumor was that Amos struck it rich in gold. Amos constantly desired gold panning and mining. He inherited much of that knowledge from his parents. His father had been sure the mother lode was somewhere in these mountains, but he never secured the findings. Amos found the rich rock outside the cave near the ledge where his father fell to his death. And now that he had conquered the mountain ledge, he was here to dig some more on his father's mine claim.

The walk continued despite the cold. Amos was eager to show Maggie his discovery. Maggie was aware of such mine, but she never saw its richness. She was excited to see this rumored claim. Amos was eager to show her that one existed.

"So, this is where the mine is. I never dreamed this place existed."

"I did tell you about my father's mine claim."

"Yes, but it was like a dream, not a reality."

"My father did embellish some, but he never gave up."

"Let's go inside!" The mine piqued Maggie's sense of adventure.

Drifter, following close behind, was having the time of his life. Maggie and Amos always enjoyed his free yet gallant show. He was unaware of being watched. At this point, Drifter did not have a care in the world. He loved Maggie being here and enjoyed her bright smile and joyous laughter. Drifter adored her. He would protect her faithfully.

The three of them would soon be approaching the mine. After finally reaching its presence, Amos uncloaked the carefully prepared covering. The underbrush blended in so perfectly. Amos didn't recognize the mine from a distance. Even up close, the disguise was a masterful job.

With a look of enchantment, Maggie felt like a princess in a fairy tale who just found a long-lost treasure. She was eager to see the opening to their mine. Amos used his lantern to look into its large oval-shaped mouth. The mine sounded back alarmingly. She often heard of tunnels like this one with its echoing tone but never saw one up close. Her eyes lit up with a curious look, excited to go exploring. He tested his tunnel many times and knew it to be secure and stable. They slowly climbed down the newly made ladder that provided a quick and safe entrance. Amos proudly gave a tour to his new bride. He showed her where he found his first trace of gold.

"When I was a boy, several things happened in his finding this vein of gold." Amos looked like a young boy ready to eat his first bite of candy, and Maggie was amused.

My grandfather claimed the mine before his father was born. It never provided much, even though my grandfather worked for years trying to find the rich vein. My grandmother kept his simple findings in a secret chamber for many years without touching them. She always felt it was his claim and had no right to it. Although my grandparents believed the gold to be there, my father never found the mother lode of gold grandfather believed to be there."

"But here it is. She is quite the beauty." Maggie, proud of her husband for finally finding the rich pockets of gold, sat down near her husband like a giddy schoolgirl.

Amos' grandparents did not have an abundance of material possessions, but their love blossomed every minute they were together. Amos' father passed away when he was sixteen from a tragic fall after his mother when he was twelve. Amos was not aware of the mine's presence when he was younger. His mother always knew that someday, when their son was born, he would want to be a part of his father's life: this claim. She often expressed her love for his father openly. She respected and admired his goals: mining for gold and providing for his family, which he cherished above all. The tenderness touched Maggie as he spoke of his beloved grandparents, mother, and father. He continued his story: "My mother kept a journal of her life with father, including his mining adventures. In reading this journal one day, he was brought to the claim," speaking respectfully. Her notes were not precise, yet Amos' knowledge of these mountains took him to the mentioned reference points.

They began their entrance to the tunnel. As Amos and Maggie sat amongst the silt and debris of the dusty, damp cave, her eyes widened with hands clasped. The lantern held long enough for them to find several turns and deep crevices that lacked oxygen. The flame flickered and almost went out, indicating carbon dioxide. They avoided those areas in the future by marking them with a solid wooden post and a piece of red cloth. The exit to the cave was visible. Direct sunlight was coming through a small crack near the opening. Maggie did not anticipate coming here so soon but wanted to know the ends and outs of the cave. She wanted to learn as much as she could about Amos' mine.

It had been a special day! A day of growth and learning more about each other. They were thankful no one had discovered the gold mine. Anyone could have found and claimed it because all the records had been destroyed. They discovered the shaft at the precise moment. God's timing had been perfect.

After their morning adventure of exploring, Maggie expressed an appetite for food. Their climb back up the entrance wall was successful. They both walked steadily, looking for Drifter, who wandered off shortly before they entered the mine shaft. "That 'ol rascal," muttered Amos under his breath.

"I wonder where he could have gone." Maggie's face showed worried frowns.

"I'm sure he'll be fine," reassured Amos . . . "He probably got bored with our little adventure or just wanted us to be alone. He doesn't like coming into this musty 'ol cave anyway."

With nightfall shortly approaching and no sign of Drifter, Amos became restless. Drifter was not known to wander off from Amos' side for an entire day like he had done today. In the distance, he heard howling, which Amos had not heard in many a year. It was a pack of wolves roaming this territory. He knew at once where Drifter went. Amos had never been aware of Drifter's heritage, yet sensed he had some wild wolf breed in him. Even though Drifter was an obedient dog that demonstrated distinguishable tenacity, he had all the characteristics of a wolf. He began to think (now that Maggie was here) that he was losing Drifter's loyalty to a wolf pack.

It had been two days with no sign of Drifter. Amos told Maggie he was going to search for him. He knew he was not lost but feared the worst: The wolves had attacked him. Skillful tracking allowed Amos to discover the wolves' territory. He came prepared for any peril with his trusty rifle in hand. Finding a stable oak tree, Amos perched himself upon its high, lofty branches. He waited until the evening when the sight of wolves would be evident. Hopefully, the wolves did not notice him. The crescent moon began forming in the sky when he heard the sounds of crying wolves all around him. He was aware his hiding place had been obscure. They did not sense his presence, but he was sure they would notice soon.

He was sitting precariously as the branch began to split from his weight, ambivalent. An ambush could be upon him the moment he fell. He tried to reach for the nearest branch and grasp hold. The reach was too broad. He held his composure. Suddenly, without warning, a large hawk swooped above Amos' head, causing him to waver and crash to the ground below.

Within an instance, a pack of wolves circled him when, abruptly, a shrill cry stopped them in dead silence. Drifter charged toward the pack. The wolf pack cautiously backed away as Drifter moved toward Amos' side, where he remained on the forest floor, gazing into Drifter's eyes.

Drifter wandered away after Maggie and Amos entered the gold mine. He was innocently playing near the creek bed when a wolf approached him. Drifter stood, gazing into his eyes as if he knew him. Transfixed by the glare of his eyes, he followed. As Drifter continued behind the wolf, he knew where the pack was leading him. He had been among this group before. As he approached the pack, he recognized many of its members. He was among the young pack from which his mother and father were leaders.

His mother was a gorgeous husky dog, and his father was an alpha male. After her master died, his mother wandered from her home. She came to this wolf pack, where the members graciously received her. Drifter's father had been the tenacious leader who accepted the lone husky as his mate, beginning Drifter's life. Drifter was separated from them when another pack attacked its members, leaving his mother and father lifeless, along with many older members. Drifter had been wandering for many months when a kindly older man found him, cared for him, and trained him as an Arctic sled dog.

After his master died, he traveled as a leader of the young pack. But soon, they were attacked again by an older, more experienced, larger renegade pack. Most of them fled. They did not have the strength to fight against their tenacious leader. Drifter was left to fend for himself. Drifter fought with all his might, but the pack overcame him, weakening him. The sad memories of his wolf heritage once again led him to another destination: The home of Amos.

Now that he was visiting with the pack again, he wondered what would become of him. He knew he loved Amos, and being away from him was almost more than he could bear. He genuinely loved Maggie and knew they would be looking for him. He enjoyed his three-day stay with his old friends but knew he belonged with Amos and Maggie, so he set out again on another journey home!

Drifter raced with velocity toward the renegade pack, which was much smaller now. That pack had given him much grief in the past, but they also knew his strength. Drifter knew someone was in danger! He charged toward the wolves, only to find Amos where he had been lying.

The renegade wolves wisely left his presence by the time he reached Amos. They knew his speed and agility were unbeatable. They respected his tenacity in leadership. The pack fled as he moved near Amos' side and rested his head on his heaving chest. That was a joyous moment for the two friends, a sense of relief as Amos reached his arms around Drifter's wide neck and lifted himself.

Luckily, no bones had broken from his fall, only a few sore muscles. They began their trek toward home.

The step into his door was triumphal as Maggie welcomed them with open arms. She threw her arms around Amos and then ruffled Drifter's hair behind his ears. He liked it when Maggie petted him that way.

She cooked up a hot pot of stew for Amos and a big juicy steak bone for Drifter. Their home was in order once again.

Indian Revival

People knew Amos and Maggie throughout the countryside for their devotion to God and each other. They were known for their generosity and overwhelming peace. Many townspeople, including other nearby Indian villages, heard of a loving God they worshipped and were curious to learn more about Him.

One day, when Amos was out gathering water at the stream running through the meadow below his cabin, he saw curious eyes peer at him through the brush. Amos observed and spied on what looked like a young Indian boy. Amused at playing this hide-n-go-seek game from behind the swaying branches, Amos soon engaged in the sport. He would turn in quick maneuvers to catch the glare of the young lad. This game continued for nearly an hour when the boy walked closer to Amos, amazed at his size and kind nature. At first, Amos pretended not to notice as the boy mimicked his every move.

Amos started to venture toward the cabin, with his new admirer following close behind. Curious about the boy's intent, Amos slowly approached the cabin door. Setting down the water jugs in front of the door, he gradually moved toward the boy to find him again behind another bush. Amos was learning some language of the Eskimo tribes and tried to speak a simple "hello." The boy's laughter told him he spoke incorrectly, yet he seemed to understand his intent.

Moving closer to Amos, the boy raised his hand to say hello, which he had learned from watching other white men before. He interpreted it as a kind mannerism. Now that they were both on the same terms, Amos gestured to the boy to enter his home. Gingerly, the boy moved toward the door.

Once inside, they began conversing through sign

language, in which they both appeared comfortable. The boy looked interested in learning more about his God as he gestured to the sky using other hand motions to indicate this desire.

As Amos spoke, the boy watched with curious eyes, trying to articulate some of the words himself. Amos was reaching the boy through patience and wisdom. He silently prayed as he spoke, hoping something would get through to him. Soon after, he attempted to speak of God's love. The boy signed the word G-O-D and pointed to the sky. He was sure he understood.

After a restful night, the boy returned to Amos' door with another tribal member. She was a small, delicate creature with long, flowing hair that ran smoothly across her shoulders. She had the same wide-eyed expression and shared the same enthusiasm as the boy. The two continued to come as each day passed.

It had been four months since they began this ritual of sign language and trying to communicate. They were becoming close friends, and Amos was ecstatic that God had allowed him to share his faith. Amos laid a firm foundation for developing close relations.

During these months, they were learning each other's language somewhat proficiently. Amos discovered that the boy's name was Running Swiftly, and the girl's name was Flowing River. Running Swiftly was his given name because of his speed and accuracy in bow hunting. Many tribal members thought Flowing River's hair looked like a peaceful, tranquil river flowing delicately through the serene valley. The two of them decided to give Honorable One a name for Amos. Amos felt humbled at the name they chose for him.

These two new friends mentioned seeing a large, broad

wolf they saw in Amos' home. They wondered if he was some spirit of guidance. Amos explained about Drifter and how he came to be with him. He helped them understand that he was his benevolent, loyal friend, not a spirit. The only spirit was the Holy Spirit that came to live in our hearts.

That was hard for the Indians to understand, as they thought ghosts lived in everything. Amos helped them to understand how the Holy Spirit knows our thoughts and guides us to make the right choices. The two mentioned how they told the rest of the tribe about this Holy Spirit, and they were curious to know more about Him. Amos welcomed the opportunity when they invited him to their tipi village. He prayed God would give him the words to speak and help them to understand God, the Holy Spirit, and God's son, Jesus.

Amos began another trip to the village. The chief requested to bring along Drifter and explain that he was not some spirit to be revered or worshipped but a friend. They invited Maggie to come along and share some of her special baking treats, which she secured in her bag, while Drifter carried the bulk of the food in packs across his broad shoulders. They left early in the morning, traveling through the night as "Running Swiftly" and "Flowing River" must have done on their walk to Amos. Their journey was to be a full day's walk. The weather was still holding up well for their excursion.

Arriving at the camp, Amos recognized the area and often wondered why he had not seen Indian tribes here before. Entering the tribe's home was a pleasurable experience. Many children came to greet this, "Oh, most Honorable One," they had heard so much about.

Maggie thought the sight to be one of the most brilliant examples of God's creativity and love. The people were splendid in form, with a color rare in beauty. Their warmth and affection were worthy of praise, an excellent example to all.

These people had charming personalities, full of courage and vigor. Their manners were impeccable as they greeted and moved them toward the chief's tipi. Although their modesty was not what Maggie and Amos were used to, their innocence touched their very lives. The tribe welcomed them and was eager to share what they knew to be the truth about their God.

Amos spoke of God's love among the people, "God sent his beloved son to take the punishment for our sins. Sins are the bad things in our life that displease God. We all have sinned and will continue to do so, but Christ's blood can cleanse the wrong actions in our lives. God requires that all sin be judged and paid for by the shedding of blood. God wants to make our hearts clean through His blood. All we need to do is accept His gift. When we do that, we become God's child, and there will not be any more punishment." Amos continued to share. "God's love and forgiveness for our sins are given to all who believe. God will provide us with peace and keep us from evil." Amos spoke of heaven and how each man, woman, and child who accepted God's gift could someday live there forever.

Wide eyes all around gave Amos the impression they either understood or were too overwhelmed to comprehend the message of truth. Questions from the chiefs began: "How did God come to be? Why did he have to die? And, how could one man do all that?" They worshiped the sun and moon and stars and every living thing, believing a spirit to live inside each of them. "How could this be?" Amos patiently answered each of their questions to the best of his ability. Maggie took many of the women aside and spoke to them similarly.

A day of sharing Christ with others passed quickly. Many people did not understand, but some were ready to accept this kind, loving God who gave this gift. Big Bear, the chief, asked more questions than any other and was unprepared for Amos and Maggie to leave. He offered them to stay the night in the chief's tipi. That was an extraordinary honor. They graciously accepted and asked if the "Great Wolf" could join them. All agreed as the night ended. The tribesmen swiftly, yet quietly, moved to their tipis to let the "Honorable One" and his wife sleep.

God's beauty filled the surrounding valley in vivid pictures. The vigorous activity all about them showed them to be hard-working people filled with wonder and innocent charm. The speed and efficiency with which they worked confirmed their idea. The women were up before dawn, progressing in all their work. They were busy scraping meat from the hides of a previous kill. They gathered the fresh water and prepared a meal like they were ready to serve a king before Maggie and Amos awoke.

The children were gaily playing. Drifter was the center of attention. He thoroughly enjoyed every minute of this loving attention he received—the "Great Wolf," as everyone called him, became the life of the party. Even the elders were enjoying his delightful company.

The camp elders moved toward Amos and Maggie as they watched and learned about the culture of the people. The men motioned for them to come toward the center tipi. Their voices expressed a solemn tone. They heard about Amos' God, his love for all people, and this gift that was given simply by asking. All night, Big Bear contemplated accepting what he felt was a rare gift. "Why weren't sacrifices needed?" questioned Big Bear.

Amos explained, "God had sent His only Son as a sacrifice so we wouldn't have to. The day he died on the cross, Christ forgave our sins. All we need to do is confess our sins, and our hearts can become clean and pure because of His shed blood. He is alive and well in heaven, while his spirit lives in our hearts, continually cleansing us." Amos prayed silently.

At this point, Big Bear thought of his only son, who died at a young age. He knew this must be a great God willing to sacrifice his only son to save all the people. Big Bear spoke to Amos in his native tongue, which Amos was learning well, and asked Jesus to be his personal Savior. Some of the elders also joined Amos in this prayer of salvation.

It had been a glorious day. Amos and Maggie knew their mission had begun. Now, to train and teach these people how to live in a way pleasing to God. They had their hearts right with Him and now needed guidance in their new faith. Amos would continue to mentor the men while Maggie worked with the women and children.

Amos and Maggie left the camp that day, hearts filled with love. In the short time of knowing these people, they developed a kinship. God's family was growing up in the Canadian hills. A revival was happening in the native tribes.

Ronny's Mission

Amos began searching for Bibles everywhere. He contacted people he knew in Pennsylvania, North Dakota, and neighboring territories. People were responding positively. He shared his experiences with Ronny in the town. Ronny had prayed for an opportunity to reach a native tribe, and now he would have a part in the mission.

The chief again invited Ronny and Amos into the native camp. Ronny prayed the Lord would give him the words to open the Chief's heart. Ronny provided the people with Bibles he brought with him from Pennsylvania. The Native tribes were learning English well, and Ronny hoped they would understand the Bible. He was beginning to learn the native tongue and would do his best to serve as an interpreter.

The next few months proved successful as their love grew. Many of the children were beginning to understand the true God. Running Swiftly and Flowing River were among them. They were learning the English language from their contact with Amos and were able to serve as interpreters for the other children.

One afternoon, Ronny was alone with these two children and saw a rare quality about them. Their desire and ability to learn were extraordinary; their patience and willingness to serve were abundant. They acquired a rare sense of knowledge in these few months.

Ronny greeted his new students, becoming more acquainted with them and their desire to gain knowledge. He taught them the letters and sounds of the English language, and they continued to teach Ronny words in their native tongue.

A young boy stood out from the rest. He was not radiant in talking like many others, but he showed humble quietness, intriguing Ronny. He would sit in the back with eyes wide open as he read the Scripture. His countenance glowed with each mention of Christ's name. Ronny watched with anticipation as he read. Never speaking a word, the boy would form shapes in the air around him. Each figure seemed to indicate he understood the spoken words. When Ronny read of the coming King and Heaven, his hands lifted in worship to the sky. His lips moved to the rhythm of his own. Yet not a spoken word came from his mouth.

One bright afternoon, Ronny made his excursion toward the Indian camp. It had been several weeks since he could visit his pupils because of his responsibilities in town. He came close to town without one child coming to greet him. That was an unusual occurrence. Finally, after a time, one of the camp elders came from his tipi to welcome him; with a sad and exhausted-looking face, he said, "Last night, a young member of our tribe went home to be with the Lord. He had been very ill for some time. None of us knew what disease afflicted him. When he first came to be with us, he would not speak. Only smiles came from the young braves' lips. He was a content young lad. He was a good hunter and served the members of our camp well. We thought at first some spirit took his speech from him. We thought his ears did not work. We knew better when he would look up when other people spoke. His keen ears could always alert us to any danger.

Yesterday, a pack of wolves circled the camp, unknown to the rest of us. The young boy came to us and signed Wolf. Sure enough, the pack was beginning to invade our territory. If it had not been for his insight, they would have overcome for sure. So, we knew his ears worked well. But never a word came from his mouth."

The elder momentarily paused as he saw tears flow from the preacher's eyes. Ronny knew of whom he was speaking. It had been the young boy who had a rare countenance about him. The young boy would sign the meaning of all the spoken words. Ronny assured the Indian elder peace now that he was in heaven with his Heavenly Father. Ronny was sure of this from the content look on the boy's face as he lay on his burial ground.

It was a sad ceremony, yet a blessed time as the Indians worshipped together. This young man, whose name was Shining Face, would be missed by all the tribe members. He had been a great help in times of distress and sorrow. Even though he would not speak, his actions and kind heart shone forth. Ronny would miss the young lad known as Shining Face.

Amos and Maggie were busy preparing the house for the coming winter months. It had been many weeks since Ronny and Amos had spoken to one another. When Ronny and his wife came calling, they were excited to hear about the news from the Indian village. Ronny shared his progress with the tribe and the one friendly boy who went home to be with the Lord. Maggie was excited about Ronny's ministry. Even as a child, he desired to serve the Lord, his heart filled with compassion and tenderness.

Once, Ronny saw an abandoned robin's nest. He took these robins in, caring for and nursing them back to health, then crying after setting them free. His tender quality blossomed as a child, never realizing the effect he would have as an adult. Amos demonstrated these same qualities, attracting Maggie to him. Maggie had seen many angry men with tempers and harsh words to say to their women. Maggie saw enough of that kind of man to appreciate Amos and Ronny more. They were both dear to her heart, and she would always treasure their closeness and love.

The winter months were now approaching. Ronny wondered about the Indian village and where the winter months would lead them. *Would their destination be close? Or would it be so far that he could not complete the mission he started?* The winters here in the Pacific Canadian Hills could be treacherous. The Native Americans had only been in these parts for the spring, summer, and fall. He was unsure of their survival in the winter. Concerned about this, he set his destination toward the village.

It had been two weeks since he last saw the people. He was missing them. His fondness for these people grew daily. He began learning of their ways and appreciated their strength and courage. He longed to continue his mentorship, guiding them in their walk for Christ so that they could fully understand God's love and grace. He gave a message of love they would never forget.

Nearing the village, he didn't see any sign of life. They had moved. The rapid speed and efficiency of the people set Ronny at ease. He underestimated their capabilities., He continued praying for their safety. He knew God would be with them wherever they set up their next camp. They now believed the Holy Spirit would be their guide.

Now that Alex's ministry was finished (for a time) with the Native American village, a new church was flourishing in town. Many modern homesteaders were making their way there. Some came from quite a distance. Many came from Europe and the bordering countries. New people could come since the town bordered the North Pacific Ocean. The dock provided large and small boats to rest there. There was still some land in nearby Canadian territories for a small fee. This land became very appealing to many with its vast beauty. There was a sense of adventure for many who came. The soil was fertile for growing a variety of fruits and vegetables. It was abundant and beautiful but could also be treacherous. Many people with high hopes would turn and go home after a few months of winter, and many more would leave much sooner.

With the new families came women and children eager to learn. Ronny approached these people, telling them of a church in town. The interest was overwhelming and very encouraging to him and his wife. Sarai had a rare gift for relating to young children. The children responded well to her creative teaching, but after several weeks of Sunday School, the one class was becoming more than she could handle.

Ronny searched in town for anyone who could help fulfill this need for teachers. He asked new settlers to help, but they were busy establishing their businesses. Some older ladies and gentlemen offered to help teach, yet many quickly became tired. Ronny was in a dilemma. He felt his gifting was toward adults. Although Ronny was very good with children, he needed help. He prayed to God to show him the answer.

Ronny woke up the following day with a comforting thought. He knew Maggie had worked with children of all ages. She successfully taught in Pennsylvania. He pondered over this thought for quite some time.

Maggie and Amos lived a full day's ride from town by carriage and a two-day walk. Taking care of her household was filling her days. Many times, Amos would leave home to trap or mine. These would be the perfect times for Maggie to come into town. She could spend the night with us and help. She has a good heart. He knew her answer would be yes.

Ronny rode to their home in the meadow near a bubbling stream to ask Maggie. Saddling his well-bred horse, he rode toward their cabin. Nearing the place, he started having second thoughts. *Should I impose on this newly married couple? But Maggie has such talent. I know she's the answer to my prayer.* Gathering his courage, he stepped off his Thoroughbred and approached the door.

Maggie was there instantly with warm hugs and kisses for her brother. Maggie could tell something was up by his strained look. It was the same look he always gave when he was deep in thought. She could read her brother like a book in which she was most affluent. She compassionately asked him about his concern. After talking about the weather and the goings on in town, he gathered his courage, "Maggie, would be willing to help with teaching in town? There are ...

'I thought you would never ask.'"

"How did you know what I was going to ask?"

"Remember, I can read you like a book."

Ronny, overjoyed with enthusiasm, reached over and gave her a bear-sized hug, almost collapsing Maggie to the floor.

"Okay, Okay, brother. I'm excited, too!" Maggie had to catch her breath after Ronny squeezed it out of her.

Ronny was about to reach for the door when Amos walked through. He was excited about the happenings in town. He and Drifter had been on one of their excursions while Maggie was preparing a gourmet lunch. "She sure does spoil us around here," Amos picked her up and swung her around. Maggie squealed!

Reaching to kiss Maggie, Ronny blushed for the newly married couple. "Before you leave, there is just one thing I need to say to you." Amos gave a teasing look. Ronny was beginning to feel nervous, thinking there was something that would prevent Maggie from serving in the church as a Sunday School teacher, "Before leaving this home, you must stay and share some of this well-prepared food with us."

Ronny felt relieved, "No one turns down one of Maggie's meals." Ronny gazed at the delectable serving of food. Ronny gave many thanks to his gracious Lord for answering his prayers. He had another mission to complete, a task to guide young children. Maggie was the perfect person to fulfill his goal. She was a loving answer from the Lord. He was eager to see her help in fulfilling his new mission.

Sunday would be Maggie's first to serve in the classroom while Amos and Drifter went to seal his mine claim. They were ready to prepare it for winter. Drifter was always a big help in this area. His strength in carrying the needed boulders, twigs, and branches would serve Amos well. The opening would need to be sealed from wild animals searching for shelter and from strangers and trappers roaming the area. Gold was a rare commodity, and ruthless men would do anything to acquire it. Even though his claim gave him the rights to the mine, many greedy and self-wanting men roamed the countryside for easy money.

Amos knew just how to blend the opening into the surrounding terrain. Amos carefully placed each piece of twig, rock, and dirt. Amos knew the territory so well that only he could recognize the opening. His father and Sam taught him well, plus Amos had a few tricks up his sleeves. Once Amos sealed the mine opening, he could venture into town. He could hardly wait to see all his loved ones and friends.

After a long, hard day's work, they welcomed the rest. Amos and Drifter spent some quality time together. They ran and leaped through the meadow. Drifter was nipping at Amos' heel, then watched him roll down the hill. Drifter chasing after Amos became more enjoyable than chasing squirrels. One forceful leap of Drifter brought Amos to his knees, laughing ecstatically. "You better go a little easy on my old bones," each pounce humbled Amos to the ground. Looking at the sun nearly fading away, Amos knew he and Drifter's time together had ended.

Upon reaching the town, Maggie had some exciting news to share with Amos about her first day of teaching, "I shared the Gospel today. The kids were enthusiastic listeners. Amos, they had never heard of Christ before."

"I'm glad you were here to help them understand God's love."

"They asked questions about who God is, where he came from, and what was in their future. They challenged me."

"God gave you the answers?"

"Yes, the exact verses came to mind." Her compassion and love for the children caused Amos to admire her all the more.

Amos did not have the opportunity to observe her in this setting but remembered her from days long ago. He thought she possessed a rare gift, given graciously by God. Amos' love grew with each passing moment spent with Maggie. He knew she was given to him to love and cherish always.

Amos and Maggie enjoyed a smoked venison barbecue, apples, and homegrown tomatoes that Sarai prepared. Upon eating their meal, they spoke of the morning's success. Ronny was excited to hear of the enthusiastic learners in both classes. There were many questions related to Science and Math. Maggie knew her responsibilities to Amos yet knew he would understand and support her decision to continue teaching each week, presenting a firm foundation for these children.

The long winter was upon them, yet Maggie wanted to teach at the church each Sunday. Her weekly travels to and from the church were enjoyable, although many times very treacherous. The blistering snow and wind were almost too much to bear at times.

As the months continued into the depths of winter, travel became increasingly complex. One time, the sleigh almost tipped from the blistering wind and hail. Another time the runners got stuck in the thick patches of icy snow. Maggie always said a prayer before she left on her journey, and God never ceased to save her.

Maggie made her journey weekly into town, but Amos became concerned for her safety. So, they both decided to make a change for the winter months. After the fourth morning's service, they visited with Ronny and Sarai to discuss their plans. Ronny, aware of the treacherous journey, suggested, "I've been very pleased with your commitment and strength of character, Maggie, yet I'm concerned for your safety. The winter is beginning to batter us hard. Would you, Amos, and Drifter enjoy staying with us through the winter months?"

"That is a wonderful idea. It will solve both of our problems."

"I've already talked with Sarai about that same idea. She would love to have some company." Sarai listened to their conversation and made preparations in the spare bedroom.

The house Maggie owned - where Ronny and Sarai now lived - could easily accommodate Maggie and Amos. There were separate rooms and a bath in the upper corner with an elegant pitcher and bowl and a copper washtub. A freezer in the back would provide storage for meat and frozen goods. The windmill would provide adequate water for them all. Sarai and Maggie worked well together in the kitchen. They were delighted to share recipes. That would be a splendid time to strengthen their friendship.

Drifter was not to be left out. There was adequate shelter behind the house. Amos previously built a nicely shaped dog house for Drifter. He was looking forward to becoming acquainted with his new surroundings and loving the attention he received from everyone. He would walk with Maggie to the church, and the children loved his presence. Maggie always felt a little safer with him around.

Now that they were living with Ronny, they could teach more about everyday life. Amos would give his lessons to the students on mountain survival and how to set traps. He would also have the children participate in finding edible herbs and what plants were poisonous. Maggie's confidence in Amos allowed him to flourish in the surroundings in which he was the most comfortable. A new ministry for both had begun.

Drifter's Rescue

Drifter was living lavishly in his new, temporary home. He didn't remember receiving so much attention since his days as the "Great Wolf" in the Indian village. Every evening after meals, Drifter devoured a hearty plate of leftovers. Ronny and Sarai grew to love and respect his loyalty to Amos. He never left his side in trouble, nor Maggie's. They were joyous to have his presence near them.

One dark, bleak night in December, Christmas Eve to be exact, Drifter never knew how much he would need to prove his loyalty.

The morning was a crisp mixture of rain, sleet, and hail. A typical morning for this time of year. The family was enjoying each other's melodic tunes as Maggie gracefully played the old-time piano she acquired from a town in Pennsylvania. The instrument was shipped by train to her sister's home in North Dakota and then transported to Canada. She struck each note carefully in a rhythmic yet festival tempo. The morning meal was about to be served before unwrapping their gifts to one another.

Each thoughtfully considered the interest of the other as they prepared to share their gifts. Amos carved a set of candle holders for Maggie. The finely shaped curves of each piece matched the feminine decor of her gracious, warm home. Sarai was aware of his carving ability and noticed the candle holders. Amos knew Sarai had become proficient at candle making and asked if she would like to make some for the holders. She agreed. The match was exquisite, with the candles highly accentuating his professional work. Amos crafted a workbench for Ronny. He also carved and designed pieces of furniture unique to the rugged land. Maggie finished crocheting a smooth, dainty table runner for Sarai's antique table brought back from Pennsylvania. The men each bought the friends a beautiful handmade hunting knife carved by the neighboring Eskimos. Neither knew the other had purchased the same gift. They were amused, laughing with delight. The morning continued, and nothing could have separated them from their joy.

After the gourmet breakfast of hot cakes, fruit, brewed coffee, and various freshly baked loaves of bread, the two men and Drifter decided to take a mid-morning walk before the wind turned into something serious. Suddenly, a gust of wind blasted through the room as they opened the door! The blast whistled through the air in a rage. It nearly knocked the men over as they reached to close the front door. The storm became too much for them to handle. The wind forced the door off its hinges, crashing through the living room entrance.

Drifter, anticipating the moment, leaped upon Maggie. She had been standing in the door's path. The blast sent her to the soft fur rug below. Maggie lay stunned on the floor, realizing the seriousness of the storm.

As Drifter covered her body with his, the door slammed into the hearth just a short distance from Maggie. Drifter continued to protect her. Finally, Amos could reach them both! Maggie looked up to her husband as he lifted her to safety.

The rest of the household headed toward shelter. The gust of wind had calmed a bit. That allowed the guests time to reach the back of the house. Perilously, another horrifying sound of wind sent small branches slamming through the window near the far wall. Luckily, each person anticipated the event. They found some tarps lying in a pile near the exit where Amos left them after his last outing with Maggie.

Usually, Amos placed the tarps into the cellar for the winter, but he left them hanging over the line drying to prevent mildew. The tarps covered their heads while the branches sailed over them.

The calm before the increasing rage was upon them. The friends quickly took advantage of the time and ran safely toward the shelter. The bulk of the storm approached like a roaring lion. Amos had never seen one with such fury before. This storm would be one with savage fierceness. God's mercy and love would be their only saving grace.

They successfully reached the outside dugout shelter. Maggie's parents dug the burrow many years before her birth, putting much thought and preparation into the construction. They designed the burrow to withstand any violent storm. It now seemed this would be that storm. *Would it be strong enough as her parents had predicted? Could it protect all who resided in it?* They would need much courage and faith as they sat in the cold, damp shelter.

Maggie's parents had placed emergency supplies on the top shelf. Among the contents was a lantern Amos used as a young boy. He gave it to Maggie one cold, wintry night. They were in their younger days of romance. She kept it safe all these years. They filled the lantern with kerosene, providing much-needed light. There was a wood-filled pit that would serve as warmth and food preparation. The warm woolly blankets, canned fruits, vegetables, and venison jerky sustained them. There were also a variety of cooking utensils and supplies. Her parents added books to help calm her nerves.

Amos' sagacity served well as he read from the Twenty-third Psalm. That had been one of Maggie's favorite verses for comfort in times of turmoil. Amos continued to read the words of encouragement when they heard an outrageous scream for help.

Sailors were sinking without warning. The fury of the storm destroyed the town's provisions. The sounds and cries for help told Amos these men were exhausted. They could hear the passenger's panicked screams. Amos jumped into action. He dove into the strong current, allowing his strength and determination to carry him.

Amos and Ronny grabbed onto the handle, lifting the shelter door. The struggle was significant as it took all the strength they could muster. The door finally lifted, only to find it crashing down again with mighty power. They continued trying to pry it open but to no avail. Success would soon be evident as Amos' perseverance took hold.

As Amos prayed, he forgot how sore his tired muscles had become. He continued prying open the small entrance. It finally gave way enough for his body to slip through. He had reached the top, heading into the relentless wind. He came to his feet when a blast of surging wind overcame him, carrying him closer to the crashing waves approaching the town.

Most townspeople were safe in their shelters and out of sight. But as Amos had not expected, many merchants and their passengers would not reach safety. Small children and their mothers from foreign lands were struggling to survive. They must have been overwhelmed with fear.

The storm continued crashing upon the sails that were becoming torn and rent. The ships had split masts. Sharp objects had punctured the hull of the ship. The waves continued crashing upon them. At any minute, the ocean waves would swallow them up.

Just as the ship filled with water, Amos saw several men, women, and children swimming toward land. Many managed to find some casks floating toward shore. The survivors were struggling to grasp the rope attached to the barrels. Mercifully, many saw the lines and held on the best they could, pulled with every wave that broke. The crashing waves seemed to force them toward land as Amos prayed. He began searching for a way to save the other people fighting for their lives.

Many frantic people were furiously attempting to escape the vicious storm, and the mighty waves swallowed many of them. The cries and screams of family members were a heart-wrenching sound. Heads continued to bob up and down, trying some way to reach safety. He cried to God for mercy, praying he could get just one soul, if not more. With its howling sound, the storm suddenly came to a calming halt, almost more frightening than a thunderous storm.

This sudden calm in the storm made it possible for some to reach land. Amos began swimming within the hand's reach of a young woman and her child. Calling for Drifter, who had not left his side, he jumped beside him. On his shoulders, he was carrying a floating device Amos attached when the storm began. Amos jumped in beside him as the waves continued to rise higher and higher. He reached across Drifter's back and untied the life-saving devices. Beginning his approach toward the woman, she reached out at arm's length to Amos, but to no avail.

The calmness was short-lived as it started to surge again. Looking out into the haze, he saw the woman and the child swallowed up in the crashing waves. Amos headed toward shore. The current pulled him away. His pounding head and cramping muscles did not stop him. He knew all would be for naught if he did not go toward the shelter. Amos dug his heels into the sand near the shore.

When all seemed lost, he saw another young child

struggling to survive. He could not imagine how this youngster managed to get so close to shore. The boy was within arm's length of Amos. He reached out to grab his arm, but the boy could not grasp his hand. The tide was too strong. He cried for help just before a strong wave swept him under.

Amos looked all around to find him. The boy surfaced once again. His head continued to bob up and down as Amos pushed with all his might to reach him. Amos could not. Each attempt and he was swept under himself, crashing to the sandy bottom. The potent taste of salt water was pungent in his mouth. He was beginning to feel faint. He knew he must hold on. This boy had held on, and so could he. The boy finally came close enough for Amos to reach but was suddenly torn away by the unmerciful waves.

When all hope vanished as the boy went under, Drifter came from under a crashing wave and lifted the boy to shore! He had been there all along. Amos reached land and picked up the helpless boy.

Amos began heading toward the shelter while carrying what appeared to be a lifeless body in his arms. He listened for a heartbeat and discovered a faint regularity. Proving success, Amos knocked on the shelter door. Ronny reached up and opened the slightly latched door. After the long-anticipated wait, he was able to open the hatch. His arrival finally came. Amos covered the young boy's chilled body and placed him in the shelter.

Before he secured the door, Amos could see the torrents blow against the building. Their entry was none too quick as water began crashing toward the shelter door! Amos and Drifter quickly handed the boy to Ronny and dove in, landing on the blankets below.

Amos and Ronny attempted to close the door when

Drifter lunged with a forceful push. The door closed, and Amos secured the latch. Once safe inside, the men could still hear terrifying sounds. The thundering sounds beat against their shelter home. The storm went on for several days that seemed to last an eternity.

The rescued family, safe inside the shelter, cared for the boy's wounds and covered him with warm blankets, opening his eyes for only a moment. His heart beat steadily with healthy vital signs. The friends in the shelter had not stopped praying since the moment they entered the shelter. God had been merciful by saving the lives of Amos, Drifter, and this young boy.

The storm continued furiously for another four hours, sending wailing tones throughout the valley. It had an unbending will. The small town was sure to be in ruins. Amos was already contemplating ways to rebuild the town. He knew the potential of the skilled workers. They had learned to survive in harsh conditions. He was sure they would be able to again. Amos believed there would be no hesitation to work together. The mill could supply lumber, and the trees in his forest could provide the rest.

These were good people, hard-working and resourceful. They were known for managing hard times and trusting each other. There were many gifted and talented residents. This community was their livelihood. God would provide for their needs.

All the friends were very thankful for their spared lives. Still, many were grieving for the poor souls who had not survived. They suddenly realized they were famished as they continued praying and praising the Lord. The freshly prepared foods from the hands of Maggie and Sarai were a welcomed relief. They heard a sigh as they began munching on beef jerky, dried fruits, and canned foods. The young boy had regained consciousness, asking for food. The women gladly granted his request.

Twelve hours since the storm had passed gave the men time to discuss ways to repair the town's damages. Maggie and Sarai spoke of the young boy. He was a lad of six or seven years. He had blonde curly hair and the face of an angel. His blue eyes looked up at Maggie's with a piercing calm. The solemn eyes melted her heart. She nearly broke into tears thinking of the boy's future.

His parents had not survived, she had guessed. Only a few passengers from the ships made it to safety. This boy was one of them. There was a slight chance the mother or father had survived, yet the signs showed otherwise. More and more time went by with no sign of his parents. She grieved for the boy. God brought him into their lives for some reason. She only hoped the boy would grow to understand and appreciate them for who they were. Maggie dreaded to think what might become of him.

Maggie fell in love with the lad when she saw his angelic face. His voice was tender and calm as he spoke. He looked into Maggie's eyes, saw her glassy eyes, and asked, "Why are tears in your eyes? Don't you know God? He is alive, and I know Him well. He saved my life, don't you know."

This boy's spoken words of faith and wisdom were beyond what Maggie thought possible. She lifted her head with glassy eyes, "These are tears of joy because of your spared life and tears of pain for you and your loved ones."

"I know I am alone. I saw my mother go overboard. I watched the storm crash on the bow of the ship. I know she is in heaven now." *Was he this brave, or was it a vulnerable innocence that kept him thinking so positively?*

Maggie grabbed the boy into her arms and hugged him, sharing a tight bond. An angel of mercy spared this boy's life, and Maggie knew why. He was to be a testimony to her and all the others of the town. All children grieve in many different ways, but this boy seemed to understand his grief, at least now. *But what about after the storm when life for everyone else returns to normal? What will he do? What will become of him?* The questions swelled up in her heart with peace and anxiety simultaneously. She knew this boy would somehow become a significant part of her life.

The storm finally ended. After more than two full days of vicious fury, they understood the storm's impact. The calm weather opened the opportunity for all to examine the destruction of their town. Many of the compassionate, well-prepared merchants were beginning to survey the damage. Maggie, Amos, Ronny, Sarai, and the young boy exited their shelter in amazement. They were ecstatic at what they saw!

Most of the town's buildings survived, but they needed much repair. Boards and broken glass filled the small, dirt-filled street. Roof shingles spread throughout the once-clean streets, and the General Store's supplies were strewn into the dark alleyways.

But all in all, the people felt blessed they had survived. It was a mighty hand of protection that covered the shelters. Amos, Maggie, Ronny, and Sarai knew who guided them. Only the mighty hand of God could have provided such a covering for the faithful town.

All the community members reached out to the foreigners with kind words of encouragement. Many of the townspeople welcomed the unfortunate, showering them with food and blankets. The local merchants provided what they could to help those who lost everything. Many rescued people offered to assist in rebuilding the town in exchange for food and shelter. People of the town welcomed anyone's help. Many new friendships were forming. God saw their love for each other and their faithful service to Him.

Even with all the help, it would take months to repair the damage. The hotel needed some repairs on the west side facing the storm. Many windows throughout the town shattered into thousands of pieces. The storm destroyed many of the blacksmith's tools. But the merchants' homes, a further distance from the raging waters, needed only minor repairs.

The people stood in amazement for many a day, thanking and praising God for his miraculous saving power. They allowed themselves a few days to rest. Then the townspeople began restoring what they could of the destroyed roofs and broken glass.

Many of the glass supplies had to be ordered by ship from the neighboring territory and would take several weeks to arrive. They covered the window openings with boards and nailed the best they could. They used the few weeks before the weather set in to chop down good trees for lumber. Dead tree branches and broken glass were everywhere. The entire town pitched in to help.

They even turned the work into a time of rekindling friendships. The women prepared food while the menfolk labored. Children ran about playing after helping with what they could of raking and cleaning trash. Even Drifter helped carry heavy loads. He helped entertain the young children when his work was through. Everyone loved and trusted the healthy dog. All the parents believed he would be gentle with their children.

After a few weeks, the supplies arrived. Amos used his skill at roofing. He also helped with the church and a few others in town. Ronny and Mike began rebuilding the tools in Mike's blacksmith shop. He observed Amos and admired his character. *There is something different about him.*

Later that evening, after the last sign of light flickered, Mike approached Amos while cleaning up his tools from the difficult reroofing job. Amos could sense a different countenance upon his face. He looked peaceful and content. Mike wanted something different in his life. He believed Amos to have those qualities he wanted. He asked Amos to show him the way.

Now that Mike had seen the light from God, he also wanted the same qualities of care and concern that Amos showed and the ability to listen and speak with wisdom. Amos appreciated and graciously accepted the compliment. The two friends would now have the same capacity for friendship as he and Jack, the Wilsons, and Ronny shared. He was looking forward to mentoring and discipling this new babe in Christ.

While the men were busily working on restoring the town, the women gathered together at Sarai's house to prepare food. These were delicacies the men were looking forward to eating. The men could smell the fresh aroma of baked bread and confectionery pastries sprinkled with fresh cinnamon. The scent was tantalizing, one they could hardly stand; with each breath, the smell filled their minds with hunger. Amos and all the laboring men came seeking the desirable scents. The women, having anticipated this moment, graciously welcomed them. Into the home, they gathered. After smelling the aroma, the men ravished in hunger — or at least they thought — said their prayers and devoured the rare feast. The women laughed in joy. Knowing their men enjoyed and appreciated them and their cooking brought pleasure.

The men, too stuffed to think of working right now, settled down upon the soft deerskin rugs and fell fast asleep; every last one of them! The women greatly sympathized with the men, allowing their much-deserved rest. The sounds of easy breathing brought peace as they began cleaning up the remains of food and utensils.

It was only a short time before their chore was complete. The sounds and stirs of waking men brought a realization that work was about to begin again. The men knew they still had another few hours of work before dusk. The rest had served its purpose, and the motivated men started on their task.

Amos and a few others gathered the travois Amos made for such occasions. While using the tool, they headed toward the forest for more lumber. Each tree was carefully chosen, sawed, shaved, and split to the proper proportions. While many merchants continued ripping the old debris from the roofs, Amos and close friends gathered wood on the travois.

Without notice, some unsuspecting Eskimos came into town. Amos had not seen them for many a season.

The greetings were as cordial as ever as they offered to help in their time of need. The help was much appreciated. The sun began falling behind the rocky crescent mountain that lies directly behind them. Their support completed the task, allowing for a fresh start in the morning.

Gathering at Ronny's home once again, Amos and the two Eskimos, Keomi and Ketami, who always traveled together, began catching up on recent events. The Eskimos explained how the storm had destroyed their village. Many women and young children did not survive. The Eskimos stayed, trying to save lives, but it had been useless. Their homes had not fared as well as the town. The grieving Eskimos spoke of their loneliness at the loss of their loved ones. Only a few families had survived. They were heading into the most northern country of Alaska, where many distant relatives had made their homes.

Amos and the others listened carefully, grieving along with them. Amos never knew other Eskimos but grew to love and admire these two. Their perseverance was noteworthy. They headed south first, hoping to find Amos, Drifter, Jack, and the Wilsons to say goodbye. They knew it would be long before they would see each other again once they headed north. It was a sad time to see them go. The friends would never forget their friendship.

The reunion became pleasant now that the storm had passed. Clear weather seemed evident in the distant sky. Jack and the Wilsons came the next day after hearing of the Eskimos' near departure. Amos sent a note with Drifter relaying the message. Their homes, still intact, needing only minor repairs, were left alone. They could travel to town to see Keomi and Ketami for one last visit.

The friends, upon arrival, gathered close to the fire Amos stoked with his flint and steel. Each played their part in boarding the windows and carrying blankets and other supplies to the shelter below. They gathered around the warmth of the flames near the stones radiating extra heat and listened to stories of their adventures from the storm. Despite the harsh wind, Jack and the Wilson's home had fared well. They had helped each other through some callous times, joining each other for comfort and companionship when the storm hit. Genuine friendship was new to Jack, and he flourished with the idea.

New Members

The town was almost back to normalcy. The men continued to work daily to repair the damages. The teamwork brought a new spirit of hope and companionship among the recent settlers. Men and women were beginning to establish a routine and commitment to one another. The hardworking newcomers were a welcome addition to the community. The men had been working faithfully, knowing winter was approaching. This disaster had been a blessing in disguise, for many men and women bonded in their friendships.

After a time, the women and men gathered in separate rooms for "men" and "lady" talk. The women listened intently to each other's stories about their firm and faithful men and how God graciously continued to bless them. There were so many young women with new children. Despite the terrible storm, they were confident they belonged to this Rocky Mountain town with its rugged beauty. They were thankful for the influence of the older and wiser men.

The younger women, about five of them, listened while Cora shared an event before the storm about Harold's faithfulness:

Each morning, Harold would get up before the break of dawn, nestle himself in front of the warmly lit fire, and sing his praise to God. His voice was very melodic, like that of a songbird singing joyfully its tune of morning bliss. After his song of praise, he delved into the Scripture, memorizing at least one verse every morning. This morning, the Lord had led him to a passage in Psalms chapter five. "But let all who take refuge in Thee be glad, Let them ever sing for joy; And mayest Thou shelter them, That those who love Thy name may exult in Thee."

Harold had become familiar with this passage but did not realize how those words would test his life. God always provided for them in the past. He had been generous to his family. His grown daughter and son were living their lives, serving the Lord as he had taught them. There had been plenty of food, clothes, and shelter for all of them. Oh sure, there had been trials along the way of raising children. Each had their path to follow, and Harold allowed the freedom for them to choose. It wasn't easy providing necessary needs during the slow work months, but God had always been faithful.

As Harold continued reading, he was also preparing himself for any trial that might come his way, ready for any task God put before him. The obedient servant never allowed an opportunity for Satan to invade his life or thoughts. As soon as he sensed fear or anxiety, he took those to the Lord in prayer. God had been faithful; now it was Harold's turn.

Cora shared this story with her friends, realizing the storm was the trial. After Harold had read Psalms, they immediately got down on their knees — as the hurricane was already brewing — asking for protection for their home and friends. Cora also had a deep faith in God. She believed her husband was a great steward, and God had proved faithful again.

Before the storm began, Harold saw the brigantine and the schooners approaching the Pacific shore. They were carrying their common consumer goods, but there were also more than a dozen passengers this time. The British Isles and French settlers were coming in. The land was ripe for homesteading, and many wanted to start over and escape the tyranny of British rulers.

Harold was on his way to greet the incoming ships, as was his usual fare when they came to shore, but the storm crept up so suddenly and violently that he had to rethink where he would go. It wasn't until the harsh waves crashed upon the schooner, capsizing it and sending goods to the ocean bottom, that Harold realized the severity of the situation. Some barrels floated toward shore, and he noticed men, women, and children hurrying to catch one. He rushed to the coast along with Amos to help. Harold reached the hand of a young man and woman as the rest plunged into the bottomless sea.

He discovered their names were Alex and Beth. They had not seen their parents as they cried out their names. Harold wrapped them in the sheepskin he had just purchased to make a coat for Cora. Then he brought them to the shelter where the town members now reside.

All the women listened to her story in awe of her amazing husband. Each woman shared at least once their husband had done some fantastic feat. They were thankful for the devotion to their families each seemed to possess. Not all the men had come to know the Lord during this sharing time, but Amos and Ronny wanted to reach as many as possible. They were sure that, in time, they would have abundant testimonies to tell.

The community welcomed Alex and Beth with open arms. They welcomed the new hardworking couple as they pitched in to help restore the town's damage. They were still grieving the loss of their parents but had help and support from Maggie and the other town women.

As the women continued to visit, Maggie thought of Joseph. He had been sleeping so soundly since the storm's calm and had amazingly survived and remained courageous. He understood the loss of his parents and was holding up well. He seemed very content to be here with Maggie and Amos. He looked so peaceful resting in the bed in the upper room of her house in town. His angelic face spoke to Maggie again as she thought of her love for him. She had only known him briefly yet recognized an innocence of faith beyond the knowledge of an average six-year-old.

Sitting on the edge of his bed, she glanced away to hear his soft voice speak.

"Thank you for caring for me. I love you too," Joseph said and then fell back asleep. His breathing patterns were peaceful and calm. He was a gifted child, but Maggie was concerned about when he would fully understand his loss and how it would become real. She had not seen him cry yet. *Would he be able to grieve properly?*

Walking from the room, she looked into Amos' eyes as he met her in the hall. Amos knew what she was thinking from the look on her face. "I love him also," Amos said in a soothing voice.

"What do you think we should do about it?"Maggie looked into Amos' eyes with concern.

"It has been several weeks with no sign of his family. He will need a home and someone to care for him. He seems very fond of you, Maggie," Amos began to consider other options.

"And he seems equally fond of you." Maggie fell into Amos' strong arms and wept.

"Surely there can be arrangements for adoption." Amos continued to hold Maggie with fierce love.

"I will talk to John in the morning. He will know what to do." Maggie knelt and prayed softly for an answer. She knew God would show them the direction to take.

John Parks, the town lawyer, was a man of few yet wise words. Everybody trusted him. He had handled any dispute in town, whether small or large, with wisdom. Maggie opened the door of this tall, slender man, who held himself with self-assured confidence. He anticipated her call. Aware of her feelings for the boy, he had researched and prepared what he would say.

Maggie shared her love and concern for Joseph. There was no question in his mind of the care they would give the boy. He knew Amos and Maggie to be honorable and respected by everyone who knew them. John believed they were the best couple to take care of him. They needed legal papers to complete the adoption procedure. The days would go by slowly while John performed a background check on the family. Some family members might have legal guardianship of the boy after his parent's death. Finding all the resources he would need for completion could take some time.

As he explained all these facts to Maggie, she understood they would need to wait. She would depend on the Lord's work to solve the situation. There was no doubt in her mind of what she wanted. Maggie thought of Amos and knew what he wanted as well. She thought of Joseph. *He cared for them, but would he be able to accept them as parents?* God would show them. He would give them all complete peace and confidence in their decision.

The days became weeks before Maggie finally heard from John. John called Maggie and Amos into his office to review the situation. Her nerves were calm for the first time in weeks. Amos, standing by her side, walked with her. Upon arrival at the office, they said a short, sincere prayer.

"I'm so glad to see you; please come in," John asked them to sit. "I have some good news and not-so-good news. Which would you like to hear first?"

Looking at each other with anticipating eyes, they spoke simultaneously, "We prefer to hear any problems that we need to be concerned with first."

John told them of his search. Upon receiving that information, he found there was an Aunt who had requested to meet with Maggie and Amos regarding Joseph. She was the legal guardian but was willing to hear Maggie and Amos' concerns and desire for adoption. She lived in the States and was unable to seek passage to Canada. She requested they meet her in Pennsylvania, and Joseph's aunt sent money for their journey.

She was quite wealthy and was willing to share this with them. She had been healthy for many years, but the past few years had taken a toll on her when she came down with pneumonia. She fully intended to care for young Joseph but did not feel she could do him justice with her failing health. Her sister and brother-in-law loved him dearly. He was their pride and joy. She loved her sister and wanted to ensure Amos and Maggie were the right people to care for their precious Joseph.

Amos and Maggie were delighted for the opportunity to meet her and travel to Pennsylvania. Amos had never been away from this country he loved and cherished. His anxiety showed in his hands, twisting his thick brown curls into tight knots. If the tour allows, we could visit the rest of Maggie's family residing in North Dakota.

They were prepared to travel by that next week. Joseph bundled up in his favorite Sunday clothes. It would take nearly a week to reach their destination. But little Joseph would have it no other way. He would have to be in his best clothes to see the Aunt he had not seen since he was four. Joseph did not remember her but hoped she looked like his sweet mother. He missed her so much but tried not to think of the past. He had two people who loved him dearly, and he loved them. The future was all he could think about now.

The trip was a long yet fulfilling journey. The three of them sang songs and read stories for entertainment. Joseph brought along his pencils and drawing paper. He proved to be exceptionally talented. He drew a picture of the cabin and Drifter. Joseph showed the sparkle in Drifter's eye and the smoke rising from the chimney. He even captured the stone fireplace with the one crack that ran through the front piece. They had exquisite detail and color for a six-year-old.

While drawing, Joseph asked about Drifter. "Who will care for him while we are gone, Amos?"

Amos answered his question with the confidence that Mike would be taking good care of him. "He will have other dogs to play with and keep him company. There is no need to worry about our special friend." Amos wondered the same thing but knew Drifter was in good hands. It was not long before Amos fell into a peaceful sleep with Joseph nuzzled close to him, dreaming about Drifter and his Aunt.

The journey seemed like it had just begun when they arrived near familiar surroundings. Maggie looked out the cab window, recognizing the landscape where her aunt, uncle, and two brothers and sister lived. They were approaching the train station not far from her relative's homes. The train had arrived at its destination on time. The city looked the same, yet very different. New buildings, restaurants, and a remodeled opera house were all in full view. Maggie took in the sights with fond memories, while Amos was overwhelmed by the city walls' vastness and the people's hustle and bustle. They all seemed to be in a hurry, but not Amos. He was never much concerned about time.

" I am looking forward to visiting with my family. I can't wait for them to hear about our adoption plans."

"I haven't seen your family for quite some time. I hope they remember me."

"They always loved and admired you, Amos. They wanted us to be together. They could never forget you."

"I know they will love Joseph. He is so personable. I hope he doesn't talk their ears off.

"And if he does, it will be good for my family to have a youngster around again."

Maggie's aunt and uncle had arrived at their new homestead shortly before she came to Canada. She loved the ruggedness of the land and was happy for her aunt and uncle to finally live in an area they had dreamed about for many a year. But it was not her home; her home was now with Amos in the Canadian Rockies. She was proud to be sharing her life with him. She loved this country and was glad to be a part of it again. They would have plenty to discuss, but meeting with Joseph's aunt was the first thing on their agenda.

The anticipation of meeting Joseph's aunt was overwhelming. This woman was sure to be gracious. The letter she had written to John was of sincere compassion and concern for this young boy. They weren't sure what to expect concerning her lifestyle. She had been a woman of considerable means and status among the rich. Even so, they were not concerned; her gentle countenance in her picture complimented a serene look about her. She had not mentioned her expectations in her letters; they only hoped they would meet with approval.

Soon, they would arrive at her home. It wouldn't be long now. They were nearing the train depot in Susquehanna. The landscape was beautifully green and lush. The air was warm yet humid. She had heard many people talk about this land, but she never dreamed it would be so lovely. She looked up from her daydream as they approached the destination of Joseph's aunt's home.

A woman in a wheelchair, indulged by two servants, approached the carriage. Maggie looked at the picture she held and then at the woman. That was the aunt they had longed for a week to meet.

Joseph awakened from his restful slumber. He awoke with excitement to see his aunt. Saying a short prayer before their descent from the carriage calmed their hearts. Joseph, an inspiring young man, introduced himself to the woman.

"Hello, Aunt. I am Joseph. Your home is a beautiful place to live." Joseph remained calm and confident.

The tears welled in his Aunt's eyes as she reached out to welcome him. Her features were light and delicate. "My dream has come true. I finally got to meet you. What a handsome young lad you are." Walking close behind her, the servants wheeled her into a private coach and escorted them to the other side; they knew this would be a pleasant visit.

The house was exquisitely constructed of marble stone lined with glimmering pillars. It was one with rare beauty. The rooms were large and spacious yet full of warm decor. In one corner of the living space were several large hand-made quilts and solid wood trunks filled with exquisite charms and treasures. A picture on the wall showed a tall, slender, handsome man with a dainty, beautiful woman with bright blue eyes. Maggie knew at once these were little Joseph's parents. He had his mother's eyes and his father's slender build and handsome face. Upon noticing the picture, Joseph silently walked over and knelt before it. His soft voice whispered words only God could hear. Maggie felt it best to leave him be. He had his way of grieving, and God had always been a part of that process.

The woman wheeled herself into the living room with a glow on her dainty face. "Joseph's mother had been a loving woman with strength and courage. His father was a man of exquisite taste. He always was a hard worker. Even though part of the inheritance he received belonged to Joseph's mother, he insisted on making money his way, and she agreed. They had strong faith. God consistently blessed them with a special love and a heart for others."

The wide-eyed Joseph listened as his Aunt shared about his parents. He wanted to hear more.

" Erick, your father, had received word from a relative in the Northern Country of free open land to claim, full of fertile soil and broad open meadows. They desired to travel to this land and homestead their place. That was their journey when the storm hit and took their lives."

Maggie and Amos knew of this area not far from their home. They could have been a part of their lives, yet God saw fit to alter the course and bring Joseph to them.

Maggie and Amos had the opportunity to share their lives and love of God. Sylvia was delighted that Amos and Maggie shared this same love and devotion. She knew Joseph would be happy and well cared for living with them.

Their visit came to an abrupt end. The longer they stayed, the harder it would be for Sylvia's emotions. They would miss their new friend. They would contact Sylvia as often as possible, for her days on this earth were short.

Pneumonia had taken more of a toll than they expected. Sylvia was frail and knew she could not properly care for Joseph. She loved him dearly and longed to have a part of her sister with her forever. She had the finances to provide for her nephew adequately, yet understood there was more to raising a young boy than money. Amos and Maggie could be that family for him.

Joseph thoroughly enjoyed meeting his aunt and loved their time together, yet his love for Amos and Maggie grew more profound. They had a bond of love that no one could take away. Their God was his God, and they would be his family forever.

The next day brought the promise of love and hope as they headed to the train station back to Canada. They expected to hear from her soon.

Amos, Maggie, and Joseph sat in the dining cart, looking out the window at the mountain scene before them. Sylvia graciously provided their tickets and one of the best rooms. Their afternoon meal consisted of a luscious piece of roast beef with a side dish of fresh green beans, jello, and rice pilaf. For dessert, a selection of chocolate pudding or fudge brownies delighted their eyes. Joseph stared in awe, unable to make a quick decision. The waitress saw his glow and generously gave him one of each. What a treat and delight it was for Joseph!

After that entire meal, it was no wonder Joseph slept through until supper. Awakening to another meal was more than he could hardly bear.

"What do I deserve to have such delightful food one right after the other?" Joseph felt sick after too much indulgence.

Amos and Maggie were delighted, knowing this gifted child would soon become their own.

Sylvia had graciously provided them enough fare to stop in North Dakota to visit Maggie's relatives. The visit to Susquehanna was glorious, yet there was a rare beauty in her sister's town in North Dakota. The farmland was exquisite, with deep, fertile soil. The weather was pleasantly cool. She knew why her aunt and uncle had chosen this territory for their home. Yet, to Maggie, Canada had a rare beauty all its own.

They entered the station, taking a coach to Aunt Carol's and Uncle George's farm. They had not been expecting them yet knew they would always be welcome.

It was a rare greeting when her older brother, Roger, and his family came out to welcome them. She had not anticipated seeing Roger. His banking business in Pennsylvania had been very successful. Was he here to stay? Her relatives lavished hugs and kisses upon them. Little Joseph received so much attention. The story of adoption and how they came to find Joseph was relayed to them, with tears in each of their eyes as they listened intently. They expressed their happiness and congratulations to their new family.

Maggie questioned why Roger was there. Maggie's aunt wired them when they first heard of their travels to Pennsylvania to adopt a new boy. Roger could hardly contain himself, so he visited his aunt, hoping to connect with Maggie and Amos and meet Joseph.

"How did you know I would be here?" Maggie pursed her lips and then smiled brightly. "We could have easily seen you while we were in Pennsylvania."

"I had an inkling you wouldn't miss an opportunity to see your family while in the States, so I took a chance that we would all be together. Besides, it has been too long since I have seen our aunt and uncle."

"I'm glad that family intuition is still with you, little brother," Maggie teased.

"How are Ronny and Sarai? Is the church thriving?"

"The congregation is flourishing. New people are coming, and the town is becoming more united than ever."

"Before too much more time passes, I can visit you all.

I have given more responsibility to my new assistant. He is quite the marvel with numbers and very trustworthy, giving me the opportunity for a vacation." Roger couldn't wait to meet with his younger brother, Ronny.

"Ronny and Sarai would love to have a visit. You can meet all of our close friends and Drifter."

"Ah yes, the infamous Drifter I have heard so much about from your letters. He seems the perfect companion."

The small talk ended when Maggie noticed the glow in Amos as he listened to Maggie and Roger. He loved that they had stayed close through all these years.

Amos now became the center of attention with Maggie's brother. Ronny and Roger had always been fascinated by this man when they were younger. They were even more ecstatic in his presence now that he was their brother-in-law. His stories of Drifter, the gold mine, and his encounter with a mountain lion and grizzly bear kept the family's attention for many an hour.

Maggie's aunt expressed her deep love for Maggie and how content she looked. "I know Amos is a good man. I can see it in your face," Carol said as the corners of her mouth tipped upwards. She knew Maggie had made the right choice to return to her Canadian home. She belonged there with Amos, and he with her. Everyone admired their love.

They said their long goodbye as the tears welled inside them, wondering when they would see each other again.

The train station back home in the Canadian Rockies brought a welcome home from Drifter and Mike. Amos missed his faithful friends and was glad to see them doing so well. Joseph ran to Drifter, nearly choking him with a firm grip around his neck. Drifter did not seem to mind, for he had missed them all and welcomed the attention.

Mike described his adventures of having Drifter and their romps in the forest. He was going to miss his company. Drifter always seemed to have a calming effect on his dogs. He demonstrated leadership ability and skill. My dogs naturally follow him. "He was very obedient. I never had to worry about anyone or any problems with my team. Drifter was a real joy to have around." Mike walked toward Drifter, who affectionately barked, "I'll see you soon ol' boy!"

"I'm glad you enjoyed his company. We'll have to get together again next dog sled season."

"You can count on it."

As the greetings ended, they headed toward their cabin. They were eager to see how things held up these few months they were away. They had hoped to see Ronny and Sarai before their journey home. They were on their way to visit them when the General Store merchant stopped them. He said they had some business with some of the new landowners. It was something that needed Ronny's immediate attention. They missed the opportunity to welcome them home, yet knew Amos and Maggie would understand.

Some new landowners needed clarification about which portions of the land belonged to them. Two of the families had a dispute, with a shotgun involved. No one was hurt, yet there were some hard feelings. Ronny had gone to talk with these two men, hoping to mend hurt pride.

Sarai was there to calm the two women who had pleaded with their husbands to give up this ridiculous talk. They had asked their husbands to review their deeds and bring them to John in town. The wives knew their husbands were proud men, neither one willing to admit a wrong; each was equally stubborn. They were strong men with high expectations of raising cattle. The land showed good promise for such a venture. Now that Ronny and Sarai were there, they were sure of a solution for both.

Alex had talked with the men. After a time, each agreed to work together and share their profits. They would provide each with the other's know-how of raising cattle. John, who had more extensive experience of how and where to sell the animals, would ensure the information's confidentiality. George, the town bookkeeper, would manage their books. After realizing each had some talent or quality the other needed to possess, they agreed on the solution.

John looked over the deeds and helped them see where the edge of their properties ran. They were satisfied and greatly thanked Ronny and Sarai for their patience and understanding.

Ronny's wisdom averted another disaster. Hopefully, this would bring new prospects into town and the church, along with many changed hearts and lives.

Adjustments

Amos, Maggie, Joseph, and Drifter finally reached the sight of their comfortable home with a fire lit promptly after entering its premises. Joseph and Drifter were so happy to be together that the cold temperatures were of no consequence to them at all. The comfort of each other kept them warm.

Joseph awoke bright and early with a sparkle in his eye. Amos promised to show Joseph the mine before a hard winter. He had already dressed in warm clothing, ready for the adventure before Amos awoke. Drifter had sensed some activity was about to happen as he sat impatiently at the front door. Amos, still slightly tired, could not win at this point. He had no choice but to get dressed and head toward the mine.

Amos kissed Maggie goodbye as she prayed for their safety. He prepared the travois with emergency supplies. The harness was securely attached to Drifter in its usual fashion. Amos packed their snowshoes to the travois, and they set out on their long-anticipated journey. "It will take nearly half a day to reach the mine," he warned Joseph.

"Will we be there soon?" Joseph ran ahead excitedly.

"Be patient, my son. The time will go quickly," Amos' soothing voice had a way of calming.

"I am ready to take on the challenge. I am seven years old now. I can handle the mission." Joseph claimed he was ready to accept the adventure, talking like a mature adult. Amos could not help but laugh at this boy's anticipation. It was nearing noon when Joseph asked if they could rest after a long haul. Amos, none too willing, laid out the blanket under a large poplar tree and handed out the sliced venison sandwiches and fruit salad Maggie had prepared. In quiet rest, they said their prayers and quickly devoured the food.

"There's no time to waste," Joseph said as Amos laughed under his breath.

"No, I guess there isn't," answered Amos, while Drifter promptly placed himself before the travois, ready to be harnessed.

The mine was within sight now as Amos guided Joseph to its entrance. Joseph hardly knew where to look because of the sufficiently covered shaft. He didn't know where to look. It wasn't until Amos removed the debris and rocks from the entrance that Joseph could glimpse its presence.

Excitement swelled within him as he lowered the ladder attached to the entrance wall. Amos ducked his head and headed in first to ensure no collapsed walls or cracks were along the sides. All looked secure. Joseph began his descent down the ladder into the dark cave. Amos lit his lantern once they were safe inside, providing a warm glow and calming peace.

Joseph had been anxious about the darkness but stood brave and tall as Amos led him to an area where he knew gold awaited.

Joseph reached up and saw some brilliant colors of silver and gold. "Is this gold?" Joseph's mouth rounded, and his wide eyes flashed bright.

"No," answered Amos. "This is called pyrite, or fool's gold. But keep looking. You have a good eye for noticing color."

Joseph continued looking, and boy, was he happy he had! Because right before his very eyes, he saw a spot of glittering gold. Joseph used Amos's pic to get at the gold and began chiseling away at the rock. A giant chunk of gold fell to his feet within minutes. "Wow!" Joseph clapped his hands, leaping like a jackrabbit. He showed Amos the piece, bouncing with excitement!

"Sure enough, son — he liked the sound of that word — this is a rare beauty . . . and for your first time out." Amos congratulated Joseph with a hearty slap on the shoulder.

"Let's go home and hurry! I can't wait to show my treasure to Mom!" Joseph wailed in a dither.

The journey home was quick, with Joseph running until he could no longer hold himself up. Taking a breath under the same tree where they had eaten lunch provided a peaceful rest. Joseph was ready to go in just a few short minutes. You could say he was running on adrenaline alone.

Exhausted, they finally reached the cabin. Drifter looked curious at Amos, wondering what the rush had been. Amos coaxed and soothed Drifter while trying to explain Joseph's findings. Drifter understood Amos' calm voice and settled himself down immediately. He could tell that something unusual happened.

Maggie saw the treasure in Joseph's hand. He hung onto it so tightly that he had to pry his fingers to get it out. Maggie said, "You must have had some day, being back so soon and with such a hunk of gold, too!"

"We sure did."Amos reached for Maggie's hand. "He couldn't wait to get home and show what he had found to his mother."

"He said that, Amos?" Maggie asked with a trembling voice.

Hearing those words meant as much to Maggie as it had to Amos. It was a blessing to have Joseph as their son.

They were glad Joseph had an opportunity to see the mine before winter. Amos knew there would be no chance for them to make the trip once winter came. It would be too treacherous for Joseph. He was an agile boy, but the Canadian winters were hard for anyone, let alone a young boy. In time, Amos would teach him all about trapping, hunting, mining, and surviving during winter in Canada. He was eager for that day but also looked forward to enjoying Joseph's young years and watching him grow.

This winter was going to be a different one. They now had a new member of their family. There were minor adjustments when Drifter first came to be with Amos and then when Maggie moved in, but that adjustment had been easy. She was easy to please, and she was born to serve. But now there was Joseph. Amos didn't regret any of them, but there would be some changes in his usual routine. He was looking forward to the challenge.

Amos was in his mid-thirties now and was feeling at the peak of his life. Waking up was a comforting thought. Before bathing or eating, he would open his Bible and meditate on the wise words. This morning came quickly, as he woke up to a young face lying beside him in bed. Still soundly asleep, the child sleeping beside them did not disturb Maggie. Amos enjoyed looking at the young face of this boy, their son. He did not lay next to them the previous night. But he was here now. It was a warm, cozy feeling. But he also knew this could not become a habit. Amos was a light sleeper. It was hard to have Joseph next to them every night.

Amos knew Joseph was still getting used to his new home. He had quite a few adjustments to make. Joseph was making them quite well. His comfort level was strong with Amos and Maggie. Amos wondered if sleeping with his parents had been the usual routine. He hoped it would not have to be a hard habit to break. Realizing he was in a new home must still be unsettling. Amos could understand that. Joseph remembered sleeping with his parents, enjoying their closeness and warmth. But, as time passed, Amos grew tired and enjoyed his space. Tomorrow, he would talk with Joseph.

"I noticed a warm, cozy young person next to me this morning." Amos combed Joseph's hair from his eyes.

"Did it bother you?"

"We enjoyed seeing your bright face."

"Sleeping with you is fun. I felt kind of lonely in that new room all by myself."

"Were you frightened?"

"No, I'm just missing my mother and father."

"Oh, I see."

"He finally understands he will never see his mother and father again. He is such a stable boy. He will pull through." *Maybe we should let him stay with us until he gets over this, thought Amos.*

"I'm sorry I bothered you." Joseph stared with strained eyes.

"Let me talk with Maggie about it. We love you very much and want you to feel comfortable with us, but it is hard for me to sleep. But don't you worry! We'll figure it out." Amos hoped he did not hurt his feelings.

"I understand, Father. I'll try to sleep in my room tonight. Will that be okay with you?"

Amos gave Joseph a big hug of approval. He would still talk with Maggie about it, but he knew, for now, Joseph understood.

After their delicate conversation, Joseph headed out the door to play with Drifter, patiently awaiting his arrival.

"Everything seems quite alright with him."

"What was that concern in your voice?" Maggie overheard his quiet remark.

"Oh!" Amos jumped with a start. "I didn't realize you

heard our conversation."

"Would you like to talk about it?"

"I was talking to Joseph about his sleeping with us."

"Yes, I felt him all night."

"You did? I didn't realize. You were sleeping so soundly in the morning."

"It was so exhausting last night; I had nothing to do but sleep."

"So, it bothered you?"

"Only a little. Joseph is a new member of our family and must have been frightened. Or, maybe he was missing his home and family."

"Maggie, you are so wise. I talked with Joseph this morning, and he said he was missing his parents. He understands it is hard for us to sleep with him next to us. He said he would try to sleep in his bed tonight."

"So, that's what concerned you. You were afraid you would hurt his feelings." Maggie understood her husband well.

"Yes, he is so content. I'm going to have to be careful not to spoil him. He might not be as easy to raise as we think with his compliant nature."

"He has a lot going for him. He is bright, speaks his mind, and doesn't seem to let other people influence him incorrectly. We have a lot to learn from this young boy." They both agreed they would have much to teach each other.

Maggie went back to her morning breakfast preparations while Amos washed up. Joseph was having the time of his life with Drifter. He was a good companion for him. Drifter didn't mind the company too much, either.

"Joseph! Joseph!" called Maggie. He quickly responded with a "Coming, Mommy!" She loved hearing those words. He sure had been raised with proper manners. His parents must have been incredible people, thought Maggie while dishing up the last portion of scrambled eggs, cheese, and bacon.

Joseph was the first to volunteer to say prayers.

"We would be proud for you to say them for us, Joseph."

They all bowed their heads to God. "This day is blessed. I have two new parents. They love me very much, I can tell. I'm going to like it here. Oh, and thank you for the delicious food Maggie made. I can hardly wait to taste it." Amen!" Joseph spoke in such a sincere tone, and it delighted them both.

After breakfast, there was a sudden change in the weather. Amos looked out his solid window frame and noticed a storm brewing. "It looks like winter is approaching, and rather suddenly."

"I can't wait to play in the snow." Joseph finished his last bite of food before charging to the window.

"I'm sure I can arrange some snow fun. But probably not until later this afternoon. It hasn't started snowing yet. But, with the way the clouds appear and the sudden drop in temperature, we will have snow soon."

"Oh, boy!" Joseph ran to his cozy room and put on his boots. Winter had always been his favorite time to play. He enjoyed the hot summers, cooling himself off in the brisk water, but the snow was his delight. "I can't wait to go sledding."

Amos hadn't thought of that one. He would need to get busy and make one. He had some pieces of wood cut from the mill in previous years. Mike, the blacksmith, gave him some solid iron rod pieces. These would be perfect for making the runners. He was delighted to get started. They stocked up on meat, canned vegetables, and fruit from the summer and fall. There was nothing to keep him from this new challenge.

Maggie knew once Amos got started on a project, it was hard to take him from it. Once he got his mind set, there would be no stopping him. "I guess I'll just have to be a sled widow for a time," she said to herself with a chuckle. *I'll work on some new curtains for Joseph's room. Those flowery curtains that are in there now will never do.*

So, Maggie got right to the task of making the new curtains. She busied herself sewing the masculine-colored fabric with brown stripes and a touch of blue to accent the quilt. She had been saving this fabric her sister gave her when she was in North Dakota, just for an occasion like this: a new son.

Winter Warmth

The sled looked magnificent! It was steady and secure, big enough to hold Amos and Joseph. An abundant supply of snow had fallen over the past few weeks. Joseph could hardly wait to go sledding. Amos planned to secure the harness to Drifter while he pulled the sled. Joseph agreed while smiling from ear to ear as he said, "Daddy, I can hardly wait!"

Joseph's eyes blazed open with the thought of the sled. "It looks wonderful, Daddy! How did you ever manage it?"

"I'm glad you like it, son." Amos's mouth turned up into a relaxed smile.

Joseph was ready at this very moment to hop in the sled. "May I go for a ride now, Daddy?" Joseph jumped on the sled before Amos could answer.

"We are about ready, my son. Drifter looks excited. I know he will give you an enjoyable ride."

Drifter wagged his tail with enthusiasm. He felt at home in this position in front of a sled. It had been a year since his last race. He contemplated what joy it brought him every time he pulled a sled. The memories of his first master, John, were somewhat faint, but his instinct told him what he needed to do.

Waiting in front of the sled, Drifter stood ready for Amos to place the harness upon his chest. He could hardly contain himself, jumping around in his usual dance.

"Joseph, you better hop on this sled before Drifter, in all his excitement, goes without you."

"I'm ready!" Joseph said, bundled up in warm winter clothing.

Jumping aboard the sled, Joseph held on tightly. Amos declared briefly to Drifter before he turned him loose. "I know you are going to look out for my son. He is very special to me. Take it easy with him. This time, it's not a race, just a casual ride near our home." Drifter seemed to understand every word Amos spoke as he approached the sled.

Joseph gripped the harness reins, ready to work them. Amos taught Joseph the commands. "Mush" or "Hike" meant to move forward. If he wanted to go slower, he used "Easy." "Gee" meant to turn right, and "Haw" was to turn left. If Joseph wanted Drifter to move past an object, he used the words "On By" and "Whoa" to tell Drifter to stop. Drifter was very skilled at his job and knew the territory very well. He would give Joseph a clean, safe ride.

"Try not to go very far. We want you home in time for lunch." Maggie leaned out the front door with floured hands after preparing her sourdough bread to give her request.

Joseph was too excited about the ride to worry about lunch at this point, but Maggie knew he would want it before too long.

Finally, the ride began. The long anticipation had been worth it as Joseph raced across the broad open field. The sound of the runners over the hard-packed snow sent thrilling shivers up his spine. The sounds reminded him of biting into a tasty snow cone his mother had made him before their venture to this new land. He loved the cold, crisp feel of the snow upon his lips. He enjoyed the sound of the snow brushing against the runners and spraying his once-warm face.

They were quickly coming to a crossing in the meadow that led to a narrow trail between a tall mountain ridge and a stream. Joseph felt the thrill of adventure yet tensed up as Drifter lunged through the narrow path. *If I get too scared, I will just say, "Whoa,"* thought Joseph to himself. But he was frozen in anxiety. He let Drifter lead the way, trying to calm his nerves. Once he trusted the mighty dog, he enjoyed his ride. Drifter began slowing down, feeling the tense pull on the reins, which Joseph did not realize he was doing. Coming to a smooth halt, Drifter looked back to see the pale white face of Joseph. He knew he had overdone it. Resting a bit, Drifter waited for a sign from Joseph that he was ready to start again.

Joseph looked around, observing the lush green hills and wildflower beds. He never realized how beautiful this country was until now. In the distance, Joseph could still see the smoke rising from the well-lit stove. He felt safe knowing he was not far off. This feeling of safety gave him abundant peace. He could thoroughly enjoy his ride. He stopped a moment and lifted himself off the sled. He approached Drifter and patted his broad neck, speaking many words of encouragement to Drifter. "I'm so happy you gave me such a safe and exciting ride. I love the scenery out here! Don't you just love it?" Joseph cuddled against Drifter's warm fur. Drifter barked his appreciation to his new, young companion.

Once finished taking in all the sights, they were ready to start again on their journey. Joseph knew if he did not head home soon, his parents might worry, and he might miss out on Maggie's well-prepared lunch. Joseph loved her cooking, which he was thinking about. Her chicken salad sandwich melted in his mouth just thinking about the flavor. Joseph did not realize his hunger until he looked back and saw the smoke rising from the cabin. Maggie was cooking something special. He stepped aboard the sturdy sled, signaling for Drifter to start his run toward home.

Drifter made a skilled turn through the narrow ridge. He was careful not to tip the sled and spill Joseph on the frozen snow. The head home was exhilarating, like the ride to the mountain ridge. Halfway home, Joseph looked to the right and saw a strange sight. He tugged at the reins, directing Drifter to halt obeying immediately.

Off in the distance, Joseph could see what looked like a dog similar to Drifter. He had never seen a creature resembling Drifter before. Drifter was such a fantastic animal. He didn't think any other animal could compare to him. He directed Drifter toward the beast.

They approached the sight cautiously, recognizing it to be what he thought. It was a giant wolf comparable to Drifter, or so Joseph thought. But once he looked closer, he knew he was nowhere near Drifter's size. The wolf was a skinny animal caught unaware of the coming storm.

Joseph, not quite sure what to do, commanded Drifter to halt. It seemed the wolf was still breathing, but he did not want to get too close, fearing the animal's snapping jaws. Thinking again, Joseph realized this animal was in pain and needed help.

Getting back on the sled quickly, he and Drifter headed toward the cabin. It was a welcome sight as he came bursting through the door.

"What is all the excitement about, Joseph?" Amos saw Joseph's face turn white.

"There . . . Over . . . There!" Joseph murmured. He was barely able to say the words he wanted.

"What is it?" Maggie tightened her eyebrows and clenched her teeth.

"There! A wolf! Over there!"

"Amos quickly fetched his coat and ran toward the direction Drifter was pulling Joseph in the sled.

"Look! Right over there!" Joseph pointed to the area where the sick wolf was lying on a thick patch of grass.

The snow camouflaged the wolf's fur. Amos saw the

wolf's faint breathing while lifting him onto the sled behind Joseph. "Don't be afraid," Amos said. "The wolf is too weak to harm anyone. I'm surprised he is still alive. He looks like he has been here for some time, maybe since the beginning of the snowfall."

Joseph reached back and gingerly touched the creature's matted fur. He sympathized with the animal and hoped Amos could nurse him back to health. While pulling the sled, Drifter howled. Amos thought of Drifter's heritage and wondered if this lone wolf could be part of his upbringing.

While Joseph and the wolf rode on the sled, Drifter pulled it quickly using smooth strides. Amos ran beside, trying to keep up the pace, although Drifter's speed was too fast for his. They arrived at the cabin with Amos close behind. Joseph stood beside the wolf and patted his fur once again. It was not soft like Drifter's but matted and dirty. He silently prayed while Amos lifted the beast and laid him on the cabin floor.

Maggie had been unsure of this venture, trying to rescue a savage creature, but she knew Amos and his kind nature would have it no other way.

Once inside the cabin with the distraught-looking wolf beside him, Joseph knew Amos would care for him. His Daddy, Amos, would do his best to restore the wolf to health.

"Maybe Drifter can have a playmate once he's better!" Joseph ran his fingers through the wolf's hair, hoping for a playmate for Drifter. He didn't realize the danger of a wild wolf.

"We'll have to wait and see." Maggie watched Amos clean the animal's wounds and bandage his broken leg.

Many hours went by without signs of improvement. Amos told Joseph the wolf might not make it. "It is in God's hands now. We know there is a reason for everything." Amos looked at his sad-eyed son and prayed he would understand. "If he did live, it might be hard for him to survive in the wild. He might be too weak to hunt for his food. He might not be able to defend himself against stronger predators." Joseph spoke these wise words, and Amos listened intently. He knew Joseph's heart was pure and could understand there would be a plan for this wolf's life.

The morning came, and Amos was nowhere in sight. Joseph asked Maggie, "Where is your Father?"

"He has gone to take the wolf to a safe place."

"Do you mean he lived or . . ."

Maggie tried to console Joseph when Amos arrived through the door.

"I'm sorry, son. The wolf did not live through the night. I buried him near the stream bed. It looked like a peaceful place for our wild friend to rest."

Joseph was sorrowful but understood. He thanked God for his short time with the wolf and the opportunity to feel the wild beast's fur. The young lad knew that even in the winter, there was warmth.

It had been an exciting past two days. Joseph loved the new sled Amos made. He was glad for a warm home he could share with his parents. Drifter was a special friend, and Joseph enjoyed his company. He knew the wolf could no longer be with them but hoped for another friend for Drifter someday.

The crackling fire that blazed forth warmed the sizable cabin. It felt delightful. The winter days could be cold and harsh, but not with family around to enjoy the winter warmth of their home. The sled was there, ready to take Joseph for another ride, although he was not quite prepared for it this time. He was enjoying his family too much at this moment.

Maggie was sitting before the fire, crocheting a scarf

for herself. Maggie had always used her hands to make precious things for others but often neglected herself. Amos insisted she take a break and work on something she always wanted. Amos was busy in the kitchen preparing the afternoon meal. Drifter curled up near the hearth, and Joseph read from his Bible while often taking breaks to observe the tranquility of his home. He felt so blessed to be here. Joseph could not always comprehend why certain things happened; he only knew he needed to trust what his biological parents taught him and how his new parents were continuing to do.

Just as Joseph was about to drift off for an afternoon nap, a knock came on the door. The sound startled him at first.

Drifter was on the alert, taking his place beside Maggie. Once he recognized the scent of the visitor, he left her side to greet their guest.

"Well, hello, Jack!" Amos had just finished preparing the last entree for lunch when he welcomed his friend.

"You always have perfect timing, Jack," Amos teased, knowing Jack's weakness in Maggie's cooking.

"I could smell her cooking from a distance . . . I knew it was time for supper."

"Amos, it seems like old times once again. Here you are at the stove, preparing your meals."

"Maggie needs a break now and then. Don't you agree?"

"She sure is a good woman. She does deserve a break. But it looks to me like she's busy working on something."

Overhearing the conversation, Maggie set down her crochet needle and greeted her guest. "Thank you for the compliment. You will be staying to join us for this fine meal my husband has graciously prepared, won't you?"

"Amos did say my timing is perfect." The three grinned

with contentment.

"So, tell us what you've been up to these past few months," Amos said, eagerly awaiting his answer.

"You probably thought I fell off the face of the earth. I haven't been around much since the rebuilding of the town. I enjoyed helping and was glad to do it. But since then, I've been hunting and trapping on my own, set for the winter months. I learned much of your skill, Amos. Thank you for teaching me more about the trade."

"It's good to hear of your success."

"I didn't see much of you, Amos . . . I mean, trapping this year."

"The Lord was good to me this past year. I have enough meat and other supplies to get us through this winter and spring. Next autumn, I will need to go out on another expedition. We can go together if you'd like."

"I would like that. You could teach me more. There is still so much to learn."

"What an alert and quick learner you are! It would be a good time of fellowship, also."

"Your beaver pelts are fascinating. Sam has many of them displayed in the Trading Post. He is quite proud of them. They are good for his business. Many trappers for miles around come into the Trading Post."

"You've seen them displayed?"

"Yep, that's a fact! they are throughout the shop for all to admire."

"Well, what do you know? Sam said he would display them last fall when I was there. I thought he was kidding. I know when he does sell them, he makes an excellent profit."

"I understand they bring in more business from groups of Eskimos in the North. It seems your name has become well known up there."

"Well, enough talk about that . . . "

"How about some fresh apple pie, Maggie," Jack stood ready to cut a piece.

"I've just been waiting to see how long it would take for you to pick up the scent." Maggie always had a quick wit about her, especially regarding Jack and food.

Jack gave a teasing look and graciously accepted the large piece before him.

"The meal was delicious, Amos. Thank you so much for allowing me to stay."

"We wouldn't have it any other way."

The two friends continued conversing about their previous adventures. The story of the wolf showed Amos' tender side.

Jack and Amos took their nightly walks through the meadow toward the river's edge, admiring the sun's view ahead. The cold did not stop them from their fellowship. Reaching inside Amos' pocket, he pulled out a small Bible his father gave him years ago. "I would like for you to have this Bible. The verses brought me through dangers and conflict."

Jack took the Bible, promising to read it daily. If he knew anything, he knew Amos to be a God-fearing man. Amos' character and handsome features caught many an eye, but he never strayed from God nor his love for Maggie. The warmth of friendship was a calming attribute of this warm winter day.

Strange Occurrence

This winter season did not appear to be a harsh one. Not like that of the previous year, with its violent torrential winds and storms. It would be a season of continued warmth and pleasure. Amos had his family beside him, and his God was always present. New friendships developed even stronger than before. Jack and he were always becoming closer, yet circumstances had not allowed them to be together much lately. The Eskimos, Keomi, and Ketami, who had traveled north with their tribe, were still close to his heart. He longed to see them again. He anticipated the long journey from British Columbia to the Yukon Territory and Alaska. He never saw the vastness talked about by the Eskimo clan, but he was eager to see it.

He knew this winter would not be the time to travel north. It would be too long of a journey for Joseph, and he would not want to leave Maggie for that lengthy period. He thought of the memories of his Eskimo friends and prayed for their continued devotion to the Lord. Before they went north, their acceptance of Jesus Christ as their personal Savior was a precious thought.

Maggie tended to Joseph's needs and began to prepare the afternoon meal. She noticed a distant look in her husband's eyes. She had not seen this look for a long time. Amos was pondering over something. Maggie wondered whether to disturb him in his thoughts or let him dwell in them some more. She decided to give him rest.

Her preparations of stew and cornbread sent a delicate aroma throughout the cabin walls. Amos lifted his longing eyes and smiled at her. He picked himself up from his solid wood chair with the soft cushion Maggie had graciously sewn and walked toward her. Pulling her into his arms, he gave her a tender kiss. She looked into his eyes and saw the longing look. "You seem so different this afternoon." Maggie clung to his solid arms of muscle.

"I guess I have been rather quiet. Haven't I."

"You are not your usual self. Would you like to share your thoughts with me?"

Usually, it was Amos listening, but today, he would talk and share his thoughts with a woman who would listen and understand.

"I do feel discontent today. I'm not sure how to describe what I am feeling. I've been thinking about people and past events affecting our lives."

Maggie was happy to hear him talk about "our" lives. She knew she was somewhere among those distant thoughts.

"Our friends are so dear to me: Sam, Jack, the Wilsons, Mike, the Eskimos, and other new acquaintances. The Lord has allowed me to minister to each one of them. But now I feel an uneasiness. Maybe there's something else I can do to help them grow. To help them understand his atoning grace. I feel the Lord prodding at my heart. I think I need to go and see Jack and then the Wilsons. Would it be alright if I went to see them this afternoon?"

Maggie respected her husband's wisdom and closeness to the Lord's leading. He usually knew what to do and how the Lord could use him. But now, she was unsure of his feelings, nor of what his feelings meant.

"Spend as much time as you need." Maggie gathered his warm woolen shirt and gave her blessing. She knelt and prayed as he left the cabin. He harnessed up Drifter to the sled, pulling the travois behind, and they rode away.

Upon reaching Jack's home before the Wilsons, he

sensed an uneasy feeling about the place. Jack, whom he had seen more recently than the rest, shared his successful hunting experience, ready for the winter. But he saw no sign of Jack or his fresh meat. Amos helped him make a smokehouse for storing and smoking his meat. He walked behind the house, cautiously approaching it. He saw the door off its hinges. It looked like someone had bashed the door with a sledgehammer. He became frightened as he opened the entrance very gingerly. He was alarmed at what he saw!

"Jack . . . Oh, Jack!" He lifted his head that had been lying in a pool of stench blood. He felt for a pulse. There was a slight one. "Oh, dear Lord, you brought me here. I felt you calling. Surely you didn't bring me here to see my friend die. Please guide my footsteps. Give me the courage I need to help. Please guide my thoughts. Help me to know the answers."

Amos lifted the limp body and carried him into the house. He pushed his head back and began breathing air into his lungs. There was still no response. "Please . . ." He tipped his head back once more and started again. His pulse was weakening. Amos felt helpless. *Please, Lord, I can't do this on my strength. I need your help.* He breathed once more, then pushed on his chest with hard pressure. Listening to his heart slowly gaining speed, he continued. There had only been a short time of doubt before he realized God was in control.

Jack looked up into Amos' caring face. He looked worn and tired. After seeing his sad face, Jack knew Amos had always been there.

Several hours went by since Amos first arrived. Amos looked intently upon Jack's face. He placed cold rags upon his fevered brow. Amos anticipated his awakening. The entire time, Amos was praying for God's guidance and care. He noticed the gunshot wound on his chest. He saw a welt upon his neck. There was a significant bump on his head.

The swelling was beginning to reduce. Amos would need to remove the bullet. Jack was still unconscious, so now would be the time. He had seen this process before but had never done it himself. Amos prepared his knife and pliers with fire to sterilize it. He tore open the wool jacket. Taking the knife, Amos carefully pried open the wound. He could see the tip of the bullet. He was careful not to hit the muscle or an artery. He was so close to retrieving it. His arm was shaky, and the sweat dripped down his brow. He had to continue. It was Jack's only chance before regaining consciousness from the unbearable pain. He opened the wound again with all his might, grasped the bullet's end, and pulled it through. He felt relieved when Jack moaned as Amos cauterized the wound. The bleeding had stopped, but Jack was weak. His pulse was slow, but he was breathing. The next few hours would tell his fate.

These were the most extended hours Amos had ever spent knowing whether Jack would live. He continued applying cold rags to his hot head. He seemed to be getting worse. Amos began doubting his efforts. All Amos could do now was pray for complete healing.

Another two hours passed, and Jack began responding with a movement of his right hand. Soon after, his eyes opened with a dazed look. He didn't seem to be aware of Amos' presence.

"How are you, my friend?" Amos said, gently.

"Where am I? What's happened?" Jack moaned as he tried to sit up from the cloth covering the floor.

"Please! Jack, you need to rest. Someone shot you, and I just removed the bullet."

"I don't understand. I was out in the front meadow

picking some wild mushrooms when out from nowhere came a burly man. I recognized him. I know who he is. I must find him. He is my father."

Amos could not understand what Jack was saying. *He must be delirious.* "Jack, please, you must not try to move; you will open up the wound. You have lost a lot of blood."

"Help me. I need to find my father. He doesn't know what he's doing. He's lost. He's more lost than ever."

Amos tried to control the irrational Jack but was unsuccessful. He was insistent on finding this man he called his father. Amos held him down with all his might until Jack's strength again left him unconscious.

Oh Lord, please help me. I don't know how to help my friend. He's talking nonsense. Jack told me his father was dead. He doesn't understand what he's saying.

He wished someone else was here to help. Harold would know what to do. Cora could be the calming influence. She could help understand what was happening, but no one was there. *The Wilsons were always home. Where could they be?*

Another hour went by. It seemed like an eternity to Amos when Jack awoke, only this time much calmer. His presence of mind was back to normal. "Amos, what's happened? Why is there all this blood?" Amos tried to answer the best he could. I arrived here five hours ago and found you lying in the meadow just below your west-facing door. You were unconscious with a gunshot wound just above your right lung. I brought you inside and removed the bullet. You have lost a lot of blood. "Can you tell me what happened?"

"I remember gathering mushrooms. I saw a tall, muscular man standing in the shadows. I began to run toward the door when he jumped in front of me. Amos, he is my father."

"I thought your father was dead!"

"No, I only wanted you to think that. Rupert is an evil man. He beat and abused my mother and me mercilessly. I ran away from home before I was a teenager. I joined up with two men who manipulated and used me when I was young and vulnerable. I thought they were kind until they used me for their purposes. They were liars and thieves. They hurt many people. I could get away from them, but not before there was much damage. You know who they are, Amos."

Jack's story puzzled and shocked Amos, but he listened intently. "The men I mentioned are the same two who attacked many settlers, robbed banks, and stole, leaving Keomi and Ketami stranded. They left them to die in the bitter cold. How could I have been so stupid to listen to those men."

"You were young. You had no proper upbringing to guide you."

"But I did. I had my mother. She was kind and generous but weak when it came to my father. I hated him growing up. And seeing him again brought back those same feelings."

Amos could tell Jack was in agony from his hate and despair. He was such a young believer; it would be only natural for those feelings to creep back up again. Amos tried to console Jack and listen to his story.

"He's back, and I fear he will cause much trouble in our town. He's looking for the two robbers, convinced I am still with the gang and know where they are. You see, my father was the gang's leader, the ruthless leader who only cared about himself his whole life. How did my mother end up with him."

Amos stopped him before he continued dredging up the

past. "Lay down some more and get some rest. We can continue talking later."

Jack agreed and rested his weary body upon Amos's soft feather pillow under his swollen head.

In the morning, Amos saw a much calmer demeanor with Jack but didn't want to push him to tell the rest of the story.

"God led me to you," Amos said while helping Jack sit on his feather bed.

"I knew you would be here." Jack seemed so confident the Lord would hear his prayer. "I looked up to the sky before I fell, asking God to bring someone before I died. I knew you would come."

Amos wanted to know when he got shot. He knew Jack was still weak, carrying a relatively large knot on the back of his head, so he gave him more time to rest before asking.

Jack gently closed his eyes and fell into another deep, restful sleep, and Amos felt content he would be back to normal soon.

Amos found Jack's Bible on the top cabinet shelf beside his bed. He found a marked verse and opened it. "Oh, give thanks to the Lord, for He is good! For His mercy endures forever. Let the redeemed of the Lord say so, Whom He has redeemed from the hand of the enemy." The Lord spoke to Jack even before the shooting. He prepared Jack for what was ahead. Amos continued reading and came across another underlined verse. It read: "He brought them out of darkness and the shadow of death . . ." So that's why Jack had mentioned it. God would bring someone before he died. He had read these words and trusted God would answer.

Jack was still a young Christian, but his faith beamed forth like a beacon of light. Jack would survive even with the heartache and the hate that crept up for a while. He was stronger because of this trial.

Jack awoke with bright, cheerful eyes. Amos sat by his side all night and through the morning. Jack could continue the story in his timing. Amos would patiently wait. "You must be starving!" anticipated Amos, ready to serve.

"I feel much better. I thought my last few moments lay in that meadow just below the smokehouse. I sure am joyous that God didn't intend to smoke ME."

Amos could see Jack still had his sense of humor. He was no longer concerned about his return to normal. He knew he would be just fine.

The next day brought more to the story as they sat down to some savory cornbread and sausage. Jack had some of Maggie's canned jams for spreading over the cornbread. The coffee brewed in the pot while they talked: "I was coming home from a visit to Harold and Cora's. They were rejoicing with me on my successful hunt. I hadn't begun to smoke the meat yet. I was excited to return home and start smoking. I wanted some mushrooms to add to the flavor. I was eager to try what I had learned from you, Amos. Harold and Cora said goodbye and encouraged me out the door."

"Take care of yourself. Don't rush. Be sure to put down the smoking lever before leaving the room."

"They were more excited to see the result than I was. Well, anyway, I reached the smokehouse where I stored the elk. I had just begun trimming the fat and cutting the steaks. I knew the meat would keep because of the cold winter weather brewing.

Above the meat rack, I saw a pair of beady eyes looking down at me. Calmly, I shined my lantern up to see what was there. A familiarity was in this raccoon's eyes as he glared down at me.

This raccoon had been in my home and helped himself to my garden before. I had grown accustomed to his presence. I began feeding him rather than having him destroy my garden crop. After a time of providing for him, he seemed to understand where and what was the proper food to eat.

Another time, he snuck into my cabin before I replaced the hole in the floorboard. He wasn't a nuisance looking up with those pitiful beaming eyes. I began to wonder how anyone could skin such an adoring creature. He became like my pet. Every day, I looked forward to his presence. When the summer ended, I no longer saw him.

"Here you are again, you rascal. I'd given up on you." I began coaxing him to come down. Slowly. Cautiously.

The animal made his descent toward Jack. He seemed unsure of his old friend but somehow remembered his kindness.

"I reached up to guide him down when the smoking lever was caught by his tail, startling the poor creature. Reaching up to push the bar down, I gained control of the poor beast, trapping him in my arms. My sleeve caught on the gear, forcing me down to the hard floor. The raccoon clung to me as if he had seen a ghost. "There, There!" I comforted him.

Taking the raccoon to safety was my next goal. He was too startled to move. I couldn't understand what frightened him so much. Sure, it was startling, but it wasn't life or death for him. A wild animal on the Canadian frontier must have been in other precarious situations. He had to be resilient to last this long. I had not seen him for several months, but here he was. *What could be frightening him so much?*

As I approached the smokehouse door, the signs of a bear answered my question. A slashing claw bashed the door, sending me again on the floor. The vision was in my mind as I saw this sandy-colored beast with its powerful jaw open wide, baring its sharp fangs. The sound was like a roar of thunder, sending chills up my spine. It was frightening realizing my doom could be near. The bent metal door was the only distance between me and the mighty beast. My feet pressing against it could barely withstand the force of his claws scraping the metal. My little friend was still clinging to my chest. My breathing was heavy, as was his. His nails were digging through my leather jacket. I felt no pain, although I was sure he was leaving marks on my chest. I would become aware of the pain later. Realizing the alternative, I thanked God it was only the raccoon. I knew one smooth swipe of the bear, and all would be over.

Please help me, Lord. I know you are my provider and guide. Please remove this beast from my presence.

My mind repeatedly raced as I tried to figure out the solution to this puzzle that involved me. I waited for the moment I could lift myself from under the door. How could I remove myself from the presence of this mighty grizzly? My strength was no match for his.

This bear was not so easily discouraged. His body was too large to fit through the small, slender smokehouse door. His claw would have been enough to swipe against me, sending deadly blows. Crouched up in the corner with the metal door as protection, he could not reach me, determined as ever to contact us. I wasn't sure if his goal was my friend or me - or if he had any purpose other than the satisfaction of trapping us.

Lying against the stone floor was protection enough, but how long could I stay here? I had to try something! Reaching up with all the force I could muster, I managed to squat under the metal door. The grizzly paused, so I took advantage of the moment. I forced the door up against its original position. The hinges had come off, so the door was no more stable than lying on the floor. I prayed he would not be around the corner. I cautiously looked about with no bear in sight. Thinking I had my chance, I tried to escape when a gunshot rippled through the forest. The man plunged out of nowhere as I crashed to the floor. The butt of the rifle above was the last thing I saw before being knocked unconscious.

Amos sat amazed as Jack revealed the past events. "Are you telling me these large claw marks on your chest are the raccoons?" Amos asked, puzzled. Not only was there a gunshot, but those terrible marks as well.

Jack could feel the pain in his aching chest. He only remembered the raccoon having dug his claws in just before there was a sign of the grizzly having no idea where the bear went. Looking down at his bandaged chest and feeling the intensity of the pain, he remembered. "Did you see any sign of my little friend when you approached the cabin?" asked Jack longingly.

"I saw no sign of him. I did see a trail of blood winding around the smokehouse."

"He's gone. The grizzly took him instead." Jack was amazed by the beast's ferociousness and wondered why the damage occurred. Taking the raccoon had sufficed the bear, or was there another reason? Contemplating the thoughts, Amos knew he was thinking intensely.

"I ran out of the smokehouse and started to gather mushrooms when I saw him. He had been watching the entire scene with no attempt to help me. He always was a coward."

The thoughts fueled Jack again with hate. These feelings were hard to overcome. He thought of his kind mother and the Lord that was now in his life. "When I didn't give the answer my father was looking for about the bandits, he fired a shot and ran. Rupert said he would find them, and when he did, he would break them out of jail."

"I will return, Jack," his father spoke with a growling sneer as he shot and ran through the dense trees.

"God was prodding me to come to you," acknowledged Amos in hushed tones. I hadn't realized why he wanted me to come, but I knew I needed to.

Drifter had been faithful beside Amos throughout the entire event. It must have been horrifying for Jack. First, the bear was attacking, then seeing his estranged father. Amos could have easily walked into the grizzly's path unaware or encountered an angry man with a gun.

He thought of this intense situation. God brought Jack into his new life and would continue to use him to make a difference. Amos was no longer a shy young boy but a courageous man. He also knew God was not finished with him yet. But he would never doubt again in his faithfulness.

Spring Allure

The winter trials were over. Signs of spring, with their fresh aromas and delicate sunbeams, filled the rooms. Maggie gathered her gardening tools and began preparing the nutrients on the topsoil for a vegetable garden and an array of flowers bordering the cabin's front steps. Maggie arranged just the right flowers, making the house a beautiful home. Her collection of wild Black-eyed Susans and purple coneflowers, lined with tulip, iris, and daffodils, were her pride and joy. The birds singing off in the near distance comforted her even more as she listened to their soft, sweet melodies.

As Maggie began her preparations, she looked up only to find Joseph standing nearby, eying her every movement. He was eager to learn the fine art of gardening, which Maggie was glad to show him. Joseph caught on quickly and showed great aptitude for color combinations. He chose a delicate assortment of violets, hyacinths, lily-of-the-valley, and soft pink tulips for his imaginary garden.

Maggie looked over at Joseph's sweet face, observing peace and contentment. But she knew it would not be long before he would need the companionship of children his age. She thought about that fact for some time. Maggie prayed God would show her a way for him to meet other children. Lifting her eyes to the hills, she thought of Sunday mornings. It had been some time since she taught Sunday school class with the journey to Pennsylvania and preparing for the adoption. *This Sunday, I will start up again. Maybe there will be some other children for Joseph there.*

God answered Maggie's prayer that Sunday morning, but not through teaching Sunday School. It happened when Ronny made mention of a new family close to town who just moved in and were struggling. Many members prepared food to bring them, yet there was never any answer when they went calling. Amos and Maggie decided they would make it their mission to try and reach this family.

After the service, they set off toward the isolated farm. The front door was slightly ajar when they arrived. Amos knocked lightly so as not to frighten anyone. When there was no answer, Amos tried again. Finally, a man in torn and dirty overalls came to the door. He had a sad look about him, yet somehow looked content.

He welcomed them and showed them to the room where a young lad lay. Thinking Amos was the doctor, the man asked what he could do for their son. He had been sick for a week now with a high fever. They knew no one in town and did not want to impose on anyone. Amos knew that codeine was good for bringing down a temperature. He immediately went to buy some from the General Store. He also meandered through the field and hoped to find willow bark sap for tea to help with his fever.

Maggie, staying close by the boy's side, looked up at the solemn face of his mother. "How old is your son?" Maggie used her soothing voice.

"He just turned seven yesterday, March 4th."

"My son is also seven. He is right around the corner," spoke Maggie. "Shall I bring him into the room? Maybe that will bring hope to your boy, knowing there is another child his age."

"That would be wonderful. My little David has been without a friend for so long, ever since we arrived here nearly five months ago. He has longed to play with someone his age. His father and I read to him and play games, but it is hard to keep up with his energy at our age. This past week, we have been wondering where all our strength went.

"Amos will be returning soon with some willow bark for making into tea. I am sure the tea will help bring down the fever. He should be feeling like new in a few short hours," Maggie looked at David's parents, reaching out to comfort them with gentle touches.

Joseph came into the room with bright eyes at the sight of another boy his age. He had been secretly praying that God would bring him a playmate. Joseph was sure they would become good friends. "Hello, my name is Joseph. I have come here to live with my new father and mother. My parents died and went home to be with the Lord after that big storm we had not too long ago. Do you know about the Lord?" Joseph asked with boldness.

"I have never heard of Him before." David rested his chin in his hands and tipped his head to one side.

"Let me teach you about Him." Joseph began to present the Gospel to his new friend.

Joseph started to think about the gold piece he discovered in the mine just a few days earlier. He told David how beautiful it was and how it shined and glimmered in the sun. He said he thought of Jesus that way, one who shone forth his love for us.

As Maggie listened to this wise young boy, she was amazed at how simple believing in Jesus was for this little man.

Joseph continued. David's face seemed to brighten; there was a new glow. Learning about Jesus could have something to do with it, or it could be that another boy was here to share and play with him. Either way, he felt assured he had found a lasting friend.

After leaving the home of their new friends, Joseph

began thinking about the latest gold piece. Thinking of it helped him remember to pray for his new friend, David. He decided then and would always keep that gold piece as a reminder to pray for others.

When they got home, Joseph polished his gold chunk and placed it securely on his shelf, and he vowed never to move it. That night, looking up at the gold, he prayed David would quickly recover from his sickness and that he would be able to see him soon.

The next week, Maggie began preparing some canned foods for the new family on the lonely farm. She noticed there were no fresh vegetables or fruit anywhere. While gathering extra jars of peaches, Maggie also picked some squash and beans from the garden that were starting to ripen. So, she decided to call again next Sunday after teaching her class.

She and Joseph arrived at the home of their new friends. They greeted Maggie and Joseph with a warm welcome. The two boys immediately ventured toward the open field and into the woods. Neither of the mothers worried about their boys, for they were aware of their surroundings and knew they would not wander far. They were both very obedient children.

Their home was a delightful place filled with love. As she looked around, a wonderful sense of hominess filled the room with scenic pictures, a cedar chest in the corner, and a hot pot of tea brewing on the stove. On the south wall, she saw a picture that resembled the family. Only one thing was different. Two boys looked the same age. She went closer to study the painting while Emily poured an exotic tea blend. While looking at the picture, she noticed the two boys looked identical.

Emily entered the room with her face aglow to talk

with Maggie. She looked at Maggie's questioning eyes as she slowly moved from the picture. "That is a fairly recent picture of my boys," Emily said solemnly. "Nearly one year ago, our family was split apart by a thunderous storm in the Nebraska territory. The wind was mighty and ferocious. The fury of the storm tore many homes apart. Our son, Lucas, risked his own life to make sure the rest of us made it to safety. The violent storm took his life.

Maggie sat stunned at the calmness in her voice. She had faced many trials, including the loss of loved ones. She thought back to the loss of her father and, not long after, her mother. As Emily continued with her story, Maggie felt deep empathy for her. She prayed silently for this woman's pain, which she could sense through her voice and facial expressions.

Emily continued: "It was a calm April morning. Clear weather appeared evident in the distant sky. I walked down the lane with David while Lucas voluntarily stayed home to hang the wet clothes on the line. Even at seven, Lucas was a vibrant son with good character, always willing to help. He knew it was a challenging summer for his Pa and me. Most of the crops failed, destroyed by a locust swarm. By the time they detected them, it was too late. The remaining fields suffered damage but not a total loss. It took selling much of the sheep and one of our milking cows to recover from the disaster.

Lucas and David tried to help in as many ways as they could. They both took jams and jellies to the nearby markets and sold them. They went to other farmers nearby asking to help rake, glean in the fields, feed the animals, and do whatever they could find to help make it easier for us. Because of their help, times were more comfortable. Our family became closer because of it until the day of the tornado. We have not been the same since.

It came upon us so suddenly. Our walk was average; we walked many times together as a family. It was a pretty lane filled with rows of oak beauties. A peaceful brook and a small meadow lined with wildflowers glistened in the distant sun. But this morning, the scene around us was different. There was no row of flowers; the clouds appeared awkwardly in the sky as we approached home. I knew a storm was brewing but never dreamed it would hit so suddenly. I called for Lucas, who had finished his chores and ventured to the nearby pond. That was one of the boy's favorite places to explore. I knew when he was not within hearing range of my voice, that is where he went. The sky began filling with a delightful purplish-green glow and then the calm. I feared the worst, a sudden attack of fury. My fears were entirely in view as I called for Lucas to come.

Our descent to the cellar took place as my husband came into view. He made it home before the tornado destroyed everything in our vicinity. In the distance, he saw Lucas running with all his might toward the cellar. He noticed a supporting bar had come loose near the entrance. Lucas ran to move it into place. He had the strength, even for a six-year-old, to secure it in the hole with his father's help, but now he was all alone. The strength of the wind had pushed Lucas away from his father's grasp. His father, calling for him to come, began running to save his son.

David and I were secure in the cellar. Carl dove toward Lucas, but to no avail. The storm kept pulling them farther and farther apart. With each approach Lucas made toward his father, the fury of the wind pulled him farther away. Carl could no longer see his son in view when the wind caught him off guard and slammed him into the cellar's entrance, closing the door behind him. Carl struggled to move toward Lucas, but the tornado kept pushing him back.

I will never forget the silent rage upon Carl's face as he thought of his son out in the storm. I knew Carl would never be the same again. He still blames himself for not saving his son.

Carl was a man of strength and courage, accepting any challenge. That day, he turned into a cold and lonely man. Maggie, he has no life left in him. It breaks my heart every day to see him like this. I have not heard him smile or laugh for nearly a year now. He loves David and tries to be a good father, but David knows his father is different. David is a very forgiving young lad and understands his father's pain. But Maggie, I am worried about him. He has to let go of this guilt soon before it kills him and us."

Maggie tried to give some words of wisdom but mostly listened with an open heart to her story.

Emily expressed how Joseph reminded her of her son Lucas, and Carl mentioned how he loved having that boy around after their first meeting. "Thank you so much for coming and bringing Joseph with you. Maybe his presence can bring some joy back into David's and Carl's lives."

"We will try to come as often as possible," Maggie said. "I know Amos could be a real help and encouragement for Carl."

"Carl is a hard man to reach anymore, but I know his heart, and he is still courageous. He needs someone like Amos to help remove the hurt and build his confidence. I would love to get them together. Carl has a talent for roofing. Maybe he and Amos could work on a job together," Emily's eyes beamed with hope

Maggie and Emily parted, feeling much closer than

before. They began to form a bonding friendship. Maggie continued to pray for their salvation and that mending could take place in Carl's heart.

As Joseph and Maggie walked toward the church where they would meet up with Amos and Ronny, they talked pleasantly about the day's events. Joseph shared a thought with Maggie. "David is a nice friend, isn't he, Mom?"

"Yes, he sure is." Maggie was thankful. "I'm sure glad you two have each other. You could be a real help to David and his family, Joseph."

"I can!" Joseph, who seemed to understand how much pain had been in their lives this past year empathized with the family's situation.

"You can be a real witness and loyal friend for David. He needs someone like you, Joseph."

"While on my walk with David, we began talking. He told me about a brother he had. He said he was his best friend. As he told the story, I saw the wrinkle on his brow. He seems so lonely, doesn't he?"

"Yes, I suppose he does, son. What did he say about his brother?"

He said, "The fury killed him."

"I asked him what he meant by a fury." He could only say, "Whatever kind it was, it greatly hurt my father. He won't talk about it anymore. I have tried to talk with him about how much I miss Lucas, but he turns away and walks out of the room. My mother says he just needs time. I sometimes feel he doesn't love me and blames me for Lucas leaving."

"His mother told me the same thing, Joseph. He is hurting now and needs time to heal. Maybe now is the time he can let go of the guilt and pain and start healing. Emily shared with me how happy it makes Carl when you come over. He says you remind him of his son, Lucas. You, Joseph, can continue to visit David and help bring joy into their lives."

Joseph enjoyed every moment he spent with David. They were genuinely bonding. Drifter played a large part in that process also. David's face would brighten every time they came to visit. Drifter helped him forget about the past and focus on the future.

Decoy

Their journey home after seeing their new friends was an exciting event. Drifter ran ahead of the wagon like he had done many times before. Joseph decided to try and run beside the moving carriage. It would be challenging for him to keep up, yet today, Joseph felt vigorous. He still had adrenaline flowing through his body from his exciting time spent with David.

Drifter eyed him with a longing look as he stepped out of the wagon in a game of chase. Drifter knew Joseph's energy was exuberant, challenging Drifter even more as he darted from his young master. He began leaping and dashing all around his young master. The game was joyful until a loud shrill in the distance caught their attention. Joseph called for Drifter but didn't receive an answer. Drifter had followed a familiar scent and ran ahead. It had been another lone wolf that wandered away from the pack. Drifter recognized this wolf as a renegade from the tribe he journeyed with last year.

As Drifter approached this rebel, he knew the wolf recognized him. The wolf snapped and snarled at his presence. Drifter looked down and noticed the hunter's trap had caught the wolf. This hunter had no regard for this land that was not an open trapping area. It was a land shared equally among the wild and free. Amos worked with the ranger to set the delegated trapping areas. The local officials warned this hunter once before, but he did not heed their warnings.

Maggie and Amos could see off in the distance that trouble was brewing. Drifter kept his distance, warning Joseph as he began jumping before him, bringing Joseph to a sudden halt. Joseph saw no immediate danger. All he wanted to do was free the wild wolf. Joseph did not realize this dog had gone mad. Drifter knew this dog to be a rebel, but how he was snapping, twisting, snarling, and foaming at the mouth told him there was more to his behavior.

Maggie stayed in the wagon while Amos approached the renegade wolf. Knowing there was no hope for a rabid animal, he went to the cart and drew his rifle. Joseph saw and knew what Amos had to do. He was brave and silent as Amos took one accurate shot and killed the rabid beast.

Amos' shot was quick and painless as the wolf fell limp on the frozen ground below. Wearing his gloves and using sticks to move the rabid beast, he began preparing a burial ground for the wolf. His shovel - as was always carried with them in the wagon - was used to dig a good-sized hole. He buried the beast out of respect for the wild and other animals' preservation from the disease's further spread.

It was against Amos' nature to shoot any animal without first trying to help. He would always try to save the poor creature in any way he could. But he had seen what a rabid beast could do and that no hope was available to an animal once he had gone this far into insanity. Joseph took Drifter by the collar and walked with him behind the wagon.

They would no longer see this wolf again. The renegade wandered off from the pack because of his sickness. Amos did not think that any of Drifter's friends who became inflicted with the disease would suffer the same feat.

The rest of the journey was not the same for Joseph and Drifter. They sat quietly and solemnly in the back of the wagon. They rested upon each other while gaining comfort from each other's presence.

Amos was very quiet. Maggie began wondering what was on his mind. She knew his tender side and asked him what was on his heart.

"I'm thinking about the wolf, yes, but more importantly, I'm thinking about how he came to be that way and where the disease started. I'm thinking of the trapper who violated the rules of this land and where he might be."

"Look!" Maggie interjected with a burst of energy. "Tracks, I see tracks!"

They could see a dozen or more wolf tracks in the distance. From the appearance of the snow-covered ground, a scuffle had taken place. Torn pieces of flesh, fur, and blood covered the small area. Amos stepped down from the wagon to take a closer look.

Feeling the ground and observing the freshness of the tracks, Amos knew it had not been long since they passed this way. The lone wolf most likely came from this pack. No other signs of dead animals were present. Amos could only suspect the rabid disease had spread among this pack. He became worried about Drifter and other wild animals in the area.

They continued their journey toward home while Amos began thinking of a solution to the problem. He would need to find the source of the disease and hunt the animal that started the spread of hydrophobia. It was most likely lying dead somewhere in the brush or rugged terrain.

After ensuring his family had reached home safely, he began his journey for any sign of rabid beasts. Even though Drifter longed to stay by his master's side, he understood the firmness in Amos' voice and what that meant. He knew his place was to stay here and watch out for Joseph and Maggie.

Amos' first inclination was to backtrack near the wolf tracks and remains. He gathered enough information from his travels back to know the rabid creature must be close.

Some prints other than wolf were sporadic in the snow like the animal had lost all sense of direction. He cleared the meadow, approaching the brush nearby. Expecting to find some creature lying dead with only bones remaining, Amos cautiously continued. With his rifle, he was ready to strike out if the animal was alive. Amos walked stealthily through the forest grounds, preparing for any possible attack.

As he continued, he wondered if his intuition was playing tricks on him. Amos followed all the signs left behind and covered the ground where raccoons left their trail, yet no animal was to be found, dead or alive. He was not about to give up. He must discover this animal he was tracking and see if it was responsible for spreading the disease among the wolves.

It was a cunning, intelligent beast, this raccoon Amos tracked. This animal was able to maneuver unpredictably. Its tracks disappeared without warning, like a hunted animal stalking at night. Amos reached a point where there was no more evidence of footprints. He realized the animal was stalking him or had crossed the nearby river, finding a peaceful, comfortable place to live out his last miserable days.

The hydrophobia can only be transmitted through saliva. The wolves could have eaten from a carcass that came in contact with the stray raccoon, or the raccoon, in its debilitating state of mind, could have bitten a wolf, leaving the wolf defenseless after encountering the animal. Amos began looking for signs that would lead him to a solid conclusion.

Amos became suddenly aware of an animal, brown in color, plunging toward him from the rear. That was no ordinary raccoon. That was a force with lightning speed and tenacity. The beast was not a raccoon but an animal as aggressive as a lion with a strength that no man should question.

He had not seen one of these in this territory since he

was a child hunting one day with his father. His father had warned him of the danger of this animal and to always be on the alert because his cunning nature was one to be feared. This beast had been stalking him. He now knew this to be accurate as he turned around only to face the gleaming eyes of the "Wolverine."

It seemed like an eternity as a fearful man and a treacherous beast glared at one another as if melding each other's minds. He loaded his "Trusty" rifle. As he leaned over to fire point-blank at the fierce wolverine, he stopped suddenly, stunned to find no sight of the calculating beast. The quickness of the wolverine amazed him as he darted out of the way in anticipation of Amos' every move. Amos cautiously examined his black powder again as he prepared for the courageous animal's next step.

The Wolverine, a direct member of the crafty weasel family, set off in the distance to plan its next move.

Amos knew wolverines to be wily, swift, and tenacious in their maneuvers. He remembered his father once told him how this beast bluffed a grizzly into leaving a carcass for the wolverine to devour on his own. This creature could be crouched and waiting in the thicket, ready to pounce at any moment. If this beast were rabid, carrying hydrophobia, it would be even more dangerous, with more strength. He would need to be on the alert.

He began to move forward more cautiously now that he knew what kind of animal he was approaching. He found a thick set of underbrush to rest securely from what he sensed was a predator approaching. He couldn't tell whether it was the wolverine he had been watching for or some other frightened creature. He peered up from the brush, trying to maintain his disguise as much as possible, only to find several squirrels flipping and twisting around in an insane yet humorous manner. These were the animals he had been tracking carrying the deadly disease, or something had them in such a shock that they could not move with sound reasoning.

Studying these creatures closely, Amos suddenly knew why. The Wolverine quickly approached. Amos could see his beady eyes as he raised his rifle again to fire. Just as Amos raised "Trusty." the animal disappeared once again. Only Amos knew this time where he had gone. In his sight, he recognized a well-covered opening he once used in trapping before the area was off-limits to trappers. It was a deep, jagged pit, and the Wolverine headed straight for it. An animal of this stature would most likely remain alive after falling into the hole. Amos hoped the beast would suffer some blow from falling so he could get a closer look. He cautiously approached the opening, finding the Wolverine clawing up the jagged wall.

Looking into the hole would now be his chance to determine whether this animal was the carrier of the lethal rabid disease. He would have to work quickly; his speed would need to be equivalent to the Wolverine's to accomplish his goal. Now was the time. His aim had to be precise. The Wolverine, stunned by the blow, fell back into the pit with a thud. Amos cautiously watched as he ensured the animal had no fight left in him. He was sure of this when the animal remained utterly still. Sometimes, Wolverines could trick their enemy by playing dead, yet Amos had severely stunned him. His attempt was not to kill the beast; he wanted to examine him to see any signs of hydrophobia before killing him.

Seeing the Wolverine up close gave him a new appreciation for the cunning nature of the beast. It was a sight to behold as he studied his stout features. The blackish stripe with a light brown band on each side of its body demonstrated the beauty of its smooth, water-resistant fur. His length was nearly three feet, extending another foot in his tail. His weight, Amos guessed, was sixty or more pounds. He would not have wanted to fight with this carnivorous nocturnal mammal known as a ruthless predator. His three-toed sharp claws reminded him of the danger this beast could produce on a man. He was revered and awed by its presence.

Upon examining him, no signs of irregular breathing patterns or foam from the mouth existed.

Amos knew that the wolverine was a tenacious creature by nature, and understanding its cunning nature, Amos resolved to believe this was not the animal carrying the hydrophobia.

Nighttime approached, and Amos knew Maggie, Joseph, and Drifter would be happy to see him. His search ended as he headed toward his home, where his family eagerly awaited.

Amos was about to enter his home when a new set of tracks appeared in the same random order as the ones he first saw. He followed the tracks that eventually led him to the same place. He was stumped, indeed. He didn't know if he was suddenly losing his sense of direction or if something was playing tricks on him. He had just about given up for the evening when an ominous raccoon glided out of the tree just above him out of nowhere as he landed near the river bed below. He was acting strangely. He was not attempting to avoid him but scurried toward him instead without fear, like a crazed predator.

Amos had already loaded his rifle. He quickly made his shot with quick precision. The raccoon lay slumped over in a heap just below his "Trusty" as foam dripped from his distorted jaw. He knew at once this was the carrier of the dreaded hydrophobia.

He eliminated the carrier, yet his concern was how far the animal carried the disease. *How many infected wolves were there now? How many wolves were spreading it to other animals in the region?* He could only hope they would die out soon or move on to less occupied territory. He feared for Drifter's life. His loyal dog is a great companion not only to him and Maggie but to Joseph as well. The thought of losing his wolf-dog friend this way would crush both of their hearts. It would be a painful and disturbing way to die.

He could now continue his walk toward home as the twilight hours began fading from existence. He couldn't help but pray throughout his entire journey home for all their safety.

Coming close to his home, he noticed an unfamiliar sight. It looked like someone at the cabin had been searching for food or shelter. A man's backpack and gear sprawled out in front of the place. He sprinted again toward the door, praying for his family's safety. He was thankful Drifter had been there. No man attempting to hurt anyone in the household would be able to succeed with Drifter there.

As he entered the door, a strange man was lying on the floor covered with blankets, and Amos draped a damp cloth across his forehead. Amos looked around for Maggie and Joseph, who came into the room with more rags. "Oh, I'm so glad you're home safely, my love," spoke Maggie in a calm, sustaining voice. "We've had quite a time of it here these past few hours."

Amos could only guess the man was the trapper whose infamous traps they passed on their way home. He figured he had come this far before collapsing at their doorstep. Amos gave Maggie a questioning look. She knew he had probably already guessed who the man was, but how he ended up here was a question to which he longed to hear the answer.

Maggie and Joseph entered their cozy cabin, ready to rest beside the warm-lit fire Amos had skillfully built before leaving for his excursion. Drifter lay down upon the warm hearth, as per usual. Joseph drew close to his favorite companion, resting his head on his soft, supple coat. Drifter sighed with contentment as Joseph lay his tired head upon the broad shoulders of his dog friend. The two of them had a unique bond. Both had been separated from their natural homes and came here to live among two of the most generous people they had ever known. They shared the bond of love.

Even though Joseph was his young companion, there was always a place for Amos in Drifter's heart. It was a love he shared with no other. Since his first master, John, there could still be no comparison to Amos. John was a kind master, yet compassion from a godly man was no match. Drifter had found his rightful home here with Amos, and nothing could or would ever change this devotion to his master.

Rupert Claas

Maggie was about to take her place beside the full flames of warmth when a horrendous knock blasted on the front door. Drifter immediately took his place by her side as they cautiously approached the door.

Amo successfully taught Maggie how to use his black powder pistol and rifle. Since Amos had his "Trusty" with him, Maggie reached for the loaded gun that Amos kept on a high shelf near the door entrance. She gingerly placed the handgun under her apron and approached the door. Before she could move toward the gun, an older man with long gray whiskers and the smell of whiskey on his breath fell through the rustic door. His rifle and backpack were askew upon the dusty ground in front of their sturdy cabin. Food and various other supplies lie in an untidy pile near the pack.

He reminded her of someone, somewhere. She could not put her finger on it. She only knew she had seen him before. Now, looking closer, Maggie wondered if this could be the trapper who killed so ruthlessly or if this was the same man Amos and the Marshal had tracked previously, one of the same men who had ransacked Keomi's and Ketami's sled. They had captured two of them but always suspected there was a third. Amos knew if there happened to be another, God would deal with him, and that was not a pleasant thought.

Looking at the face closer, Maggie felt sure this was the same man she had seen before. His face was longer than she remembered, and his eyes squinted in hate. His stubby, bristly whiskers were much fuller on his face. This man's hands looked rugged and muscular; they remained clear in her mind as she remembered a deep-set scar running across his right hand, stretching from his thumb to his ring finger. There was a look about him, the same look she had seen from a man: a man running desperately for his life. He looked lost and fearsome, kind of paranoid. She couldn't put her finger on it but was sure she had seen him before. Yes, he was the same man who came right up to her, reaching out his hands in desperation as if looking for someone to show him peace, and then he ran away.

Whether they could trust this man was not determined at present. Drifter remained by her side and helped her maintain composure. Realizing the condition of the man, she knew he wasn't about to harm her. Maggie placed the pistol, unseen by the stranger, safely behind some large books on the shelf directly above them. Leaning over and feeling his forehead, she knew he was in no shape to move further yet harm anyone. He was boiling with a fever, reminding her of a gust of steam from a well-heated boiler. She carefully unbuttoned his jacket, allowing him room to breathe more comfortably, which he was having difficulty with now.

Joseph helped like a real trooper preparing the cool, damp cloth to place upon his forehead, as Maggie directed. The man slightly shifted positions while Joseph set the cool rags upon his head. Drifter discreetly examined the man's movement, assuming his role as a protector while Amos was away.

While Joseph continued replacing clean, cool rags upon the stranger's head, Maggie prepared some of her special chicken broth that helped in times of sickness. She carefully measured and blended spices that people could smell for miles around. Maggie looked closer at the man lying on her once-clean floor. She contemplated which form of treatment she could use for his ailment. There were no signs of blood or open wounds. The only prevalent signs of sickness were the man's high temperature and unconsciousness.

After approximately two hours, the man started to speak. "Where am I? What is that strange smell? Who are all these people staring at me? From where did all these strange animals come? Help! Help! No, No, get off me. I must get away from here. Help! Help!"

His words were irrational and incoherent. Maggie's thoughts were now of the dead wolves caught in the traps far from their home. *Could this be the man who set them? Those wolves suffered from hydrophobia. Isn't that what Amos told them before they buried the lone wolf?* All these thoughts wandered through her mind, and she suddenly became panicked - untrue to her character - thinking of Amos and what fate he might be facing in the wild, alone, away from home, and without Drifter.

Oh, why hadn't he taken Drifter with him? She knew Amos would not risk his life, for Drifter was at much more risk than he for catching the deadly disease.

But right now, all she could think about was Amos. Maggie desired to see him. She wanted her courageous man to walk through that door; how she longed to see him. She regained her presence of mind and recalled what Amos would do in times of stress like this. Pray! Pray! That is what she needed to do. She knelt near the table and asked God to guide Amos while caring for the stranger.

Just as she finished her prayer, Joseph spoke in calming words to the man lying on the floor in a still, unconscious state. He placed his hand upon the stranger's head and told the man not to be afraid; God was watching over him. "My mother and father will help you get better and do everything they can to help."

Maggie was truly amazed at this boy's strength and

ability to think in times of stress. She provided him with warmth, clothes, food, love, and guidance while he reassured her that God was always alive and present. Maggie was humbled and greatly appreciative to God for sending them this wise little boy.

The unusual individual on the floor gave a few moans and groans. The man tried to raise himself when Joseph gently touched his head, calming him. He immediately opened his eyes, looking about without the panicky look in his eyes. He seemed aware of his surroundings. Maggie leaned over to ask him his name.

"Rupert, ma'am. My name is Rupert."

"Do you realize where you are?" Maggie's soft voice comforted the man.

"I think I'm in a cabin somewhere in the Canadian Territory. I know I have been on a long journey, and circumstances haven't gone as planned. Now I am here, away from accomplishing my goal. My wife is gone, and my son has grown up resenting me for my foolish past."

Maggie felt deep sympathy for the man. He seemed sincere in wanting a different life and to change from whatever haunted him. She recognized that same look of loneliness and discontent she saw in his eyes before, but she still couldn't remember exactly where she saw him.

He continued to explain how his greed and drunkenness drove his family away. He had been too proud ever to admit he was wrong or say he was sorry. "I have been traveling in this vast country for some time. Time allows a person to think and reexamine his own life. I know I have been wrong, but I don't know where to go from here."

Joseph picked up on the man's sorrow and what appeared to be a repentant heart. "Have you heard of Jesus?

You know he is my friend and helped me through a tough time when I lost my family in a storm."

Maggie heard Joseph share what was deep within his heart with this stranger. He always was such a courageous, content boy. But there was something Joseph was holding inside. She often tried to get him to open up about having lost his parents, but he never went into his feelings as he was doing with this man.

Joseph continued, "I lost my mother and father in a storm. It was a very nasty storm. I could tell by its fierce anger. I couldn't understand why the storm was so upset at us. My mother and father and I were very close. They loved the Lord very much."

The man looked up into the young lad's eyes with crocodile tears of delight at how he spoke. "You have shown such courage, young boy," he deceitfully declared while thinking of a way out of the situation.

"I was angry at God at first. I never wanted to talk to Him again. I thought he was angry at me, and I wanted to be angry back," Joseph said.

Maggie never realized this anger. He always talked so calmly and lovingly about God and his family.

"As soon as the waves tossed me about, I thought God would take me like he took my parents. I thought they were gone. I couldn't see them anywhere but knew they would never leave me alone. Then I realized something terrible happened." Joseph wept with tears cascading down his face.

Tears welled up in Rupert's eyes, thinking of this young boy's sorrow. He never cried a day, at least when anyone could see him. Sudden emotion somehow gave him the strength to lift himself. Maggie thought he would decide for the Lord when the truth of who he was became revealed.

" . . . but I know now." Rupert readily grabbed his things.

"Know what?"

"I know I never want to be with someone like this God of yours. He ruined my life. Get me out of here. I want to leave now." Rupert stormed out of the house. Joseph sat awestruck as the man gathered his things and ran like a banshee.

Maggie remembered where she had seen this man before. She was in town gathering supplies to come and visit Amos before they were married. He was vicious and sneered at everyone he passed. She tried to smile at him, but he raised his hand violently to hit her if he dared. She ran to the nearby sheriff and told of her experience. The sheriff darted out of the office, but the man was gone. He descended upon his horse and stormed out of town.

Maggie described the rebel's features, and the sheriff was sure it was Rupert Claas, the third member of the bandit's gang. He was the leader. The sheriff believed he was here looking for ways to free his fellow gang members. The men were captured over a year ago and transferred to a more secure facility. It would be some time before he could contact them. "Be on the alert, Maggie." The sheriff warned them.

Moment of Reconciliation

Maggie and Amos were alert, watching for Rupert and the other two gang members. Amos left the homestead to check his traps and scout for pheasant and turkey. Joseph stayed home this time, recovering from a flu bug. He didn't want it to worsen and enjoyed his time alone with Maggie. Joseph loved how she told stories of herself, Amos, and her brothers. He loved the time they spent with them after his finalized adoption. His aunt's recent passing only brought him closer to his new family.

While walking toward the smokehouse, Joseph suddenly uttered a horrendous cry of fear. "Mommy, come quickly."

Maggie darted with the speed of an antelope and approached a man lying near the smokehouse entrance. She called for Drifter to come. He obeyed immediately.

"Please help me take this man inside. He needs our help." Maggie grabbed both arms.

Drifter used his powerful jaw to latch onto the man's torn jacket, and with Joseph and Maggie's help, they successfully carried him into the house.

The man had the whiteness of a sheet, and he was unresponsive. He looked up for an instant and moaned, falling back unconscious. Joseph had a plan, and it would begin now.

Joseph's wisdom went beyond his years, sharing with a stranger. He was saying things Peter learned as a young boy from a preacher he knew back in the old country, but he didn't have the same sincerity in his heart as Joseph. He wanted to learn more. "Please tell me more about this special friend of yours. Was his name Jesus?"

Peter had been wandering through the thick forest in

desperation for food. He ran away from home at the age of twelve. His home life brought terror to the young man. His mother became a drunkard, and his father suffered from a weak heart. They adored their young son until tragedy brought them to drown their sorrows in unhealthy ways.

Charlotte grew up in an elegant home with many amenities and only knew the life of servants and pampering. She did not know how to work for herself, often wondering what having a different way of life would be like. Somewhat spoiled as a child, it taught Charlotte she could do anything she wanted. Luke was a new boy in town, and they immediately became attracted to each other. They were married against her parent's better wishes and moved to Canada. His homestead was waiting, so they made the venture. It wasn't an easy journey after sailing for a month, but her love for him was more substantial than anything she ever experienced.

When she met Luke, he was in good health. He was robust and handsome, the envy of many of her childhood friends. He did everything for her. She couldn't ask him anything he wouldn't try to accomplish. She was pleasant, and her demeanor commanded respect and honor. She had an excellent upbringing and was brilliantly strong-minded. Luke wanted to please the woman he loved and adored.

After two years of marriage, Peter was born. He was the delight of their hearts. They always wanted the best for him. They both took part in his schooling, and Luke would also care for the house and the farming chores. Charlotte learned to cook, launder clothes, and help with the family vegetable garden. She was a delicate woman loved by all. She fell in love with Luke, knowing this new way of life would bring many challenges, and was willing to do anything for him.

Eight years after Peter was born, the Scarlet Fever epidemic ran throughout the town and neighboring areas. Luke became seriously ill with a fever when he encountered some local merchants. With the help of wise doctors, he miraculously recovered, but his health deteriorated.

Charlotte spent many years after that caring for her husband and raising Peter mostly alone, becoming bitter, lonely, and depressed. She could not manage anymore on her own. She wanted Peter to work so she didn't have to and expected him to cook, clean, gather eggs, and sweep the floors, all while his mother went for her walks, bottle in hand.

Her depression sent Charlotte searching for peace outside of the home. The nearby town led her to the saloon. That is when her trouble turned for the worse. She began meeting men who flattered her and gave her the attention she missed from her once loving and capable husband. She was never the same after that. Remorse and guilt had finally set in, but the damage had already been done.

Peter's father gave up on life, so in his weakened state, he died alone in his bedroom while Charlotte was out on one of her escapades, and Peter, being only a lad of twelve, farmed the land.

His father's passing and his mother, who was never home, brought him to a dark place. The only option he could think of was to find a new way of life. He needed something to take him away from the pain.

"Yes, He is my best friend. He loved me so much that he died for my sins. My mom said everyone is born a sinner, but we don't ever need to die because Jesus died in our place on the cross at Calvary overlooking the city of Jerusalem."

Peter was a little puzzled by the words. The preacher he knew as a child never presented the gospel like this. Church had not been a regular attendance for him. Joseph seemed to have a personal relationship with Jesus. He understood and talked to him like his best friend. "Why did he die?" Peter wrinkled his forehead and sat back with crossed arms.

Maggie sat back and listened to her wise son answer his questions with the heart and innocence of a child. She realized how important his love was for Jesus. It seemed so easy for him, never doubting his presence. Maggie had grown up with this knowledge and heart for God, yet as a child, she never seemed to understand the depth of this child. His parents must have been extraordinary to have taught him such a deep love and devotion for the Lord.

Again, she sat amazed, listening to his heart as he spoke. "He died so we wouldn't have to. He has a place for us right now in Heaven. I'm going there to see Him someday. Would you like to go with me?

Peter was astonished by this. He wanted the peace of this young child. "How can I go there?" he asked, willing to listen and understand. Feeling that if a child as young as Joseph could understand, so could he. He was willing to learn. "I'd like to go there. Can you help me?"

Joseph helped him with a prayer, asking Jesus into his heart. He told him to bow his head and admit to Jesus he was a sinner and wanted a clean heart. "Now, ask Jesus to come into your heart; he will always be there."

Peter prayed the prayer and felt a sense of peace. He didn't quite understand all the details about what this meant, but he knew someday he would go to a better place. He also realized his life would somehow be different because of the young boy's strength and courage.

Joseph continued placing cool, damp cloths on Peter's forehead while covering him with warm blankets. He was still relatively weak, yet a surge of peace filled his face. Whether he would recover completely was unknown at this time to Maggie.

Amos listened intently to the details of the past few hours, marveling at the wonder of it all. He looked at Joseph and Maggie, praising God for his answered prayer.

After seeing the man's gear, Amos confirmed his suspicion of Peter being the trapper. He had several traps lying on the ground next to his pack. They were identical to those removed from the illegal trapping area. After listening to the appearance of a changed heart, he prayed the man would change his ways.

Maggie had questions about Amos' and the Marshal's knowledge of the whereabouts of Rupert. She would ask him about the details later. Now, there were more important matters to attend to at present.

Peter fell into unconsciousness once again. There was a fear he would not come back this time. Joseph continued kneeling by his side, praying. He felt a warranted burden for this man—the long night drug on with no appearance of recovery from Peter. Joseph fell asleep by his side, resting his head on his shoulder. He grew very fond of this man and greatly loved him. He felt hopeful.

Peter dreamed of his past. His life seemed to flash before his eyes, revealing all to him. He had always been a beloved son but became self-sufficient, not needing anyone. The relationship between his wife and children had been right until memories of his past took over. He was beginning to fall on the same path as his mother. He remembered her as never having been there for them. Even though, as a young child, life was much different.

Adrianne had been a helpful wife to Peter. She often waited many long hours for his nightly return, where he was most likely returning from a brawl at the local pub. She had been there to nurse his wounds, forgiving him as no one should. His drunkenness had taken over his life. He let her and his children down.

When they finally had enough and left, he turned his energy to any immoral act he could imagine. He felt no regard for anyone, only himself. Animals were of no importance to him, and he just showed cruelty. He began his illegal dealings with some local trappers who had no respect for the law or the protection of animals. It was an easy way for him to fulfill his selfish desires. When trapping did not work for him, he gained money and what he thought of as respect from a gang of criminals. These criminals left him to die in the wilderness when he became ill. He crawled to the first sight of a home, which was Amos' cabin.

Maggie and Amos listened intently to his story. Amos still knew nothing about his running with the two bandits and Rupert. She was not sure of whether to tell him. Peter had changed. He was no longer the same. God was in control. The Lord would show her the right time to tell Amos about the recognition of the man whom she now knew was a part of Peter's life.

Amos already said God would deal with the third man in his justified way. He had no idea Peter was now a fourth man of the gang.

The past began flashing before Peter's eyes; however, other peaceful thoughts brought contentment to his soul. They belonged to him and the young boy, Joseph, who led him to the Lord.

At the moment of his consciousness, he thought about these great thoughts. He longed to begin his life anew and put the past behind him. He was ready to move on to a new way of life and change in every way possible. Somehow, he knew a long road was ahead, but he now had the Holy Spirit's power. Joseph and Amos were also there to help guide him. Funny, he thought, that a seven-year-old boy could bring a sizeable husky man to his knees, but Joseph changed Peter's life forever.

As he awoke, Peter met the eyes of his young friend, Joseph. They developed a unique bond of love in a short amount of time. He knew there would always be a special place in his heart for a strong friendship between him and this little man.

Maggie and Amos began to prepare a delicious combination of vegetables and rich chicken broth for the recovering trapper. Joseph helped him sit and placed a soft pillow behind his head before serving him a portion of his favorite soup. He served the soup in the handmade bowl and spoon Amos carved. Peter was grateful for their kindness and compassion. They were such warm, accepting people who treated him like family. After spending time with the family, he knew their faith was strong. He longed to learn more but was still too weak to comprehend too much now.

"I am so delighted to see your eyes," Amos said. "We weren't sure if we would ever see them again. You were restless there but finally settled down with a more relaxed look. We weren't sure if that was the end or just the beginning."

"I must have looked a sight," Peter tapped his fingers on the table.

"Oh, no," answered Joseph. "You just looked like my Daddy sometimes looks after he is away from home on a long hunting trip."

Everyone laughed delightedly, especially Amos. He had seen Peter lying there and looked at his expression. He now thought he must have often looked a sight.

"What you said about this being the end or just the beginning . . ." paused Peter while tears welled up in his eyes once again. He had not been one for crying much, but it seemed it was all he could do to control the tears from coming. "I know this is just the beginning. I have done some terrible things, and it seemed they continued to get worse instead of better. There was a point when I felt it was no longer worth living. Joseph, your young son, helped me to see there was more to life than cheating people and going against God's law."

Amos and Maggie looked at each other simultaneously. They both had seen many people come to know the Lord, and they had all been unique, yet this one touched their hearts in a glorious, if not miraculous, way. Their son had led him to the Lord. He had opened up to the hurt he had been feeling since losing his parents and had completely healed. He was home, and that is what was needed.

Reunion

Joseph left the room briefly to walk with Drifter. While walking, he sang songs along the way. It was his way of talking to God. God was as natural to him as any Pastor. God touched his heart and used him to affect others. He thanked God for helping him learn wisdom and making a new friend in Peter.

Drifter and Joseph headed toward the creek that ran behind the cabin. It was a place of solitude and comfort. Drifter always enjoyed being with Joseph and protecting him from any possible danger. While they were there, an unusual thing happened. In the distance, Joseph could hear the cry of a lone wolf. Drifter noticed immediately and ran toward the howl. "Drifter, Drifter . . ." called Joseph. He didn't quite understand his sudden leaving, nor what had gotten into Drifter. Soon, Drifter was by his side once again. The puzzled Joseph looked at Drifter, who seemed happy to be by his side yet somehow anxious.

Drifter's excursion lasted nearly thirty minutes. He recognized the howl and knew he needed to see the problem. He bonded with his fellow kind when he traveled with the pack that short season. He was still loyal to Joseph and Amos, even with the eagerness to be with those of his breed.

One of the elder wolves and a new leader had taken over the pack. Since wolves form strong social bonds, a dominant leader is needed to keep order. That leader had shown his dominance by howling for all the pack members to hear. Drifter felt it necessary to prove his devotion by joining the group. He had been well known; he was hopeful the new alpha male would welcome him as a group member. Wolves will defend their territory from intruders, and Drifter did not want to be one of those. Keeping a good relationship with the pack would be healthy for him and his ability to protect Joseph, Amos, and Maggie.

Maggie and Amos became concerned for Joseph when he did not return by the twilight hour. Amos was going out the door when he saw Joseph and Drifter sauntering up the valley toward home. Joseph yelled, "Hello, I'll be there soon," to Amos. That brought peace to his heart that all had been well.

"I'm starving!" Joseph rubbed his growling stomach. Peter seconded the motion, and Amos was ready and eager to eat. Maggie knew she would have three hungry mouths to feed. She started preparing the meal the minute Joseph left. Serving the extraordinary men in her life was a pleasure, and Maggie was thankful for every opportunity. She enjoyed working in the kitchen and preparing meals. God developed this strength in her as a young woman. Maggie used her Godly gift by taking care of her family for many years.

God allowed Maggie's talent of working with children to disciple Joseph. God brought Amos to her at just the right time. She knew God planned for her to marry Amos, raise Joseph to be a Godly child, and help the people in her life. She wondered whether she had done the right thing, leaving Amos many years earlier, but she felt peace these past few years. God was in control and had been all along.

The meal was complete, and no one argued. Maggie's family and a newly acquainted friend sat with comforting smiles, "The meal was wonderful. Thank you for your hospitality."

Peter was gaining his strength thanks to Maggie's well-balanced and delightful-tasting meals. He could not express his gratitude in words, but Maggie understood.

"Shall we bow our heads and thank God?" Amos

asked. "Would you, Peter, like to do us the honor?"

"I'd love to . . . Dear Lord, I know I'm new at this sort of thing, but I know I can change and become a vital person in your kingdom. Please help show me the way. And Lord, thank you so much for this wonderful family that has helped me see the right way to go. Thank you for this meal we are about to eat. Amen."

"That was wonderful," Maggie said.

"Now, let's eat!" Amos and Joseph held their forks eagerly.

The meal consisted of smoked elk from the smokehouse, applesauce previously canned in October, fresh garden vegetables, and some of Maggie's titillating sourdough bread. The aroma filled the air with a delicate scent of freshness.

They were ready to indulge in their feast when a faint knock came from the front door. Amos walked over anxiously to see who it might be.

"Jack! It has been a while since we've seen you. Please come in and join us. We are just about to feast on a well-prepared meal." Before Amos could finish his sentence, Jack found a finely carved piece of furniture and took his place at the table.

"I thought I smelled Maggie's bread. Who could pass up an offer like that."

When he looked up, he was stunned to see who was sitting at the table. His hands began to tremble. Amos noticed a peculiarity about Jack but proceeded to introduce Jack to Peter. The conversation started as they both looked at each other sheepishly. Having traveled together in Rupert's gang brought back bad memories for Jack. They had been together briefly before Jack dared leave, and Peter replaced him. But somehow, he looked different. The roughness around Peter's eyes had softened.

Peter hardly recognized Jack and did not indicate he had known him. He had a new life now, and his past way of life vanished. Peter went on to explain his faith. He knew his life had changed for the better.

Jack had not been surprised by Joseph's ability to witness. He considered him a prodigy with moral character qualities for a seven-year-old. Joseph was like his father, Amos, who saved him from darkness and shame. He taught him what it meant to have peace and joy and how to be bold about his faith. He owed everything to Amos for showing him the way.

Jack was amazed at Peter's transformation, but with Amos, Maggie, and Joseph around, who could resist the power of the Holy Spirit in their lives?

Amos thought back on his past few years of life and was truly amazed by God's tender care for all of them. He was starting life as a wise yet timid child who had turned around, now a man of inner strength and a bold witness. He was thankful for his new family and close friends all around him.

The Wilsons showed up shortly after Jack.

"I'm so glad you came," responded Amos with a twinkle in his eye. "We have two seats right on the end of the table."

"We wouldn't have missed out on this for anything. Thank you for the welcome invitation. We hoped you would be home. It has been quite some time since we've seen you. We have all been so busy. Cora brought along some of her famous fruit pies."

"That fits in perfectly with the meal Maggie prepared. Your company is quite a welcome surprise. Please join us!"

Harold and Cora sat at the end of the table, eager for their time together.

Jack was somewhat disappointed in himself for not asking Harold and Cora before coming. He should have known Maggie and Amos would be thrilled to see them.

"I'm so sorry I didn't think to ask you myself," Jack repented.

"It's alright," they expressed. "We are here together, and that's all that matters."

"Ronny and Sarai should be here shortly. We invited them last week. They said to go on without them if they were late. They had a special surprise prepared for us, which might take some time.

"I wonder what it could be?" they all spoke in unison.

"Well, this is quite the family reunion. It's funny how the Lord always works things out."

"Not funny at all," Amos looked at all the peaceful faces. "The Lord always has a way of bringing his people together.

"I'm glad he chose to have us meet through a meal," Jack teased.

"We all know the best way to Jack's heart is through his tummy." The friends laughed together as Amos looked at Jack with a friendly smile.

Prayers were about to be said when a knock came on the door, and not only Ronny and Sarai entered, but Emily, Carl, and David. Joseph was so delighted that he jumped from the table and rushed into David, nearly knocking him over. "It is the best surprise I could ever have. Thank you so much for bringing them, Uncle Ronny and Aunt Sarai."

Much time had passed since they had seen each other. It was unlike Carl to leave his home. He was such a homebody.

Ronny had been ministering to them these past few months. They were accepting their loss and moving on with their lives. God came to mean something special to them. They were beginning to rely on Him alone.

The reunion was a special blessing. The friends took turns sharing the many blessings in their lives these past few years. God brought them all together in such a unique way. They would always stay faithful to each other.

Everyone graciously ate the tantalizing prepared meal. Happy faces filled the room. They gathered around the fire to sing songs of joy and praise. Amos looked around curiously for a moment. Then they all realized Drifter was nowhere around. They hadn't seen him all morning. "Where could he be?" thought Amos.

"I'm sure he's around somewhere. Please don't worry," Maggie said in her comforting voice, reassuring them.

It was unlike Drifter to wander off, especially when his favorite people were around. Amos looked away for a moment and went to the window. He looked around for a sign of Drifter, anticipating his soon return. Amos began to think of when Drifter wandered off once before when the wolves attracted his attention. Amos was worried for a short time that he had lost Drifter. After all, Drifter was half-wolf. He had some wild instinct bred in him. He might have to accept that someday *Drifter might choose to follow his instincts and not return. Now that most of the friends had settled into their lives, Drifter may feel unnecessary. He might need to be with his fellow kind.*

Amos didn't want to think about it anymore. He gathered his thoughts and joined the group in merriment and fellowship.

"We were talking, Amos, about these past few years.

The area out there is still so desolate. Yet, all our friends are still close enough to fellowship often. Let's make sure we always stay in touch," Ronny said.

Ronny appreciated everything Amos and Maggie had done for him. He loved seeing how happy they both were together. He often thought of Maggie and how committed she was to her family and how she sacrificed everything to care for others. She deserved to be here now with the man she loved and longed to be with all those years while caring for their parents. She was a marvel to behold. And Amos, words could not express how much he meant to Ronny and the rest of the family.

Harold and Cora were becoming acquainted with Emily and Carl. They related to their hurt. They remembered the past pain when their children turned from the beliefs Harold and Cora taught them and moved away to start living independently. It brought back some painful memories of when they would see their children again. They knew it would all be in God's timing. It also brought them joy to know that this family finally escaped the slump of mourning after losing David's twin brother, Lucas.

Meanwhile, David and Joseph were having an adventure outside. They were running free in the broad open meadow near the cabin.

"Don't you love it here, David?" Joseph asked contentedly.

"I love it because you are here. I miss my brother greatly, but I am glad I have you."

"Would you like to hike up to that small ridge just ahead?"

"Okay, you show me the way!"

The small ridge was very familiar to Joseph. He knew

it almost like the back of his hand. Maggie and Amos said it would be alright and went on their adventure.

It was a beautiful afternoon. The sun was at its peak. The fresh smells of wildflowers in full bloom brought a delightful sensation.

"The ledge is not far now. Look, it's just up ahead."

The two boys ran with vigor and energy. David had never seen anything so beautiful in all his life as the view from the mountain ledge. He loved being on that ridge, looking across the meadow at the smoking cabin in the distance. He felt safe and secure knowing his family was close by.

"This scene is so beautiful. I love it up here. Thank you for showing it to me."

"It has always been one of my favorite places. I come here often with Drifter. Where is Drifter? I haven't seen him all morning."

"I was wondering about that same thing." David scanned the area. "It is very unusual for him to wander off for this long. Isn't it, Joseph?"

"Yes. I wonder where Drifter can be?"

"One other time, Drifter wandered off not too long ago, but only for about a few hours. I wondered where he could have gone. Now I'm beginning to wonder what is going on with him."

"I'm sure he'll be home soon. Try not to worry," consoled David.

"I'm sure you're probably right. Let's go. Let's walk a little farther, then we better head for home. We don't want to worry our parents."

Walking together, the two boys came to a cave, one Joseph had seen before but had never entered. David gathered up his courage and asked Joseph to go inside. They examined the area and decided it would be alright.

"We better be cautious. You never know what you'll come across in a cave."

"Maybe we better not right now." David became frightened by the distance from home, peering into the dark cave.

"Don't worry! I'm sure it will be fine. Amos says there are hardly any wild animals this close to the cabin.

Their fear was subsiding, and they dared to enter. Once inside, the boys could hear some squealing and whining. "I'm scared." David quietly responded. "Let's get just a little closer," Joseph bravely conquered his hidden fear. Once inside, he felt an animal brush up against his leg. He began to move away. Only a vague sense of danger slowly surrounded him. He recognized the scent of the animal. Turning on his flashlight, he saw the animal's large face eye to eye.

"What is it? What is It?" David was almost in a state of panic. "GET ME OUT OF HERE!"

"David, wait a minute." Joseph grabbed David by the arm and pulled him closer.

"It's Drifter. Drifter, is it you?"

Standing in astonishment, David was scared half out of his wits. He was ready to go home, running full speed ahead but realized he was too frightened to move.

"David," called Joseph. "Look, it's Drifter."

Once David knew he was out of danger, he calmed down, breathing regularly.

"Drifter, what are you doing here? We have been looking all over for you."

Joseph was astonished to shine the flashlight on three young cubs below his feet. Joseph was dumbfounded, unsure of what just happened and what to think about it all.

"They are young wolf pups!" David squealed with delight.

"But . . . but . . ."

"Oh, Joseph, I have never seen you without speaking cleverly. They are beautiful."

"But where is the mother? If she returns, we might be in danger."

"Drifter will protect us." The two boys trusted Drifter would save them.

Now I know why you have been wandering far from home more often. You have a mate and babies!" Joseph could hardly hear what he was saying. *Does this mean that Drifter won't be a part of our family anymore now that he has his own family?*

"As much as Drifter loves your family, Joseph, I don't think he would leave you for good. But now that he does have a family, you might not see as much of him."

"You're right. I'm acting selfishly, thinking only of myself. We must go back and tell Amos. He will be fascinated to see Drifter's cubs."

The two boys darted off, only to find them FACE TO FACE with a she-wolf. Just as the wolf started to show her fangs and charge, Drifter came blasting out of the cave toward her. She knew Drifter would not allow the boys to harm her or the pups. Drifter had shown her that. Drifter was her mate, and she knew he would handle everything. She still feared the two boys, so she quickly moved toward the cave exit.

Amos and all his friends were having an enjoyable fellowship. They were sharing past experiences, helping them learn more about each other. After they talked for a while, they tried to play some games. They were just about to start their card game when Joseph and David burst into the room, all out of breath.

"What's all this about?" The guests stood up with worried frowns.

Joseph and David came running from quite a distance without stopping. "There is . . . something . . . you must see." Joseph was barely able to get out the words.

"What is it? David's father said. He was somewhat worried about what happened on their outing.

"Here, rest a minute, you two. Let me get you some cool water. And please try and catch your breath." Amos was just as anxious as the rest of the group to find out what they had seen or done.

"Are you feeling much better now?" Maggie reassuringly asked the two.

"We were hiking to the ridge not far from here. You know, Daddy, the one with the cave. We have gone there many times. You said wild animals rarely came there. But I remember you telling me a story about wolves living near the cave."

Amos was becoming concerned now. He hoped the wolves were not going to be near their home. Especially now with Joseph here. He loved to roam this country and had always been careful not to wander far. Up until now, there was no concern.

"You said it was rare for wolves to live this close to humans. But Daddy, there are wolves here."

"Are you alright, my son?" Emily squinted her eyes.

"Oh, yes! It was quite exciting! We walked up the ridge and saw the cave. I was hesitant to go in at first. Joseph talked me into it. I was quite frightened when we felt the fur."

"You were that close to the pups?" Emily held her breath.

267

"Yes. But when we turned on the flashlight, we recognized him."

"Recognized who? What are you talking about?" Everyone was becoming entirely enthralled by the tale.

"We knew he wouldn't harm us. He knows us."

"Drifter. Is it Drifter?" Amos asked. He thought about him all day. Amos hoped no harm had come to him. He was becoming more independent these past few months and wondered if he might have found a new home. Drifter's distance answered his fear.

"He has a wife and babies," Joseph said in his innocent voice.

"Really!"

"Yes, three of them!"

"This is indeed a surprise." Maggie was fascinated by the story and concerned. She wondered if they had lost Drifter for good. The family had become so close. She had grown quite fond of Drifter. She could see the concerned look on Amos' face. Losing Drifter would be tough for both, but if he decided to leave and join his wild family, they would have to let him. But it was something they must all accept. They would have to face the fact they might never see Drifter again.

"His mate was afraid of us. We ran into her on our way out of the cave. Drifter came from the cave and showed her there was nothing to be afraid of."

What a calm, controlled son they had. He was growing up so much in the few years they had him. Amos was amazed at his confidence and self-control.

"Is there anything else you can tell us?" Amos feared the answer.

"He didn't seem to mind much that we were there. Drifter welcomed us into his home. He seemed proud to show us his new family. I don't think he would mind if we went to see him."

"Well, son, he might not mind, but his mate would. Wolves are very protective of their young. It would be better for us to let Drifter come to us."

"But . . ."

"No, Joseph, I still think it would be best. I know you saw him, and he didn't harm you, but you might not be so lucky next time."

"Do you think Drifter would harm us?"

"No. But his mate would. She doesn't know us. And as you said, she was frightened of you. She only submitted when she knew Drifter would do the protecting. She might be the one you run into first next time. It could end up in disaster for all concerned."

"Yes, Father, I understand."

"We wouldn't want to lose Drifter's trust or have any harm come to the pups or you, my son."

"I guess you are right. It will be so hard. What if Drifter doesn't return?"

"That will have to be Drifter's choice. He has been our friend for a long time. He has served me well. We can pray for God's help in the situation. God knows what's best for Drifter and us."

So, that's what they all did. All the sympathetic friends knew how much Drifter meant to them. The story was hard to hear, so they all bowed their heads and lifted their concern to the Heavenly Father.

It ended in a rather solemn evening after all the festive mood earlier. Amos shared his concern about the situation after the two young boys slept for the night. He was concerned about more wolves coming close to their homes. He hated

269

chasing them off, maybe even shooting to protect his family. There had been signs of wolves earlier near the area, but nothing came from it. The wolves had left until now. Maybe Drifter chose that cave because it was so near home. Amos hoped he could establish a link between his new home and theirs.

Amos mulled these ideas over in his mind, hoping they were correct. He knew he would have to wait for Drifter to make the first move.

The friends knew the day had ended as the midnight hour approached. The two boys slept soundly from their frightful excursion. The rest of the families hardly noticed the passing of time.

"Thank you for opening your home to all of us."The Wilsons paid their respects and headed toward their cabin.

"Yes, thank you for your hospitality," Jack repeated the sentiment.

". . . and on such short notice," quipped the rest.

"It has truly been an enjoyable evening. One I shall never forget."

Amos loved his family in Christ. They were compassionate friends and would always be there for him, and they would be able to comfort and disciple Peter. They would remain close until God chose a different path for their lives. But whatever the outcome, he would be satisfied and content. God taught him through the years trusting was the best way. Through all his trials in life, that was one lesson he learned; many times, he had to learn it the hard way, but Amos did learn, and he was thankful for God's constant provision.

Rupert's Revenge

The night dragged on as Rupert waited for the opportune moment to make his move. The Marshal had taken the rest of his gang to prison and was scouting where to find them. He was not about to give up on his way of life, so rescuing them was necessary. *I will show Jack how dominant I am when I break them out. I will show the world and those who tried to change me. My son will regret the day he left home. Jack will regret ever having been born.* After seeing Jack and how Amos' character changed him into a weak son, he hated Jack's mother even more. *Jack is just like her.* Was it out of guilt or pure hatred he felt this way? It didn't matter. Their end would come. *I will get my revenge.*

"If only that grizzly bear had not been there. If I could have had a better aim." Rupert's face grimaced with sweaty palms. *Get ready! I'm coming for you.*

Rupert knew the whereabouts of Jack's estranged son. The courts had taken Jack's son from him during his downward spiral. Rupert found him when traveling with his gang on one of his robbing escapades. A family in Massachusetts adopted him. The only thing he cared about was this boy. The regrets stayed with him. He was now a young teenager and doing very well with his family. The boy knew nothing of Rupert, and he suspected he knew nothing of Jack nor where he was now.

None of that mattered anyway. Rupert was bent on revenge. His son left the gang, and no one did that to Rupert. Even though he had some sense of admiration for his son for having the backbone to leave, he resented Jack for deserting his son. He was better off with his family in Massachusetts. He was much better off than with him.

Jack enjoyed his time with all his friends, especially Peter. He could relate to his way of life and how easy it had been to follow the wrong directions. After Jack left the gang, he knew someone would be there to take his place. Peter was about the same age, and his father preyed on the young and vulnerable. Peter had been the naive one he could take advantage of. He knew Rupert would return at some point and feared for Peter's life. The thoughts of his father took him to a dark place. He knew he would finally need to approach Amos and tell him the whole truth about his father and estranged son.

Rupert approached stealthily toward the prison. The moon was high in the sky, filling it with darkness. The townspeople were safe in their homes, secured for the night. The local pub's raucous behavior blared through the town. Any noise from him would be innocuous. His eyes beamed with a glare of vengeance. He glanced around to see any sign of life. The deputy was within the prison, guarding it carefully. The Marshal stepped out for a moment. Rupert would move as soon as the deputy walked away from the door to secure his prisoner.

Rupert loaded his rifle, ready to fire. The time was ripe for Rupert to approach. He planned this day to the last detail. He had studied the townspeople's habits and the night guard's routine. The residents were too trusting, and the deputy needed his sleep and the visit from his young bride. He would wait a few more minutes until the opportune moment.

In the morning, the two convicts would go to a more secure location, so he had to make his move tonight. Once inside, he would do whatever it took to move the deputy from guarding the convicts. If it meant killing him, then so be it. Rupert had no reservations about proving he was the best outlaw feared by all.

The evening was splendid with all the friends. Jack finally had a moment with Amos after all the other friends left. Amos sensed a restlessness in Jack and approached him kindly. "What is on your mind?" Amos put down his brewed coffee, ready to listen.

"It amazes me how you always know. You can read me so well."

"I am ready to listen now. I'm all ears!"

"You know, Peter. He is the young man that took my place."

Amos did not fully understand what Jack was implying at first. It was hard for him to understand this man had such a past.

"My mother was kind and loyal to my father, even though he was ruthless. He didn't start that way. He used to be a banker and was very good at his job. But he was too preoccupied with making money. He was impatient and mistreated his fellow employees. One day, he got an idea that would make him prosperous. He unethically pursued the plan, taking advantage of what he knew about newly produced products. He kept them secret from the public. He embezzled money from the bank to pursue his dream of becoming rich. When the local sheriff finally found him, he raged, threatening anyone that got in his way. He escaped from the law before they were able to convict him. He came home to take me with him. I refused to go — he left, threatening me with my life. I stayed to care for my mother and fled after she passed away. The grief was too much to bear, and I didn't want to be near my father.

"Who is your father?" questioned Amos.

"You know him, and so does Maggie. He is the outlaw

bandit you served in your home. He is Rupert!"

Amos and Maggie were shocked. *How could a man like Rupert be part of Jack's life?* It was hard for any of them to imagine. They remained silent, gleaning a better understanding of Jack's past.

"I know what you must think of me. I am ashamed to call Rupert my father."Jack whispered while shaking his head in disgust.

"We know who you are now, Jack, and that is all that matters."

"How can you love me the way you do with knowing about the evil in my past?"

"Jesus has cleansed you, and you are like fine gold in his eyes. Never forget that, Jack," Amos reassured.

Rupert slammed through the jail's door, guns blazing. The deputy had no chance of drawing on his quick and accurate aim. He went down without a second of pain.

The Marshal had only a second to pull his gun before he shot him in the chest. His breathing was heavy as Rupert laughed with a sneer. "Get out of my way," Rupert incessantly blared as he kicked the dying sheriff out of his way. He grabbed the cell keys, dangling from the sheriff's belt, and unlocked the cell door.

Out jumped the two bandits. They were free, and their terror would never end unless someone stopped them. After Rupert and the two bandits ran out the door, a brave citizen came around the corner and shot the younger of the two. Rupert and the older outlaw ran toward their horses and began to ride away as this same man took careful aim, landing a bullet in the backside of Rupert's left shoulder, heading toward his heart. They continued galloping through town, leaving a trail of blood.

The sheriff brought the younger bandit into the nearby clinic for questioning. Rupert's gang showed no mercy as many of the townspeople remembered them reigning terror there before. "Where is your leader going?" They screamed at him. "Tell us now, or we will leave you here to rot!" One citizen roared with hate.

"The outlaw only looked with a glare as they continued to prod, poke, and yell at him for answers. "He's not going to say anything. Let's throw him back into the jail cell, but he will have to talk eventually, or he will die." Vengeance was on their mind.

Rupert was in unbearable pain but continued riding far enough to escape deep into the vast forest. The older of the two bandits slowed long enough to see Rupert still alive. "You're on your own now, Rupert," The bandit rode off to save his selfish hide.

Rupert remained to lie in his blood, seething with pain and hate. "After I risked my life to save you worthless . . ." Rupert faded into unconsciousness.

When Rupert awoke, two citizens, who were with Jack and Amos, surrounded him. Jack and Amos left their happy reunion when they heard of the breakout. Jack knew his father was involved and wanted to confront him.

He saw the men glaring at Rupert, and the two men hoisted him onto the Wilson's wagon. If it had not been for Amos and Jack arriving when they did, the citizens would not have been so merciful.

Amos and Jack took Rupert to the nearby town clinic. He looked over at Jack, seeing only a smile on his face. That made Rupert more callous of heart. "I know who you are and where your son is."

Jack sank back with a heavy beating heart at the mention of his son. "What do you mean, you know where my son is?"

"You will never have your son for leaving him like you did. He was my only reason for living." Rupert's vengeance came with the force of a jackhammer.

Jack remembered the past and the lovely maiden he met on one of his wild escapades. She fell for his dignified demeanor and was fascinated by his strength and stature. Liza was a quiet daughter and naive. She trusted Jack and believed he would always be there for her. He had only used her and taken advantage, and now all the regrets were coming to the surface with a sense of anxiety and bewilderment.

"Where is he? What have you done with him?" Jack put his hands into a fist and yelled.

"He thinks you are dead. I filled out a death certificate for you and signed it by a court judge. To me, you were dead."

"I always knew you to be a mean, cruel person but never dreamed you would stoop so low." Jack never felt such pain in his life as now. He wanted to raise his fist and punch him with all his might. All the feelings of hate were rising to the surface. Amos could sense the look on his face and pulled him back just in time before he planted a massive blow on his father's face.

Liza, the lovely maiden, did not tell Jack she was pregnant. When Liza died in childbirth, a close friend contacted Jack and told him he was a father. *She died from a broken heart during delivery,* said the message written in a letter that he still carried with him years later until he could not handle the pain anymore. Jack reached out to find his son, whom the courts placed in an orphanage. He was too young to remember or know his father, but Jack at least saw his son. Now Rupert is telling him where his son is. He didn't realize his father knew he had a son, but outlaws that travel about find ways. They listen to others' gossip and pay attention to minute details. Rupert kept the knowledge of his son to himself. The only care he had in the world was for that boy. Jack didn't quite know why. Maybe it was regret for losing his son or guilt for his actions. Even a man as ruthless as Rupert had to have some goodness in him.

"If you have any mercy, tell me where my son is." Jack requested with a much calmer spirit.

Hate consumed Rupert. He could not answer Jack. His breathing became more vital as he pulled himself up, yanked a hidden knife from his back pocket, and began swinging it around, cutting Jack in the arm. "Rupert is delirious," Amos said as Rupert lunged forward, forcing Amos to the ground.

Rupert would not give up. He was bent on destruction, being his demise as he picked himself up from the ground, darting again toward Amos, landing on the hard, dirty ground. The lawman grabbed his handcuffs and slapped them on his wrists as he wriggled about so violently that two men had trouble holding him down. "I will never tell you where your son is," Rupert viciously blurted.

Amos tried to calm him down when he reached around with the strength of a she-bear and screamed out without thinking as if some force had awakened him. "The Wilson's daughter, she has your son." Rupert bent over and collapsed into oblivion, and his breathing was no more.

Jack was unsure whether to be relieved or distressed as he heard the news. *Did the Wilsons know? They couldn't have. Indeed, they would have said something.* The anger toward his father had not subsided; now, it was too late. The realization hit Jack as he knelt on the muddy mess in anguish.

When Jack and Amos came through the rustic door, Maggie and the Wilsons were cleaning up from the previous day's events. Jack had a sullen look about him, and they both looked exhausted. "We were so concerned about you. Did you find the bandits?"

"Why didn't you tell me? You had to know. All this time, I could have been with him." Jack ran out of the cabin toward the spring well to clear his head.

Cora looked at him perplexed. They all stood in contemplation, trying to make sense of Jack's comment. Amos told them the previous day's events while Jack walked out the door toward his cabin.

"I knew my daughter adopted a young boy, whom they call Justin, but I heard his father had died. It always seemed curious to me. No one seemed to know about his parents. There was only the story of a young mother who died during childbirth. The attendants at the orphanage found a young boy on the doorstep in Massachusetts. When they discovered they could not have children, Jane and Luke jumped at the chance to adopt him. That is all I knew."

Harold came beside his wife and comforted her, knowing the pain she must be feeling right now. They loved Justin. They were looking forward to a visit from them after all those long years of estrangement. Jane never accepted their religion. They went their separate ways until Justin came into their life. Jane wanted him to grow up knowing his grandparents, so she made the trip to help mend their hearts, but their careers and the distance kept them apart.

"What will I tell Jack?" Cora prayed for a way to make things right with him.

"He will come around, Cora. He needs time to process all that happened. It has been a rough few days for him. Anyone would be distraught over what he has heard and seen." Amos gave Cora a gentle nudge.

Jack crouched down, knees to his chest, as he prayed to God. "What am I going to do, Lord? My son is alive, and he is so close to his family. I still have this feeling of hate toward my father, and I regret never having been with my son. He is a teenager who will probably resent me and never want to see me again. Please help me through this. Lord, give me the strength to make it through. Help me to forgive my father."

Amos and Maggie discussed the situation and decided to give Jack time before trying to confront him. "He is still a young babe in Christ, and he will need time to heal," Maggie said.

They went about their daily chores, and after completing their tasks, they traveled toward Cora and Harold to see where they could help. They saw the family were dressed formally, ready to take their wagon to meet Jane and Luke at the train station. "We are so excited for this moment, Amos and Maggie, but I am a little nervous." Cora and Harold strolled toward the door."

"Is there anything you want us to do while you are gone?" Amos and Maggie chimed in together.

"Can you let Jack know? We would love to have him meet our children and grandchild, his son."

"Are you sure that is a wise move right now?"

"There is no better time. The longer we wait, the harder it will be. I have already spoken to Jane, and she is ready for Justin to meet his biological father. He had been asking about his parents for the past few years now. I think he will be ready."

"Do they know about his outlaw past? Yes, I have informed them. And they also know about his new life in Christ. They have found the Lord through the help of a close friend of Justin's from school. It should be a wonderful reunion."

"We will pray that Jack can be receptive."

The train arrived just in time for Cora and Harold to greet their daughter and son-in-law. The blessed reunion occurred as they all fell into each other's arms with gladness. "It has been way too long," Jane said repentantly.

Cora and Harold locked arms with their grandson, Justin, and walked toward the carriage. "You are such a handsome young man. You look just like your father." They thought of Jack's handsome features. Justin anticipated meeting his biological father but was nervous at the same time. *What will I say to him? I know about his past, but Christ has forgiven him, so I must also forgive him.*

Justin was innocent of the world's evil ways, having been guarded by his parents, knowing about his father's and grandfather's past. They had seen Rupert only once when he was first born but heard rumors of him being near their home often. They feared for his life and held him close. He went to school and had friends like any young boy. Justin did not know about his biological family until recently. Justin was a mature young boy, so Jane and Luke felt he could handle the desire to meet him now.

Jack apprehensively awaited his son's arrival. He was unsure what to say to Cora and Harold. He was still perplexed by the entire situation. But he thought about meeting the Wilsons and how their lives intertwined. That was not a coincidence. He did not believe that way anymore. *I will do my best to stay positive.*

Their meeting went much smoother than anticipated. Jane and Luke were excellent parents, and Justin was a young man with courage and strong moral character. He was proud to know him.

"I have wanted to meet you for a year now. I have been preparing for this very moment." Justin prepared what he would say. He longed to see his father and be a family.

"Can you ever forgive . . ."

Even before the spoken words, Justin lunged forward and gave his father a manly hug, holding him tightly. Jack was now seeing signs of complete healing. He and his son would have a future together.

Jane and Luke had agreed to allow Justin to stay with Jack, Cora, and Harold for the summer, praying they would bond.

Drifter's Decision

Several weeks passed since Drifter left home. Joseph and Amos were worried.

"Joseph," Amos called. "I'm afraid Drifter may not be coming home. I wanted to talk to you about his background and new family of pups to prepare you if he chooses not to come home."

"I thought about it, Father. I know he has been gone for a long time. I feel confident he will see us again, at least if nothing else but to say goodbye."

"Well, I hope you're right, son."

The rainbow's colors brought new promise as they could hear the howls in the distance. They were coming from the cave. But Joseph did as his father said and did not go near it. Coming home had to be Drifter's decision. He would have to return on his own.

". . . but the howl can only mean one thing. Drifter is missing us. He has mixed feelings about leaving. I know he'll come home."

"Please try not to think about it right now," quieted Maggie. "I have some errands for you to run. Please take this bucket to the stream and bring me some fresh water. The pump is not working, and I need some water for washing and preparing the meal. It will also give you time to pray to God and let Him know the desires of your heart. He may see fit to answer your prayers quickly."

"Okay, Mother, I will go."

Joseph knew his mother was right. He hadn't prayed since Drifter left. Joseph knew God had taken care of things before and would take care of things again. He needed to trust. "Please, Lord. You know how much Daddy and I miss our friend, Drifter. Please bring him home soon. Please take care of him. Keep him healthy and safe. Amen.

Joseph felt much better. He enjoyed his walk in the spring. It was a beautiful day. He approached the water, lifting the bucket to his shoulders. *If only I could see Drifter now.* It was always so much easier to carry this load with his help. He knew he had to put that thought out of his mind. Drifter was not here. He would have to make the best of the situation.

Looking down in the water, he could see a shadow. It took his breath away for a moment. He was afraid to turn around for a moment, fearful of what he might see or, in his case, what he might not see. He thought it was Drifter and hoped he was right. Slowly catching his breath, he turned around. His mind played tricks on him. It was only his shadow flowing in the tiny ripples below. *It is unbelievable!* He had to think of something else. He would never get anything done that way. He asked God to help him concentrate and focus on his task.

Filling the water was easy, but getting it home was another story. It would not be too much farther now. He could do it. He had to. His mother depended on him.

While Joseph walked, he thought of the beauty around him and the gracious way God cared for him, bringing him into a family who loved and cared for him. He could hardly remember how his biological mother and father looked, but it didn't matter. Joseph would never forget the lasting memories of them. Maggie and Amos had filled any void he would have had. God miraculously sent him to them and saved his life. Their country was beautiful each day, and he knew who was responsible for it all.

Maggie watched her young son, who looked increasingly like a man, carry the heavy bucket through the meadow. "Look!" she spoke. "He managed to carry that water from the creek. I didn't expect he would choose such a large bucket."

"Why was Joseph down at the creek? We have plenty of water in the reserve barrels."

"I wanted to give him some chore to take his mind off Drifter."

"He misses Drifter, as I do. Doesn't he?" Amos knew his son's heart was breaking, as was his own. It had been four weeks since they had last seen Drifter. He only hoped after the pups had grown, he would come home. He also knew his loyalty. He was devoted to him for many years. He would not abandon his new family.

Drifter was in the cave raising his pups, as a loyal father should. But during that time, he was thinking of Amos and Joseph. Drifter missed them and longed to see them again. He knew his place was with his mate and the pups. He could not leave her. She was his mate for life.

The young pups were quickly maturing. Soon, they would be ready to enter the pack. Drifter knew there would be many trials for them. There would be many challenges they would have to face. They must prove themselves to be worthy of the pack.

Drifter, having been one of the pack's largest and most respected members, helped show his young pups how to hunt for their food and protect themselves from invaders. He knew they needed to know how to survive in the wild. Now that Drifter and his pups were with the pack they had no choice.

Amos, Maggie, and Joseph headed into town for the last time before the big winter storms hit. Because the snow

284

was already beginning to fall and fill the meadow with white flakes, Maggie's open carriage, converted into a sleigh, was used and would be loaded with necessary supplies.

The ride to town was an enjoyable one. The family laughed and shared as they rode. Joseph jumped down from the sleigh to see if he could outrun them. Falling many times, he jumped back in, willing to try again later.

"You have such fast, speedy legs." They loved his enthusiasm, laughing a little at his determination.

"It shouldn't be long before we enter the last stretch of the meadow. I will be eager to see everyone."

"Maybe you will be able to see David." Maggie hoped the family would be available.

"Yes. I hope David can play for a while."

"I don't see why not. I'm sure he will be glad to see you also."

Maggie and Amos dropped Joseph at David's house. David waved after seeing him near the front gate.

David's mother offered them some tea and fruitcakes. Amos and Maggie only stayed for a short time. They had plenty of jobs to do in town. They arranged to pick him up after their errands were complete. They knew it would be good for Joseph and David to play. Joseph needed another distraction.

Maggie ventured into the General Store while Amos spoke to Mike for a few short moments. Maggie suspected they would talk about Drifter but hoped something more exciting would take his place.

"Hello, Mike!"

"Well, it sure is good to see you. It has been quite a while since I've seen you. Where is that faithful companion of yours? I never see one without the other."

"I'm afraid one without the other is what will happen more often." Sadness was evident on Amos's face.

"What happened to Drifter? Has he wandered off with the wolf pack again?"

"I'm afraid it's more than wandering this time. Joseph spied him in the cave near our home. Drifter has a family — three pups."

"Why, that 'ol rascal. I knew he had more wolf in him than Husky. An animal like that has an instinct for his kind."

"That's not very comforting, but I know it's true. He was loyal until we saw that band of wolves near our house. You remember the rabies scare?"

"Oh, yes, that's right. You tracked down the rabid beast; something about a squirrel, wasn't it?"

"It was a wolverine that gave me more of a scare. After that, it seemed like Drifter was never the same. He longed for his kind. He wandered off several times but always came home within a few days. Now I wonder if I will ever see him again."

Mike could tell Amos was deeply affected by the unforeseen future. It was not like Amos to be down. "I know with all his love for you, he will come home again." Mike tried to distract Amos by taking him to the local mercantile.

"Yes, but it may never be the same again. Drifter has a family of his own now." The two talked while looking for some sweet treats to bring home. Maggie would love the dark chocolate chunks.

Well, enough of this kind of talk. How are you anyway? Here I am going on about Drifter, and we haven't even shaken hands." They gave each other a big hug and talked of days in the past.

Mike had been keeping very busy. His business was booming, with many people wanting parts for sleighs, sleds, fireplace tools, and animal pelts. He almost mentioned the thought of Drifter joining up with them again for another sled race this coming winter, but Amos knew he couldn't. It would be sad enough without Drifter, come this winter, without mentioning a thought of the race. The conversation, unfortunately, had to end suddenly.

"I promised Maggie I would help her with grocery supplies, and I see her leaving the store now. Thank you for your friendship and support. God Bless. We'll talk again soon."

Mike watched Amos lovingly caressing Maggie's shoulder, taking the packages from her hand. She sure was a rare beauty. Mike wished for a woman like her. Amos was a lucky man. Mike let out a peaceful sigh and continued with his work.

Joseph was having an enjoyable adventure with his good friend, David. They romped in the field behind their house, diving into the snow without care. Finally, the boys decided they had enough. They went toward the house just as Maggie and Amos were arriving.

"It sure is nice to have a warm greeting, with two boys running to see us just as they see us arrive," Amos teased. He guessed there must be some other reason they arrived at that time. He knew how those two boys could get going in their adventures.

"Would you like to stay for supper?" asked Emily.

"Oh, we don't want to impose. Besides, we do have some groceries that need attention. We really should get going before the light disappears. Luckily, it's no longer snowing. There is enough snow to glide upon with the newly polished runners on the sleigh. We have a long ride ahead, but thank you so much for inviting us."

The ride home was pleasant, except for one lost family

member. Amos loved the visit, but he missed his home away from the busyness of town.

They could make it much faster in the sleigh than on foot, but still, the evening was gone. The morning came with the hint of dawn approaching. Maggie fell asleep with her head on Amos' shoulder while Joseph looked up at the stars in the back.

"What are you thinking about, my son?"

"I'm wondering where Drifter is."

"I thought you might be thinking of that. He is on our minds a lot these days."

"It has been longer than a month now. Why does he have to be gone so long, Father?"

"He has a family of his own. The pups will need some training from him before they are ready to join the pack. It could be some time before we see him again, if at all," Amos reluctantly added.

"I miss him. I miss him so much. He knows how much we love and need him. Why did he go? Why did he?"

"We must trust the Lord, Joseph. He will take care of everything. Try to get some sleep. It will be a little while before we are home."

"Okay, Father. I will try."

Joseph prayed briefly, closed his eyes, and quickly fell into a deep slumber.

Time is what they both needed. Time and trust would be the healing measure of their pain.

Amos didn't know what Drifter was feeling at this moment. He loved his pups and was a caring parent. Deep inside his soul, Drifter longed to be with his master again. He knew he would have to wait. The pups were too young to mingle with the pack. It would be a few more months before they were ready. No, he must wait.

The winter months were in full swing with still no sign of Drifter. Amos almost gave up any hope when he noticed a significant, broad-shaped resemblance to Drifter. He stared at the animal with a longing in his heart. The creature stared back for quite some time. He looked as if he would dart toward him but then resisted. He was sure it was Drifter. He wanted to call for him — run to him — and bring him back home. He knew he couldn't. Drifter knew Amos wanted him, and he wanted to go. Amos knew Drifter, out of a sense of loyalty for his family, would not come. Deep sorrow hit his heart like a sharp-edged sword. He had seen Drifter and knew the result; he would never see him again.

He would not tell Joseph what he saw; it was not the right time. It had been four months since they had Drifter in their home. Amos held up little hope of his ever returning. He also knew the pups would be ready for the pack at six months of age. Maybe Drifter would come home then. Amos knew that if he did come back, he would still long to see the other wolves; it would not be permanent. He prepared his mind once again for the possibility.

The smokehouse was almost out of supply. Amos hadn't done any trapping for several months. He hadn't gone hunting for just as long. It was time. The elk and deer would be down from the high hills looking in the meadows for patches of green grass showing forth through the winter snow. Maggie packed his food in tight containers, making his load light. He would be gone for one to two weeks. Maggie and Joseph would stay busy making bread and mending clothes.

"Please be careful, as I know you will be. I will miss you. Be home as soon as possible. I will light the warm fire at your return." Maggie's tone was light, yet Amos could sense a heavy heart.

"Don't worry, my love. The event is a welcome change for me. The Lord will provide."

"I know, my dear. I'm concerned about the other matter." Maggie did not want to mention Drifter with Joseph there to bid his father goodbye.

"The Lord will take care of that as well. I love you."

"Goodbye, Father. I wish I could go with you."

"It is too late in the season for you to come. Maybe next year when so many other events are not happening."

"How will you do without Drifter, Father," asked Joseph.

Amos hoped he would not ask. It would be hard for Amos without him.

"I used to hunt and trap without him before we met. Indeed, he was a great help, making it much easier for me, but I will have to do as I used to without him." He took Joseph into his arms, holding him tightly. "Please pray for me. You have always had incredible strength and faith in God. I'm counting on you."

"I won't let you down."

Amos left and headed toward the full meadow a few miles from the cabin. He wanted to avoid traveling too far in case he did find a large animal. It would be quite some chore getting it home. He knew what it felt like and began missing Drifter more.

The first day of his hunting experience was unsuccessful. He hoped for better circumstances the next day. He built a blazing fire, allowing plenty of warm coals inside his tent for a long, cold night.

After the first day of hunting, he held more promise to find his elk. There were fresh tracks and signs of elk nearby.

He began tracking. It had been a long, arduous trek. In the distance, he saw an animal dart toward the deep mountain range. He followed curiously to find a dead elk down the ridge. It had been a fresh kill. If the wolves were nearby, he would not want to come in contact with them. He would not be able to ward off an entire pack. He would wait in the distance.

A few hours of daylight were left. Amos could neither hear nor see any sign of wildlife nearby. If the wolves attacked this animal, they would have returned by now. He didn't think he could have scared them. He began to wonder what all this meant. He cautiously walked toward the elk, rifle intact, ready to fire. He started skinning the beast and prepared to take it home. His skinning efforts were successful. He set down his knife momentarily and looked up on the ridge. He could see Drifter standing broad and proud. They stared deep into each other's eyes. He understood the look. It had been Drifter who had made the kill. He made it for Amos.

Someday, Drifter would come home. Amos could sense it. Eventually, they would be together again. Even if for a short time, and then back into the wild with his pups. Drifter had given him the sign. He still cared and longed to be with Amos.

Next year, circumstances will be as they should be. Drifter by his side when Amos needed him, then back to the wild with his family of wolves. He knew now that Drifter had been with him all along. Drifter had still been his loyal friend. He had not forgotten him. The love they felt from the beginning would never diminish. They were soul mates and would be forever.

THE END